"Get your damn foot out of my door."

This time it was a subdued roar, delivered from a twisted face of anger. "Do I have to call the sheriff to toss you out on your fanny?" He looked her up and down. "Though unless my eyes deceive me, it might take two husky men to do the job."

Alicia felt the flush climb her cheeks. It was an insult, delivered honestly—but an insult, nevertheless. And as the town's schoolteacher, she had until this moment been accorded the courtesy due to her position. She gritted her teeth. That her weight was, and always had been, a problem was neither here nor there. But this blatant intention to offend her had touched a sore spot, one she guarded closely.

"Two husky men?" Her brow jerked upward. "More like three," she answered crisply, "unless the blacksmith is one of them."

D0683897

Acclaim for Carolyn Davidson's recent titles

The Marriage Agreement
"Davidson uses her considerable skills
to fashion a plausible, first-class
marriage-of-convenience romance."
—*Romantic Times BOOKclub*

Colorado Courtship
"Davidson deftly mixes courtship
and a marriage of conveniece with the intrigue
of gold hunting, robbery and murder."
—*Romantic Times BOOKclub*

Texas Gold
"Davidson delivers a story
fraught with sexual tension."
—*Romantic Times BOOKclub*

A Marriage by Chance
"This deftly written novel about
loss and recovery is a skillful handling
of the traditional Western, with the
added elements of family conflict
and a moving love story."
—*Romantic Times BOOKclub*

The Tender Stranger
"Davidson wonderfully captures gentleness
in the midst of heart-wrenching challenges,
portraying the extraordinary possibilities
that exist within ordinary marital love."
—*Publishers Weekly*

CAROLYN DAVIDSON

Redemption

HQN™

If you purchased this book without a cover you should be aware
that this book is stolen property. It was reported as "unsold and
destroyed" to the publisher, and neither the author nor the
publisher has received any payment for this "stripped book."

ISBN 0-373-77149-5

REDEMPTION

Copyright © 2006 by Carolyn Davidson

All rights reserved. Except for use in any review, the reproduction or
utilization of this work in whole or in part in any form by any electronic,
mechanical or other means, now known or hereafter invented, including
xerography, photocopying and recording, or in any information storage
or retrieval system, is forbidden without the written permission of the
publisher, Harlequin Enterprises Limited, 225 Duncan Mill Road,
Don Mills, Ontario M3B 3K9, Canada.

All characters in this book have no existence outside the imagination of
the author and have no relation whatsoever to anyone bearing the same
name or names. They are not even distantly inspired by any individual
known or unknown to the author, and all incidents are pure invention.

This edition published by arrangement with Harlequin Books S.A.

® and TM are trademarks of the publisher. Trademarks indicated with
® are registered in the United States Patent and Trademark Office, the
Canadian Trade Marks Office and in other countries.

www.HQNBooks.com

Printed in Canada

Also by Carolyn Davidson

†*Big Sky Rancher*
Texas Lawman
One Starry Christmas
"Stormwalker's Woman"
The Marriage Agreement
††*Colorado Courtship*
Texas Gold
Tempting a Texan
The Texan
A Marriage by Chance
†*A Convenient Wife*
The Seduction of Shay Devereaux
Maggie's Beau
One Christmas Wish
"Wish Upon a Star"
**Tanner Stakes His Claim*
*The Bachelor Tax
The Midwife
The Tender Stranger
The Wedding Promise
Runaway
The Forever Man
Loving Katherine
Gerrity's Bride

*Edgewood, Texas
†Montana Mavericks
††Colorado Confidential

This story is dedicated to all those wonderful readers who took time to write me after they'd read *The Wedding Promise*. And to those who asked why I hadn't given Jake, a strong secondary character, a book of his own. I agreed with them, and found myself thinking often of Jake and wondering what had happened to him. This is it, ladies. Jake's story, which in my humble opinion is the best story I've ever written.

My dedication would not be complete without mentioning my manager, the wonderful Mr. Ed, who is my other half, my inspiration and my love.

Redemption

PROLOGUE

Green Rapids, Kansas—Summer 1877

THE GRAVE GAPED, an obscene rectangle wherein lay a simple coffin. Lorena McPherson, wife of Jacob, mother of Jason, lay beneath the scattering of flowers the mourning family and townsfolk had dropped into the grave.

Whether to relieve the stark presence of death, or to send a final assurance of love to Lorena, the effect was the same. But since the flowers would soon be covered by six feet of dirt, they failed to offer any comfort to the man who watched.

Jake McPherson sat in his rolling chair, his only form of transportation since he had lost parts of both legs, courtesy of the war. A familiar figure in Green Rapids, Kansas, he was pitied beyond measure today. Beside him, his son, a boy of six—who would grow up motherless from this day forward—stood dry-eyed, with shoulders straight. The boy's gaze was focused intently on the open grave.

Across the grave site, Jake's brother, Cord McPherson and his wife and children watched, Rachel shedding tears but standing erect and strong beside her husband.

The sun shone brightly, and Jake thought with macabre humor that it should have, at the very least, been raining the proverbial cats and dogs. But the heavens had not even had the decency to lend their tears to the event.

He'd shared almost nine wonderful years with his Rena, had discovered a life worth living with her at his side. Now it was all for naught. Life would never be the same.

Two men picked up shovels and began the slow, methodical rhythm that would fill the grave, leaving it mounded and barren of grass. Rachel carried a basket of flowers to strew over the surface once the men were finished, an attempt to conceal the scars of a fresh grave site.

Jake hoped it would bring Rachel comfort, this final act of love for her dearest friend. He would not deny her any solace she might gain, but knew that nothing could ease the stark despair that gripped him. He was alone, again. It seemed he'd been a solitary man for most of his life.

Until Lorena...

CHAPTER ONE

Spring—1880

No Visitors. No Peddlers. No Admittance.

Clear enough, Alicia thought, even as her fist pounded loudly on the solid oak front door. For the third time, she delivered four resounding thumps, then caught her breath as the door opened far enough for her to see the man facing her.

One hand lifted and the index finger pointed to the hand-lettered sign.

"Can't you read plain English?"

That the man was in a wheeled chair came as no surprise, but his total lack of courtesy took Alicia's breath away. As did the sight of dark brows and a cynical frown that seemed intent on frightening her off his porch. "Can you *speak* English?" he asked, his tone only marginally less rude.

"Yes, of course I can," she answered crisply, determined not to backtrack. Indeed, had she done so, she'd have landed in a fine crop of tall weeds, just to the left of the rickety steps. She'd noticed them as she made her way up the sidewalk, before her attention was drawn to the porch stairs that sagged in the middle where a board was broken.

"You have a step in dire need of repair," she pointed out. "You're lucky I didn't fall and break a leg."

"At least you have one to break," he growled, his lips drawn back over his teeth.

He'd actually *snarled* at her. There was no other word for it. Until this moment she'd never realized that a human voice could mimic that of an angry dog. Perhaps he had good reason, after all, she thought.

"No, I have two," she said, correcting him mildly. "But since I need them both, I'm just as glad I didn't have an accident making my way onto your porch."

"You needn't have bothered to come visiting," he said harshly. "As the sign clearly states, I'm not receiving callers." One large hand lifted to halt her words as she inhaled and prepared to explain the reason for her visit. "I *never* receive callers," he reiterated. "Not today. Not any day in the foreseeable future."

He pushed his chair backward and prepared to close the heavy door.

Alicia was quicker than he, and her sturdy, black, buttoned-above-the-ankle boot jammed into the space before he could slam the solid chunk of wood in her face.

"Get your damn foot out of my door." This time it was a subdued roar, delivered from a face twisted with anger. "Do I have to call the sheriff to toss you out on your fanny?" He looked her up and down. "Though unless my eyes deceive me, it might take two husky men to do the job."

Alicia felt the flush climb her cheeks. It was an insult, delivered with scathing honesty—but an insult, nevertheless. And as the town's schoolteacher, she had, until this moment, been accorded the courtesy due her position. She gritted her teeth. That her weight was, and had always been, a problem, was neither here nor there. But his blatant intention to offend her had touched a sore spot, one she guarded closely.

"Two husky men?" Her brow jerked upward. "More like three," she answered crisply, "unless the blacksmith is one of them."

Jake McPherson bowed his head, and Alicia wondered if it could possibly be a gleam of amusement she caught sight of, as one corner of his mouth twitched. Then he offered her his full attention, once more delivering a measuring look at her person.

"I don't entertain," he said, his mouth firm, his eyes dark as the coals she'd shoveled into the potbellied stove this morning. "I bid you good day…madam." As if he could move her foot by a glare, he stared down at it again.

"If you don't mind, I'd like to be given the privacy I'm entitled to," he told her sharply. "I've wasted enough time on you already."

"Not nearly enough," she said firmly. "I think you'll find you need to listen to what I have to tell you, Mr. McPherson."

"I don't need to listen to anything anyone has to say," he answered. Then, as he would have forced the door closed, never mind the presence of her shoe, he halted, his hand touching the knob. "How the hell do you know my name?"

"It happens to be the same as your son's. McPherson," she said. "I'm Jason's teacher. I really need to talk to you," she added, and then awaited his cooperation.

"I doubt that. I don't *really need* to talk to anyone, lady." He looked beyond her to where two women stood at the end of his sidewalk, just beyond the gate that sagged on one hinge. "Did you bring a whole contingent of cackling hens with you? Or did they just happen by for the show?" he asked.

"I didn't intend to perform for you, sir," Alicia told him, wishing fervently that she were anywhere else in the world right now. Back in her tiny bedroom or even in the cold schoolhouse, where her desk awaited her attention and the floor still needed sweeping due to the broken glass that littered it. Not to mention that the blackboard had not yet been wiped clean of today's arithmetic problems.

"I doubt you could do any tricks I haven't seen at one time or another, anyway," he said. "Now, take your damn foot out of my door and leave my house off your list of places to visit. Mind the step when you leave. I can't come to your rescue if you fall."

"If I write you a letter, will you read it?" she asked, desperate to be heard by this man, in any way available.

His look in her direction bordered on crude, his words derisive. "I don't accept love letters from strange women."

If he was trying to be offensive and rude, he was certainly succeeding, she thought glumly. If the man thought he was going to get the best of her, he had another think coming. She hadn't gathered her courage in both hands to be turned away at his front door. Besides, there was some indefinable look in his eyes that compelled her to continue this discussion. Her response was quick and to the point.

"*Love letters?* I doubt you'd ever get one," she snipped. She watched him frown and look surprised at the same time, then she leaned forward and shoved the door, causing his chair to roll backward toward the wall, where it tilted precariously for a moment before it settled back down.

With a quick movement, she slid through the opening and glanced back out to the sidewalk in front of the house. One of the spectators had her hand over her mouth, the other was leaning forward as if to look beyond Alicia's sturdy figure. She'd managed to draw enough attention to herself to last a long time, she thought resignedly.

There was nothing for it but to face the man in his lair, and hope he didn't have a gun handy. If looks could kill, she'd be six feet deep in the churchyard tomorrow. Fortunately, she'd faced down more angry opponents in her life than Jake McPherson. She'd survive this encounter. One way or another, she'd speak her piece before she left this house. Some way, she vowed silently, she'd make him smile before she was done.

He trembled with anger, his hands gripping the tires of his chair. Unless she was mistaken, his first inclination was to run her over where she stood. Perhaps he was having second thoughts, she decided. Having gotten a good look at her, he might have recognized that she was not a woman to be trifled with.

Taller than most women, she stood eight inches over five feet. Blessed by her family background with an ample backside and a bosom to equal it, she was a match for any average man. Any *average* man, she thought, beginning to rue her actions. She blushed anew as she recognized her brazen behavior, aware that she had crossed the boundary lines of good conduct.

"I apologize, Mr. McPherson," she said quietly. "I've been rude. If this matter weren't so important, I wouldn't have come calling without first requesting an appointment."

"*Rude* doesn't begin to describe you, ma'am," he told her. "You've forced your way into my house, attacked my person and now you refuse to leave."

From the rear of the house, a door slammed and Jake's head turned in that direction. "You'll have to excuse me. My son has come in, and he'll need help with fixing supper."

"Jason fixes the meals?" she asked. The boy was only nine years old. Certainly old enough for chores, but far too young to be entrusted with cooking on a stove he could barely reach with safety.

"As well as you'd expect," Jake answered, "our housekeeper quit."

Alicia tried in vain to hide her smile. "I heard from one of the ladies in the general store that you have a difficult time keeping any hired help."

"That's none of your damn business," he told her. "Now, just leave, if you please. That's about as polite as I'm going to be today. You'd better open that door and walk across that threshold right now, or I'll send Jason after the sheriff."

"Oh, I think perhaps the sheriff would be eager to see your son, Mr. McPherson," she said quietly. "However, I doubt that Jason is interested in showing his face anywhere near a lawman right now."

Jake's hands moved up to grip the armrests and then, as if he sought a distraction, he smoothed the lap robe that concealed his lower limbs. What there was left of them. One was longer than the other, Alicia noticed, for the small quilt outlined Jake's right knee and draped from it. The other leg was even more damaged, it seemed, missing above the knee.

She felt a surge of pity for the man who displayed such bravado, and yet recognized that he would not appreciate her softening toward him. "I really need to talk to you," she said after a long moment.

"Jason!" It was a bellow that would have done credit to a bull, she thought, as his voice reverberated from the bare walls and floors of the hallway. "Come here," Jake called, no trace of patience marring his sharp tones.

"I'm fixin' supper, Pa." Thin and reedy, the boy's voice held apprehension in its depths, and Alicia knew, without a doubt, that he was aware of her presence.

"Shall I come get you?" Jake asked, his voice a harsh whisper now, a sound that was more awe-inspiring than the bellow had been. It had the desired effect, for the narrow-shouldered lad who pushed open the kitchen door and stepped into the hallway did so with haste.

"Are you in trouble?" Jake asked, leaning forward in his chair as he turned it to face his son, using swift movements of both hands.

"I dunno," Jason said, his jaw set, his dark eyes flashing defiance.

"Do you know this lady?" Jake asked.

The boy nodded, tossing a look of appraisal at Alicia before he studied the floor at his feet. "She's my teacher," he said sullenly.

"Why is she here?"

Jason's head came up abruptly and his eyes widened in surprise. "Ain't she told you already?"

Jake shook his head. "I'm waiting for you to tell me."

"Let her do the talkin'," the boy said, and Alicia thought that, for one so young, he wore an immense chip on his shoulder. He spoke almost as an adult, uttering more words in these few moments than he'd delivered in her classroom all week. The boy was bright, there was no doubt about that, for when he deigned to turn in an assignment, it was far superior to the other two boys of his age. Not only was he bright, she thought grimly, he also was in trouble—of that she was dead certain.

Jake looked at Alicia again. "You've got one minute to talk," he said gruffly. "If the boy's done some mischief, you'll have to take care of it. That's your job, lady. You have him seven hours a day. If you can't control him, it's not my fault."

"But his behavior *is* your problem, Mr. McPherson," she returned bluntly. "And he is definitely a behavior problem."

Jake cast Jason a long look. "Back in the kitchen with you," he told him. "And close the door."

Without an argument, Jason did as he was told, but his parting glance in Alicia's direction was filled with defiance and, she thought, a touch of fear. She'd never attempted to instill fright in a child, and she didn't plan on starting with this one, but he must learn respect.

"He needs some sort of guidance," she began, unable to speak the words that would condemn the child, that would make his life any more difficult than it already was. Having Jake McPherson as a father was problem enough. Motherless, and part of an unstable household, the boy didn't stand a chance of making anything of himself. Unless Jake took hold and changed his style of fathering.

"He gets guidance." Jake looked at her from dark, angry eyes. "He doesn't need any Goody Two-shoes coming around trying to reform him. He's a boy, and boys get in trouble once in a while." He settled back in his chair and his chin jutted forward. "What's he done?"

Alicia felt like crying. For no earthly reason whatever, she felt tears burn against her eyelids and she turned aside, lest they be visible to the man before her. Not that he'd be able to make them out in the dim hallway, where tall, narrow panes of fly-specked glass on either side of the front door provided the barest minimum of light.

Beyond the wide parlor doors only gloom existed, apparently, for the curtains appeared to be closed tightly. At any rate, the man would have to peer intently at her to notice whether or not her eyes were shiny with tears.

This house…this man…the boy in the kitchen—all merited her concern, and that rush of emotion that threatened to melt her reserve held her stock-still where she stood.

HE WAS A MAN ISOLATED by his own choice. He admitted it freely to himself, and knew that the people who lived in Green Rapids were fully aware of his desire for solitude. Seldom in the past had anyone crossed his threshold, only the train of servants he'd hired intermittently, and then watched depart.

Housekeepers were hard to come by, a fact Jake was only too aware of. A decent cook would come in handy. As it was, his only household help was a widow lady who picked up their laundry once a week, then delivered it back to them a day or so later.

Beyond that, he and Jason were on their own, except for the occasional visit from his brother's family. That the boy needed a woman's touch was true. That he was likely to be the beneficiary of such a luxury was out of the question, unless some miraculous creature turned up on their doorstep and waved a magic wand over the household.

The woman who stood before him did not fit that description. Yet, she held his interest, as had no other woman in his recent past.

"I repeat, madam—what's the boy done?" Hearing the harsh tone of his own voice, Jake restrained himself a bit. If Jason was really in trouble, he needed to know. "I'm sure I can handle the problem, once you fill me in on the details," he continued, forcing his voice to be civil.

From the kitchen door, a scurrying sound that might have been mice, but was, no doubt, Jason's attempt at eavesdropping, caught Jake's attention. It was just as well, he decided, that the boy hear what his teacher had to say.

"He broke the windows in the schoolhouse today," she said quietly. Her eyes offered a mute appeal, glancing up at him, shining with a film of tears, unless he was mighty mistaken. "Not all of them," she was hasty to add. "But the two closest to my desk."

"Where were you when it happened?" he asked, his gaze focused upon her person.

"Sitting at the desk, going over my pupils' work. I'd just let school out for the day." She looked at him directly. "Before you ask, I have to tell you that Jason did not attempt to hide his mischief. He stood not more than ten or twelve feet from the building, and when I looked out through the first broken window, he lifted another rock and threw it at the one closer to where I normally sit."

"You're telling me you saw him break the windows?" His heart sank within him. Jason was belligerent at times, hard to handle for the past year or so, but his actions today went beyond *mischief.*

The woman only looked at him, as if she would not further verify the story she'd told. It was no doubt true. She had no reason to lie, or even stretch the truth. "What do you want me to do?" he asked.

She shook her head. "I don't know. The boy needs help, and he won't accept it from my hand. He resents authority."

"I'll talk to him," Jake said. "I'll find some appropriate punishment to deal out, and settle the matter."

"At least he'll know you're paying attention, won't he?" she asked quietly.

Jake's head came up abruptly, and his glare dissolved any small amount of amity he'd projected. "And what is that supposed to mean?"

"He seems to be asking for you to notice him,

and he doesn't care how he accomplishes it, Mr. McPherson. This isn't the first time he's been in trouble."

Jake winced inwardly. She was right. He'd received a note from the sheriff, asking for reparations when Jason had ruined the flower bed in front of the bank. The boy had come home with a black eye more than once, and his trousers were continually needing repair, where he'd fallen in the dirt, tussling with several boys in town. But then, fighting was something all boys indulged in, Jake had told himself.

Now he viewed the signs he'd ignored—and didn't relish the picture they drew.

"Do you have another idea, Miss…" His voice trailed off, wondering for the first time just who this woman was.

"I'm Alicia Merriweather," she said. "I teach the first six grades at the schoolhouse. Jason has been a student in my classroom for almost two years."

"You've been in town that long?"

Her smile was cool. "You don't get out and around much, Mr. McPherson. I've lived here for a bit over two years."

"My social life has nothing to do with you," he said harshly.

"I've had articles in the weekly newspaper," she said. "I'd have thought you read the *Green Rapids*

Gazette, and might even have recognized that there was a new teacher at the school."

She was smart-mouthed, he decided. A woman who spoke her mind. He could just imagine the sort of articles she wrote. A smile begged for existence on his lips as he considered her. Her writing was no doubt aimed at cleaning up the saloons and driving the women who worked there out of business.

"Get to the point, Miss Merriweather."

She inhaled and her ample bosom rose in response. He'd never been overly fond of women so well endowed, but she was well-formed, if a bit too full-figured for his taste. Even so, the dress she wore concealed a shape beneath its folds that would bear further study. And suddenly that idea appealed.

"I think Jason should be made to come to the schoolhouse, and at least sweep up the mess he made, and then help me board up the windows until I can get Ben from the hardware to replace the glass."

"You're going to board up the windows?" he asked. "And you want Jason to clear up the broken glass?"

She shot him a level glance. "He broke it, didn't he? He needs to learn that there are responsibilities that go along with his actions."

"And if he cuts himself in the process?" Deliberately, he was making this difficult, but the woman was persistent and he was rising to the challenge.

"What if he burns himself cooking on your stove, Mr. McPherson?" She pursed her lips and then lifted a brow as if she awaited a reply.

"Well, you have me there, ma'am," Jake answered. "The difference is in who takes the blame for his injury."

"In the case of the windows, he takes the blame, sir. Both for the damage he wrought on the school, and for any harm he comes to in the resolution of the problem."

"He's only nine years old," Jake said, intent on continuing the argument, the best one he'd had in a month of Sundays. This woman knew how to hold her own.

"He may never reach his tenth birthday if he doesn't learn some rules of decent behavior," she said firmly. "He has half the parents in town out for his hide. There isn't a boy in school safe from his fists, and the little girls have suffered ink splattered on their dresses and skinned knees from being pushed down in the schoolyard."

Jake was silent, absorbing her words. If it was indeed as bad as all that, the boy had to be taken in hand.

"I'll agree to him cleaning up the mess," he said grudgingly. "As soon as he's eaten his supper, I'll send him on over."

She gritted her teeth. He saw her jaw clench and noted the militant gleam in her eyes as she defied him again. "He'll do it now. I won't be eating my supper until the windows are boarded up and the school is back in shape for tomorrow. He can just do without his meal until that's been accomplished."

"Do you always get your way, Miss Merriweather?" Jake asked, fuming inwardly, yet aware that the woman had a point.

"Only when I'm right." The words were a taunt, delivered with a smug smile. Then she clutched her reticule and stiffened her spine. "Now, will you tell him to come along with me? Or shall I go out into your kitchen and drag him out the back door?"

"It's against the law to manhandle a child who is not your own," Jake told her.

"I have the right to discipline the children in my classroom," she reminded him. "The school board has put that into my contract."

He might as well let the creature have her way. She was going to go over his head if he didn't give in gracefully. Or at least without a fuss.

He raised his hand from the arm of his chair and waved toward the closed kitchen door. "He's on the other side of that, ma'am," he told her. "I'll warrant his ear is glued to it, in fact."

"Call him in here," she said, moving to plant herself halfway down the hallway. "He needs to know that you're aware of what he's done."

"Oh, I doubt there's any question he hasn't already heard every blessed word you've spoken, ma'am,"

Jake said harshly. Then he raised his voice a bit. "Jason, come on out here."

The door opened after a few seconds and the boy sidled into the hallway. His face was pale now, and Jake felt a moment's pain at the look of confusion his son wore.

"You'll go with Miss Merriweather and clean up the mess you made, Jason. You'll help her board up the windows, and then you'll do extra chores to earn money for the new glass it will take to repair the damage."

Jason's eyes widened. "I have to pay for new windows, Pa?"

"You broke the old ones, didn't you?"

For a moment a look of despair came over the small freckled face, and Jake felt a pang of guilt. When had the boy gotten so far from his reach? Then Jason's head lifted and a look of defiant pride touched his features.

"Yeah, I broke them."

"'Yeah' is not an appropriate word to use, Jason," Alicia said quietly. "You may change your statement, please."

He shot her a resentful look, then turned as if to seek out Jake's opinion in the matter. When nothing was forthcoming from his father, the boy nodded.

"Yes, ma'am, I broke them," he said, and for a quick

moment Jake thought he saw a bit of himself in the boy. Given to impetuous behavior, frustrated by authority and determined to flaunt his shortcomings in the face of others, he was indeed a problem.

But one, it seemed, Alicia Merriweather could handle.

CHAPTER TWO

JASON MCPHERSON WAS A capable child, Alicia admitted silently. Obviously aware of the purpose of a broom and dustpan, he swept up the broken glass without a murmur, then dumped the shards into her wastebasket. If he still wore the chip on his shoulder, at least it didn't appear to be quite so large a chunk of wood, she thought.

"I'm finished, ma'am," he told her as he returned the tools to the cloakroom.

"No, Jason, you're not," she said, contradicting his statement. From the quick look he shot in her direction, he'd expected the reprimand, and she noted the taut line of his jaw.

His sigh was exaggerated. "Now what do I hafta do?"

"You know very well what comes next, young man. You had your ear plastered against that kitchen door when I told your father what I expected of you."

He shifted uncomfortably, standing first on one leg, then the other, as if he readied himself for flight. "I suppose you think I'm gonna carry in all that wood you got layin' out in the yard."

"No," she said, disputing his idea. "You're going to go out there with me and hand me one board at a time while I nail them in place. If it rains tonight, I don't want the schoolhouse open to the elements."

"Elements?" he asked, his look skeptical. "You mean the weather?"

"You know what I mean," she told him. "You can't play dumb with me, Jason. I know exactly how intelligent you are."

His shoulders slumped and she decided it was a ploy, a means to get her sympathy. It would never work. He was slick, but she was ahead of the game.

"Come along," she said, walking briskly toward the door, hammer in hand, a small brown bag of nails in her pocket. Outdoors, the sun was hanging low in the sky, and she looked upward, thankful that the clouds were not heavy as yet. The idea of working in a downpour didn't appeal to her, and sending Jason home all wet and soggy might only irritate his father more.

Although that seemed to be an unlikely thought. The man could not be more irritable if he truly put forth an effort.

Jake McPherson had a reputation around town. A widower for well over two years, he had become a recluse, mourning his wife, folks said. And well he might, Alicia thought. The woman had no doubt been a saint to put up with him. A more miserable man would be hard to find.

Yet there had been something about him that appealed to her. Some spark within the man had spanned the gap and touched off an answering response in her soul. Pity? Doubtful, although she respected his need to mourn his wife. Respect? No, not that, for he'd allowed himself to become a hermit and had kept his son apart. Not only from those in the community who might have helped the boy, but from himself.

He'd built a wall of grief and stubborn pride. Even his own child could not surmount the obstacle of Jake McPherson's hibernation. And yet she'd been drawn to him…perhaps as one weary soul to another.

The hammer was a tool she was familiar with, but the boards she nailed in place were heavy and, as a result, her fingers bore the brunt of several blows that she knew would leave bruises behind.

"You're not very good at this," the boy observed as she held the last board in place and took a handful of nails from the bag. "I guess women have a hard time doing man stuff, don't they?"

She turned her head, caught by the scorn in his remark. "'Man stuff'? Hammering a nail is something only the male gender is proficient at? I think not," she said stiffly, holding the nail firmly and raising the hammer. The head caught the nail off-center and the hammer careened onto the board, bouncing off her thumb in the process.

Alicia's murmur of pain was not lost on Jason, and he leaned forward, as if to offer sympathy. Instead, his words only served to insult. "If I couldn't do any better than that, I'd find someone else to do the job."

She inhaled with a shuddering gasp, the pain in her thumb holding all her attention. Extending the hammer in his direction, she turned the tables on the boy. "Here you go, sonny. Have at it." She placed the bag of nails in his palm, the hammer handle in his other hand, and she stepped back from the partially covered window.

It took all of her pride to keep the throbbing digit from her mouth, and she almost smiled at the thought. As if warming that thumb between her lips would make the ache disappear. Instead, she shoved her hand into the pocket of her dress and watched as Jason fiddled with the bag of nails, extracting a handful from its depths and then placing them between his lips.

The bag hit the ground with a muffled clatter, and as she watched, the boy held the board in place with his elbow, then somehow balanced it as he pounded the first nail into it. That it took almost a dozen thuds with the hammer to accomplish the task was immaterial, she decided. That the nail sat at an angle mattered little.

The fact remained that Jason had accomplished what he set out to do.

"Bravo," she said softly, and as his features assumed a quick look of surprise, she clapped her hands together in a semblance of applause. "I didn't think you could do it," she told him.

His shoulders straightened a bit as he took another nail from his mouth and held it immobile. The hammer rose and fell, the muscles in his upper arms flexing like two halves of an orange.

"You're stronger than I gave you credit for," Alicia said. "Why didn't you tell me you could have done this job better than I?"

His grin was cocky, the sullen look in abeyance as he shot her a look of satisfaction. "You were doin' all right, Miss Merriweather. For a woman."

For a woman. Tempted to scold him for his attitude, she instead chose to change the subject, thinking it the better option. There was no point in alienating the boy unduly.

"Do you handle the repair work around your father's house?" she asked him, and wished immediately that she'd not chosen to mention his home. For his mouth drooped and he turned back to the hammering, making enough noise to prohibit him from a reply.

She bent to pick up the bag of nails, collecting three that had dropped beside her and adding them to the assortment. Knowing she was out on a limb, she back-tracked. "I'm sure you're a big help to your father."

"He don't need any help," Jason said beneath his breath. "He says we can get along just fine by ourselves."

"Nevertheless, I'd say it's a good thing he has you." She watched as he finished pounding the last nail, and then moved to stand behind him, admiring his work over his shoulder. The board was just a bit skewed, the nails perhaps not lined up perfectly, and two of them were at a slant and couldn't be straightened, but he'd done the job, and for that he'd gained her respect.

"Here's your hammer," Jason said, handing her the tool and then stepping away from her. "If you're done with me, I'm goin' home."

She needed to take a stand, Alicia thought, as he turned his back and walked away. "Jason?" He halted and stood stock-still.

"I hope there won't be a repeat of this sort of behavior. The next time I'll probably have to involve the law. And I don't think it would be any help to your father if you were called before a judge."

"You won't need to worry about that," he said glumly. "My pa will likely find enough for me to do at home to keep me busy."

That seemed to be exactly what the boy needed, Alicia thought. And what he asked for every time he misbehaved. Getting in trouble was an obvious ploy to gain his father's attention. For a man of Jake McPherson's intelligence, he seemed to be lacking common sense where his son was concerned.

She watched as Jason plodded away, wincing as she imagined his pain. Abandoned by his mother, although the circumstances had not been deliberate, he'd become a boy who was starving for that which the woman had provided in his life.

"JAKE?" The man who poked his head through the back doorway called out in a familiar voice, and Jake frowned as he turned his chair in that direction. "Are you home?" he asked loudly.

"You know damn well I'm home. Where else would I be?" Jake answered, shoving the kitchen door aside as he rolled across the threshold. "What do you want, Cord?"

"Just came to town to run some errands and I thought I'd drop in and see if there's anything I can do for you while I'm here." Jake's brother was tall, muscular and walked about on two legs, a fact Jake had been able to set aside for a number of years. Now the difference that he'd once accepted seemed insurmountable.

"I'm doing just fine," Jake answered gruffly. "Take a look around, brother. See anything that needs attention?"

Cord winced as he gave the kitchen a cursory once-over. "Several somethings, actually," he said mildly. "You need a good housekeeper."

"Tell me about it," Jake answered with scorn. "There aren't any women in this town ready and willing to put in a solid day's work and follow orders. Must be they don't need a few dollars a week to keep them going. Probably finding other work to do."

Cord raised a brow at that. "You're kinda sarcastic, don't you think? I've heard that you've already gone through the available widows and older ladies who might take such a job. You're difficult to work for."

"How do you figure that?" Jake's jaw jutted forward as he faced off with his brother, almost relishing the foray. It broke the boredom to have a good argument— such as the one he'd indulged in with the schoolteacher.

"You're a hard man to please," Cord said. "You're determined to sit in this house and keep the world away. You haven't got any draperies open, and this place smells stale. You need to open those windows and let the breeze blow through. That would help, for starters."

"Well, you find me a woman who'll open my windows and keep my house clean and I'll hire her." That should shut the pompous fool up, Jake decided.

"And how long will that last? Until you decide it's too much effort to be pleasant to another human being?"

"Some days that's more trouble than it's worth," Jake muttered.

Cord leaned against the sink board. "I heard you had a visitor the other day. It seems a couple of the ladies saw the schoolteacher force her way into your house. It was all the talk at the general store. She caused quite a flurry, it seems, coming to visit you." Cord grinned. "*That* bit of information has brought the gossips a new bone to chew on, and they're settling down for a real meal, at her expense."

Jake bristled at the thought of the meddling female who'd invaded his home, thus causing the old hens to peddle their stories about her behavior, and in turn about him.

Cord grinned. "Then your boy spread it around that he'd managed to show the woman how to pound nails in the boards that are currently covering the school-house windows."

"Jason said that?" The boy certainly hadn't shared that bit of information, Jake thought. He'd only come home and sullenly done the chores assigned to him over the past days, earning the money to pay for panes of glass.

"Yeah, your boy said that," Cord repeated. "But the rest of it came from a couple of passersby, I understand." He straightened from his relaxed stance and faced Jake head-on. "Jason needs a haircut, Jake. He needs some new clothes that fit. His pants are too short and his shirts are either ripped or missing buttons. He doesn't wear stockings half the time, and I doubt he's washed his neck in a week."

"He's a boy." The words hung between them, and Jake felt a moment of shame as his brother listed Jason's shortcomings. And yet, they weren't of Jason's doing. They were items that Rena would have tended to, had she not been lying in the churchyard under six feet of dirt.

"You know, Jake, what you really need is a mother for your son." With those words, Cord walked away, out through the back door and down the steps.

Behind him, Jake sat in his chair with a grimace of bitterness painting his features. A mother for Jason. That was about as likely as snow in August, to his way of thinking. He couldn't even find a decent house-keeper. How the hell would he go about finding a mother for his child?

"Pa?" From the front hallway, Jason's thin whisper reached Jake's ears and he spun his chair around to face the boy. "What was Uncle Cord talkin' about just now? Was he tellin' you to find a new woman to get married to?"

"That's not about to happen," Jake said, dodging the query. "Who do you think would marry a man in a wheelchair? A man without any legs?"

"Mama did," Jason answered quietly.

"Your mama was one in a million," Jake said gruffly. "There aren't any more women in the world like your mama." And wasn't that the truth. He lost himself for a moment in the memories that were stored in a part of his mind he no longer visited. Rena had been the sweetheart of his youth; and when they'd brought him back from the war without his lower limbs, she'd made it her business to crawl beneath his skin.

So well had she accomplished the task she'd set for herself, that he'd capitulated to her demands, believed her promises of forever, and married her. Now look where he was. Alone again, left to mourn.

Rena had taken ill and then succumbed to pneumonia during a week that would remain forever in his memory as the most horrendous time of his life. Pneumonia was a winter disease, and Rena had contracted it in midsummer, her stamina reduced after a cold had dragged on for three weeks.

He'd entered this house the day of her funeral determined never to leave it again. And except for a few memorable occasions, he'd kept that vow. Jason had been stuck with the most disgusting tasks imaginable, performing menial work that would have been more appropriate for a housekeeper or nurse.

Now he'd been told by two different people during a span of a few days that his son was lacking in the basic essentials of life. The love and attention of a parent and the chance to live as a child.

He rolled to the door and shut it, tempted to slam it, but leery of breaking the glass. Jason had already been responsible for repairing two windows this week; he would not add to that count. Behind him, he heard the boy's dragging footsteps as he left the kitchen, and Jake turned the chair and followed the boy into the hallway.

"Come into the parlor, son," he said quietly, and noted the startled look the boy shot in his direction. Had he not spoken to his boy in a decent tone of voice for so long that it would take him by surprise?

"Sit down." Jake waved at the couch, where books lay in disarray and two dirty plates sat on the middle cushion.

Jason moved the plates and settled onto the seat, and Jake wondered that it was such an automatic gesture on the boy's part. Used to the clutter, he didn't seem to notice that the house was in havoc.

"I'll try again to get us a housekeeper," he told his son. "I'll send you with a note to the newspaper office and have an ad put in this week. Maybe we can find someone who'll suit us both."

"I don't want some strange lady tellin' me what to do," Jason said stoutly. "It'd be better with just you and me here, Pa."

"It isn't better, though," Jake admitted. "You need someone to take you in hand, son. Someone who can take you out and buy you clothes that fit and see to it you visit the barbershop."

Jason leaned forward on the couch and spoke eagerly. "I can do that, Pa. I can go to the barber by myself, and I'll go to the general store and pick out some stuff. Can we afford all that?" he asked, almost as an afterthought.

Jake nodded. He'd been living without dipping into his savings, Cord depositing a quarterly amount from the family ranch into Jake's account at the bank. The house was paid for, thanks to Rena's thrifty nature, and food for the two males in the household was the largest expense he had.

"We can afford whatever you need, son," he said, wishing that he'd noticed for himself the boy's general appearance. "But I'd feel better if someone went with you."

"Can you go?" The look in his blue eyes was hopeful as Jason focused on his father, but Jake retreated quickly.

"No. You know I don't go out."

"You need a haircut, too, Pa." Jason looked at his father with eyes too old for a lad of nine. "You're not in much better shape than me."

"Well, the difference is that you have to be out in public and I don't," Jake told him firmly. Then he heard the distinct rap of knuckles on the front door.

"Somebody's here," Jason said, rising quickly from his seat to head for the hallway.

"Wait," Jake told him, calling him back with a single word. "Let me see who it is first."

"You can't see any better than me," Jason told him, standing to one side to peer through one of the long panes of glass that trimmed the door on either side. Glass that was dirty, with cobwebs hanging from the upper corners, Jake noted.

"It's Miss Merriweather," Jason said, his eyes seeming to darken even as his face paled in the light from the narrow windows.

"What have you done now?" his father asked, and knew an unexpected moment of pleasure at the thought of once more fencing with the woman.

"Nuthin'," Jason answered sullenly. "Why do you always think I've been bad?"

"Bad?" Jake repeated. That his son should use that word in connection with his own behavior was telling. "I'm sorry," he said, meaning the apology from the depths of his heart. "Open the door, Jason. Let's see what Miss Merriweather wants with us."

A NARROW FACE PEERED at her from behind the dirty windowpane, and Alicia caught her breath at the apprehension displayed on the boy's features. Fixing a smile on her face, she waited for the door to open.

"Ma'am?" Jason watched her warily as he stepped back, allowing her entrance if she wished.

"Is your father—" At the sight of Jake McPherson behind the boy, almost lost in the shadows of the wide hallway, she halted her query and nodded a greeting.

"I'm here, Miss Merriweather."

"I noticed the sign is still there, but I wanted to talk to both of you about something, and this seemed like the best way and time to approach the subject."

Jake's hand sliced the air, effectively halting her explanation, and he glared in her direction. "Get to the point, ma'am. Is there a problem?"

She spoke with haste, lest he be angry for nothing. "No, of course not."

"I've found there's no 'of course not' with you, Miss Merriweather. There is still something on your mind."

"Well, in this case you're wrong, sir," she said, standing outside the front door, feeling the air of dislike that emanated from the man. "I simply wanted to talk to you about something."

Jake waved a hand at her. "Well, unless it's a topic you think the whole neighborhood needs to be privy to, you'd better come on in." He regarded her as she hesitated. "My brother tells me you've already done damage to your pristine reputation with your interference in our lives. Might as well do it up brown."

And wasn't that the truth? She'd heard the murmurs

behind her in the store yesterday, and noted the sidelong glances of ladies as she passed them on the sidewalk. It could not be helped, she decided. The welfare of a child was more important than any gossiping females.

Jake turned his chair and rolled it toward the parlor, Jason scampering ahead of him, and Alicia followed in their wake. The boy was industriously picking up an assortment of objects from the couch when she stepped into the room, and he dropped them with a total lack of ceremony onto the floor in one corner.

Jake looked her way and for a moment they seemed to be in tune, both aware of Jason's meager attempts at straightening up the room.

"Have a seat, ma'am," Jason told her, waving at the couch, where an unoccupied cushion awaited her. Even as she watched, his eyes filled with hesitant light, as if he feared her mission might prove to be not to his liking. "I haven't done anything bad this week, have I?" he asked.

She shook her head and smiled, sensing that he'd feared that very thing. "No, you've been an exemplary student for the past couple of days, Jason. I appreciated the papers you turned in to me. They'll help your grades enormously."

"What's *exemplary?*" he asked with a frown.

"It's a word we're going to use in our spelling lesson on Monday," she told him. "If you know the meaning by then, you'll receive extra credit."

She looked at Jake McPherson then, wondering if he saw the boy as she did. If he noticed the ragtag appearance of the child, or if he just didn't care. If he took note of the extraordinary intelligence that gleamed from his blue eyes when they weren't dulled with unhappiness. Then she steeled herself, putting her plan in motion.

"I received a visit from your brother," she announced tentatively. "He told me you were looking for someone to help out with Jason. A woman who would see to him choosing new clothing at the general store, maybe arrange for a haircut, or whatever else he needs."

And for the life of me, I don't know why I volunteered for the job.

"Cord told you that?" The subdued tone of Jake's voice was a cover for anger. She could see it in the flush that touched his cheekbones, the flaring of his nostrils and the glare of fury that shone from his eyes. He wouldn't be smiling today.

"Well," she began, hedging a bit. "He didn't say it in so many words. Just suggested that you might be amenable to accepting my help."

The man looked her over then as if he saw her as a slab of meat in the butcher shop on Main Street. Disdain marked his face, disapproval glittered from his eyes. She felt the brunt of both as if a sharp knife had stabbed her, slicing her good intentions to ribbons. She was no raving beauty—her own mother had told her that more than once—but she was presentable.

"And you think *you* qualify as an expert when it comes to young boys?" Jake asked with a cynical smirk. "How many children do *you* have, *Miss* Merriweather?"

She dropped her gaze to her lap, noting that her fingers were twisting together in an agony of embarrassment. She lifted her chin and met his eyes head-on. "None, of course. As you very well know. But I've worked with children for almost ten years, Mr. McPherson. I'd say I have a fair amount of experience."

"Enough to take on the raising of my son?" he asked.

"I'm not asking for that position," she told him forcefully. "I have no intention of interfering with the job you're doing. I only thought to lend a hand."

"You don't have enough to keep you busy at that schoolhouse?" he asked sharply. "You need to spend your leisure time offering to tend to your pupils in lieu of finding a husband and having your own crop of children to raise?"

"The chances are very slight of my finding a husband and having a family of my own, sir," she managed to say with a reasonable amount of clarity. "I'm sure you don't mean to be insulting, but your remarks are venturing in that direction."

Jake tilted his head and looked at her as if she were

a specimen under a microscope and he was trying to distinguish her species. "Do you always talk that way, Miss Merriweather, or is it just with me that you use such highfalutin language?"

She bit at her lip. "I speak the way I was taught to speak," she told him. "My parents were educators and raised me to be a schoolteacher. I had a good education in preparation for my life's work."

"Didn't your mother ever consider the idea of you getting married and having that family we spoke of?" He leaned back in his chair and watched her closely, deciding that the flush she wore made her look almost...*pretty.* He cleared his throat and looked down. Damn, sharp tongue and all, she was more appealing than he'd thought.

Alicia felt heat climb her cheeks, knew she was blushing furiously and yet refused to look away from the man. "I think it's an insult for you to even suggest such a thing," she announced.

His gaze found her again. "You're a woman, aren't you?" His eyebrow twitched, and his mouth followed suit, as if he mocked her. Not quite a smile, but almost.

"A woman, yes. But perhaps not the sort of female who appeals to men who are looking for a girl to marry."

"What sort of female are you?"

As if he cared, she thought. The man was being

downright rude, perhaps wishing he could push her from this room, out the front door and away from his house merely by his behavior. She would not allow it. Not until she'd had her say. If he refused her help, so much the better, as far as she was concerned at this very moment.

"What sort of female am I? I'm a schoolteacher-sort, Mr. McPherson. I've never planned on marriage. At my age, it's out of the question, anyway."

"How old are you?"

Rude. The man was rude beyond belief! "How old are *you?*" she countered smugly.

"Thirty-nine," he said. "Not that that has any bearing on the subject."

He looked at her expectantly. "Your age, Miss Merriweather?"

None of your business. The words were alive in her mind, but refused to make their way to her lips. Instead, she found herself obediently blurting out the truth. "Thirty. I'm thirty years old," she said firmly. "*On the shelf,* I suppose it's called."

"Surely there's been some farmer in need of a *woman,* or a parson looking for a *helpmate,*" he said, emphasizing the words that he obviously thought described her best.

"Apparently not," she said, refusing to rise to his bait. "Had such a man offered for me, I doubt I'd have accepted. My future does not lie in raising a brood of children whose mother had the good sense to desert them, and leaving myself open to being used as a slave by their father."

"Not all children left alone have been *deserted* by their mothers," Jake said harshly. "On occasion, such women are stricken by illness, and they've been known to die, leaving their households without a woman's touch."

Alicia felt pain strike her, the aching knowledge that she'd hurt another person with no reasonable excuse. She'd spoken out of turn because of her anger with this man.

"I apologize, Mr. McPherson," she said quietly, unable to look into his face but unwilling to remain silent when an apology was in order.

"I'm not sure why you think I merit such a thing," he answered. "It seems we strike sparks from one another, Miss Merriweather. I was equally at fault."

She looked up at him then, shocked by his words, stunned by the reasonable tone of voice he used. His face had lost just a bit of its stony demeanor; his eyes were narrowed as he looked her over. The change was quite disarming.

CHAPTER THREE

THE WOMAN HAD DUG DEEPLY beneath his skin. He'd been angry for three solid years, yet the emotion he'd bent in her direction today had made his fury during that time seem as nothing. Still, she'd tossed his anger back at him, as if she were untouched by his words. As a result he'd been unkind and insulting, to use her own description of his remarks.

Alicia Merriweather rubbed him the wrong way, and yet he felt a sense of anticipation as he thought of her next visit. Perhaps she would not return, and at that notion, he rued his bad temper.

Never in Jake's life had he been so abrupt. Except for the early days, before the time when Rena had come back to him—those days when he'd made Cord's new bride the target of his anger, reducing her life to a living hell for a matter of long weeks.

He thought of his brother's wife, of the changes she'd made to his life, and then his mind compared her to the woman who had so recently left his home.

Rachel was sweet, caring and petite, a woman who inspired a man to watch over her, as did Cord. Yet she was feisty, as Jake had reason to know.

On the other hand, he'd seldom seen so capable a woman as Alicia Merriweather. She was tall, big boned, and bore her weight well. He'd had a second look today. The dress she'd worn had fit somewhat better than the one she'd had on the last time she'd been here. It wasn't too difficult to acknowledge the fact that there was, indeed, a waistline beneath its enveloping folds. Her hands were capable, her nails short, her fingers long and tapered. Her hair was nondescript in color. Brown was as close as he could come to describing it. Yet he wondered if it wouldn't gleam with red undertones in the sunlight.

Jake shook his head. Of all the foolishness in the world, this really took the cake. Miss Merriweather was a self-proclaimed spinster. And yet, he vowed the next time he saw her, he'd coax a smile from those soft lips. *Soft lips?*

He shook his head at his fanciful thoughts. After all, her one redeeming feature was the fact that she seemed to truly like Jason. Make that two redeeming features, he decided with a satisfied nod of his head. She knew how to argue, and wasn't afraid to open her mouth. A quality he admired in any human being. Rena had never allowed him to run roughshod over her, had always been vocal about her views and opinions.

Rena. My God. He bowed his head. He hadn't known he would miss her so much. His teeth clamped together as he fought the sudden despair that gripped him.

"Pa?" From the doorway behind him, he heard Jason speak to him, and he blinked against the hot tears that threatened to unman him.

"Yes, Jason?" Was that his voice, that calm uttering of his son's name?

"Pa, how come you and Miss Merriweather were fighting all the time she was here?" Jason sounded almost…bereft, Jake thought. And that would never do.

He turned his chair and fought for a smile. "I've always enjoyed a good argument, son," he said. "I suspect Miss Merriweather does, too. I know it got a bit out of hand, but it's all repaired now."

"Pa? Have you thought about what she said? About taking me to the store for clothes? And to the barber for a haircut?" He thought a note of pleading touched Jason's words, and he shot the boy a long look. Jason slouched in the doorway in a casual manner, but beneath his spoken queries lay a hope he could not hide.

"I've thought about it," Jake answered. "Is that what you'd like to have happen?"

Jason shrugged as if it were of no matter to him, one way or the other. "I guess I wouldn't mind if she took me, so long as she walked behind me or in front of me, or some way didn't let everybody know she was takin' care of me."

The boy looked so earnest now, Jake almost smiled.

"I wouldn't care, not for myself, but I wouldn't want folks to be thinking she was trying to act like my mother. You know? They might not be nice to her."

"Let's send her a note, Jason."

In an attempt that appeared aimed at hiding his pleasure at Jake's announcement, Jason merely shrugged. "I'm goin' outside, Pa. Just call me when you've got it ready, and I'll take it to her," Jason offered. Quite a turnabout for the boy.

Jake thought of what he might say in such an epistle. Something that would signify his change of heart, without letting her know he'd be beholden to her should she accept the task. He wheeled his chair to the dusty desk in one corner of the parlor. The rolltop slid up readily and he found a writing tablet there. A small bottle of ink and his pen lay beside it, both of them unused for so long. He'd had no reason to write a note to anyone in that length of time. Perhaps the ink had dried out.

He drew the paper before him and dipped the pen into the inkwell, pleased that it came out stained darkly. How to begin? *Dear Miss Merriweather...* Perhaps. Then again, she wasn't his dear anything, now that he thought about it.

Alicia. There, that looked fine. Not that she'd given him leave to call her by her given name, but he'd managed to fight with the woman. Twice, for pity's sake. That ought to entitle him to some small bit of intimacy.

And at that word, he stilled. *Intimacy.* He'd only thought it, not spoken it aloud, but the result was the same. How on God's green earth could he think of Alicia Merriweather and intimacy in the same breath? She was a female intent on spinsterhood, a woman determined to make inroads on his life, and more frightening yet, he was on the verge of inviting her to do that very thing.

Jake pushed his chair away from the desk and looked across the room. The draperies were closed, only a crack of sunshine peeking through a place where the two panels didn't quite cover the window. Cord's words reverberated in his mind.

You need to open these windows and let the breeze blow through.

Rena would be heartsick if she could see her house as it was today. Just three summers past, the windows had gleamed from her efforts with vinegar and water. The floors had been burnished to a fare-thee-well, and even when the wheels of his chair had sometimes marred the surface, she'd only brought out her cloth and worked for scant moments on the trail he'd left behind, and then bent to kiss him as she passed his way.

He rolled closer to the window, tugged ineffectively at the heavy drapery and watched as a cloud of dust rose in the air. Another tug brought the rod tumbling to the floor and he winced as bright sunlight flooded the parlor.

Now, isn't that better? He looked around quickly, for a moment convinced he'd heard her beloved voice. And then a flurry of movement from the yard caught his eye and he groaned aloud. Mrs. Blaine, a widow who had worked for him for all of three days, was marching with a militant stride up his front walkway. Even as she halted before the door, just out of his sight, he heard the back door open stealthily and his hackles rose.

"Mr. McPherson! I know you're in there. Come and open this door."

The woman had a voice loud enough to wake the dead, he thought, his ever-present anger fueled by the demanding tone. His chair rolled across the parlor floor and into the hallway. The doorknob turned at his touch and he looked up at the Widow Blaine's furious face.

"Your boy has really done it this time!" Mrs. Blaine announced, her nostrils flaring, her teeth set rigidly. "If you don't do something about him, the law is going to get involved."

Jake sat glumly in his chair, wondering what Jason could possibly have done to infuriate the woman so. He raised his hand to cut her off mid-tirade.

"What did Jason do, ma'am? And when did he do it?"

"What did he *do?*" Her voice elevated with each word.

"That's what I asked you," Jake said softly.

"I don't need to listen to your smart mouth, Mr. McPherson. I worked in this house. I know the sort of man you are and what you expect of your help. And I certainly know that your son is capable of any number of pranks."

"What did he do?" Jake asked again, his voice a bit stronger, his anger beginning to match that of the woman before him.

"He tore up my vegetable garden. That's what he did. The tomatoes were just about ready to put in mason jars and the corn was ready to pick." She took a deep breath. "On top of that, he tore down my scarecrow."

"When did he do this?" Jake asked mildly, hoping against hope that Jason was not the culprit, and fearful that he was.

"Just about an hour ago," she said.

Relief ran through his veins. "How do you know it was my son?' he asked.

She sniffed, her gaze triumphant. "I saw him myself, a boy with a blue shirt and brown hair. Watched him run from my backyard, I did."

Jake smiled grimly. "I'll warrant there are a number of boys Jason's size with blue shirts and brown hair."

He looked back over his shoulder, and his voice rose as he called his son's name. "Jason? Come out here."

Wearing a brown shirt, Jason came through the kitchen door and down the hall.

"Did you tear up Mrs. Blaine's garden?" Jake asked him.

"No, sir," the boy answered. "I've been here since school got out." He looked at the Widow Blaine. "You can ask my teacher. She was here and we was talkin' for a long time with my Pa."

"Did you change your shirt within the past thirty minutes?" Mrs. Blaine asked, her eyes moving over the boy's form.

"No, ma'am," he answered politely. "I've worn this one all day long. Yesterday, too." He thought for a moment. "Maybe the day before, too."

Jake winced at that revelation. "Does that answer your question, Mrs. Blaine?" he asked, motioning Jason to step closer. From his chair he drew the boy to his side, his long arm circling the narrow shoulders, his hand gripping Jason's upper arm. "You're welcome to check with Miss Merriweather if you like. I think you'll find she'll verify my son's story."

"Well, I know what I saw," Mrs. Blaine said with a good amount of righteous indignation. Turning on her heel, she stepped from the porch, almost tripping over the broken step. Only a quick grab at the railing stopped her from landing head over heels on the sidewalk.

She turned back and shook her finger at Jake, a good imitation of a schoolmarm if he ever did see one. "This place is a disgrace. You need to get it fixed up."

"Yes, ma'am," Jake called after her as she stormed off. "Just as soon as I get my new legs I'll do that very thing."

"What new legs, Pa?" Jason asked softly, bending to look into his father's face.

"I was being sarcastic," Jake told him. "Joking."

"You never joke around, Pa." The boy looked dubious and Jake reached up to touch Jason's face with his fingertips.

"Do you know that I love you, son?" he asked. "I know I don't tell you often, but I do."

"I don't remember you ever tellin' me that," Jason said bluntly. "You just holler a lot. Especially when we get a new housekeeper."

"Yes, I suppose I do," Jake said. Frustration struck him a low blow as he shut the door, lending it a push that vibrated through the floorboards. He turned his chair back to the parlor and rolled to his desk. The single sheet of paper lay there with but a single word written on the top line. Without a word, he picked it up and crumpled it in his hand.

He would not, could not ask the woman to take

Jason in hand. It would not only ruin her reputation to be hanging around his house, but make him look like an absolute failure as a father. He could not transfer his responsibility so readily, let her take the boy shopping, tend to his needs. Some way, he'd figure out another plan.

"I KNEW the meaning of it, Pa." Jason's eyes were bright with the joy of accomplishment as he waved his spelling paper before Jake's face. "See, there it is. *Exemplary.* I knew how to spell it, too."

The moments spent with the boy late last evening had borne results, Jake thought, and for a moment he shared Jason's exhilaration. The spelling paper bore a bright red score at its top. An *A* was written with a flourish there, and Jake looked at the precise lines of the grade Miss Merriweather had given the boy.

"I'm proud of you, son," Jake said, holding the paper in his lap. He wondered when he'd last said those words to the boy.

"Are you, Pa? Really?" The brown shirt was dingy from wear. How many days had Jason donned it early in the morning. Four? It exuded an odor of boyish sweat and a definite doggy smell.

"I think you might want to put that shirt in the trash bin," Jake told him. "How about you taking a bath today?"

"A bath?" Jason cringed. "It's only Thursday, Pa. I took a bath last Saturday."

"No," Jake said, correcting him. "It was a week ago Saturday, I believe."

"I don't think it's healthy to be scrubbin' up all the time," Jason said earnestly. "It lets all the germs into your skin."

"What do you know about germs?" And where on earth had he gotten that idea?

"Miss Merriweather has been teachin' us about science stuff."

"Well, if you ask your teacher, I'm sure she'll tell you that a little soap and water never hurt anyone." His words were firm, implying a stance he would not budge from, and Jason appeared to get the message.

"Do I hafta get the tub out? Or can I just wash in the basin like you do?"

"I wash in the basin because I can't get in and out of the tub easily," Jake told him, and wished for a moment that he might soak his body beneath hot water and allow the warmth to penetrate his skin.

"I could help you," Jason offered, and Jake was hard put not to smile at the eager offer. The boy would collapse under his father's weight should he attempt such a project.

"Let's just concentrate on your own."

Jason's shoulders slumped as the ultimatum was

delivered, and he trudged away toward the kitchen. "I'll get out the kettles to heat the water," he muttered.

Then Jake could only hold his breath and watch as his son poured the hot water into the round wash tub. The chance of Jason being scalded was slim, since they only heated the water until it was barely hot enough to allow steam to rise. The danger was in the kettles, and the fact that Jason was not tall enough to handle them readily.

Another housekeeper was becoming a necessity, Jake decided. The boy was in need of help. He scanned his mind for another prospect for the job, and came up blank. As Cord had said, he'd already gone through all the widow ladies and the women who were willing to work outside their own homes. His reputation had been blackened by the stories those women told—tales of his foul moods, the angry tirades he'd aimed in their direction when they'd attempted to open the windows and doors.

Jake looked now out of the single window that bore no covering to soften the glare of sunlight through fly-speckled panes. Rena would be aghast at the sight.

His chair rolled across the bare, wooden floor to the second window and he grasped the draperies in his fist, and tugged them from their moorings until they landed with a muffled thud on the floor. Somehow the act was satisfying, as if he rebelled against the darkness that had gripped him for so long.

"What'cha doin', Pa?" Jason stood in the doorway, wide-eyed and pale, as if the disturbance in the parlor had frightened him.

"Your uncle Cord told me we needed to open the windows in here," Jake told him. "Do you think you can push them up? Let some fresh air in?"

"I can try." And wasn't that the crux of the matter? Jake thought. If the boy was willing to try to change things, how could his father do any less?

"Let me know when the water's hot and I'll come out to the kitchen and help you," he told Jason. "In the meantime I'm going to write a note to Miss Merriweather, and once you get cleaned up, you can deliver it."

"I'm gonna get new clothes?"

Jake looked at the shaggy locks that covered Jason's head and hung against his collar. "And a haircut," he said firmly.

CAN YOU COME BY to talk with me?

The note was brief and to the point, Alicia thought, and looked into Jason's face, aware that his eyes shone with a hopeful light. The man hadn't even had the courtesy to sign his name, she thought, exasperation making her cross. It would do no good, though, to take it out on the boy.

"Tell your father I'll come by tomorrow at suppertime." A sudden urge prodded her to action. "Tell him I'll bring a picnic with me. We can eat in the parlor."

"A picnic?" Jason's mouth curved into a smile. "I can't remember havin' a picnic since my mama died, ma'am. We used to go to the celebration on the Fourth of July when I was real little. Mama got someone to help and my Pa would go, too."

Real little? The boy was far from grown now, she thought sadly. And living on memories of a better time in his young life.

"Do you like fried chicken?" she asked, and at his enthusiastic nod, she determined to borrow the kitchen of the house where she resided and make the most mouthwatering meal she could put together. There was no time to waste.

Friday was Alicia's favorite day of the week. Two whole days, in which she could please herself, loomed ahead. She'd sometimes found herself walking beyond the town and exploring the countryside during the nice weather. She had a lonely life, but had learned to enjoy her own company. A light quilt tucked under her arm, she frequently took her current volume of history or novel of adventure, finding a tree under which to sit, the book on her lap. Pure heaven, she thought. The whole of an afternoon in which to enter another world, where her imagination could run riot and her mind be refreshed.

Today was Friday, and for another reason she felt the swell of anticipation. A stop at the butcher shop gained her a plucked chicken, one the butcher was happy to cut into pieces. The general store yielded a supply of small new potatoes, fresh from some industrious soul's garden. Early carrots and a large crimson tomato for slicing filled her basket and she set off for the house where the parents of one of her students had offered a room for her use.

Her landlady, Mrs. Simpson, was willing for her kitchen to be used for Alicia's project. By the time the chicken was fried and the potatoes made into a salad, Alicia was ready to walk out the door.

Her meal was packed into the market basket and covered with a clean towel. She set off at a determined pace down the street toward the big house where Jake McPherson lived with his son. The front gate sat permanently ajar and the yard was still weed-infested, but the front parlor windows were barren of covering. She looked at them in surprise, noting the shadow of a man in a chair almost out of sight.

Edging past the broken step, she climbed the stairs and crossed to the front door. Before her knuckles could rap, announcing her presence, the door was opened wide, Jason standing before her. His hair was combed, still wet from the dousing he'd given it, marks of the comb he'd used still apparent. That the part was crooked and the dark locks hung to his shoulders was of little matter; the boy had made an effort.

"Come on in," he said. "My pa's in the parlor." He lowered his voice and bent closer. "I don't know if he's happy about this or not, ma'am. He looked kinda cross when I told him you was bringin' supper with you."

"It will be just fine," she said, offering assurance and wishing she felt some of the same. The basket was heavy and she sought for a flat surface upon which to deposit it. A library table stood near the door and she placed her bundle there and then turned to face Jake. "I hope I didn't intrude with my offer," she said, addressing the man with a confidence she did not feel. "Jason thought a picnic would be nice."

"I don't go outdoors," Jake said flatly.

"We'll have it in here," she answered. "Jason and I can sit on the floor on a quilt and you can join us from your chair."

"You've got it all figured out, haven't you?" he asked, and she took note of the burning resentment in his dark eyes. "Did anyone ever tell you you're a managing woman?"

"Yes, as a matter of fact, I've been called even worse than that."

His mouth twisted in a sardonic grin. "It doesn't bother you?"

She met his gaze head-on. "Do I look bothered?" She turned to Jason and issued an order. "Please go and find a quilt we can sit on. I'll get the food ready." That she'd brought napkins and plates was probably a good thing, she decided. Three forks and a salt shaker made up the rest of her supplies.

Jason carried a folded quilt into the parlor. "This was in the airing closet," he said, breathless after his jaunt up and down the stairs. Eyes glowing with anticipation, he spread it on the floor and sat on one edge. "Now what?"

Alicia arranged the small tablecloth she'd brought, then placed the bowl of chicken, the potato salad and the carrots and sliced tomatoes in the middle. A loaf of bread, freshly baked only this morning and sliced into thick slabs, was wrapped in a clean dish towel, and she opened it, tucking the edges beneath the offering. Butter in a small bowl completed the arrangement.

"Oh, dear. I forgot to bring knives for spreading the butter," she said softly. Her gaze flew to Jake's. "May I send Jason to the kitchen?"

He nodded curtly, and Jason rose, almost trotting from the room, so anxious did he seem to get this meal under way.

"Don't spoil this for him," she said, warning Jake quietly. She bent to arrange the food on their plates.

"I do own some semblance of courtesy," he told her harshly. "I don't need a lesson in manners from the schoolmarm."

"Well, that's encouraging," she shot back, looking up as Jason skidded to a stop just inside the parlor door.

"Here you go," he said, a grin bringing to life a dimple in his left cheek, something she'd never noted up until now. He handed her the three knives and she inspected them with a cursory glance and deemed them clean enough to be used.

She sat on the edge of the quilt, across from Jake's chair, and folded her hands in her lap. "Shall we say grace?" she asked, and then at Jake's snort of disbelief, she offered a glare in his direction. "You needn't join us," she said politely, "but Jason seems to understand the concept."

For indeed the boy had folded his hands nicely, waiting for her to speak the words. "My mama used to pray before we ate," he told her, and then looked up at his father. "Remember, Pa? I always liked it when she did that."

Jake nodded curtly. "Go ahead, if it gives you pleasure, ma'am."

His words were brief, and her mind churned as she attempted to decipher his mood. The man was angry again, probably as riled as he'd been on their first meeting. Unless she missed her guess, he was not about to accept her help with Jason.

"What part of the chicken do you prefer?" she asked her host.

"Whatever's left," he said. "It's all food."

Jason bit into a drumstick. "This is *good* food, Pa," he said, the words muffled as he chewed. Some potato salad followed and he relished it for a moment, then swallowed. "My mama used to make stuff like this. Does it have eggs in it?"

Alicia nodded. "And mayonnaise and a touch of mustard and a big onion."

Jake accepted his plate from her hand and their fingers touched during the interchange. His were warm, hers chilled, and he raised a brow as he looked down at her.

"Surely you're not cold, Miss Merriweather?" She thought a gleam of satisfaction shone from his eyes as he spoke, and rued the apprehension she'd tried so hard to hide. The man was enjoying her discomfort.

"No, just afraid that I've offended you, sir." She bent her head and took up a wing in her hand, breaking it apart and nibbling at the sparse amount of meat it held. The bones were placed neatly on the edge of her plate and she speared a slice of tomato, shook salt over it, then cut it up with her fork.

"I'm surely more offensive, than offended," he suggested, and she looked up quickly, catching him with a look of appraisal alive on his face.

His gaze was warm and she shifted uncomfortably under it, feeling self-conscious. Her black boots were large, her hips wider than most women her age, and the size of her bosom was "magnificent," a gentleman caller had said, long years ago. Back when she had thought there might be hope of a man in her life, and children born from her body.

"Well, you do know how to cook," Jake conceded reluctantly. "I'll have another piece of that chicken, if you don't mind."

She offered him the bowl and he took a thigh, then glanced at the potato salad. "Would you like another spoonful?" she asked, and lifted it within his reach.

"Maybe a slice of tomato, too." His voice softened as he grudgingly asked for her help in serving him, but she refused to feel triumph at his expense. The man was making a stab at good manners, and she subdued her own natural inclination to gloat.

"Do you cook often?" he asked, wiping his mouth with the napkin she'd provided. She'd already noticed Jason copying his father's example, placing the napkin across his lap before he began eating.

"Not very. I don't have a kitchen of my own."

"Miss Merriweather lives with Catherine Simpson's mama and papa," Jason offered. "Catherine thinks she's real smart because the teacher has a bedroom next to hers." He looked gloomy, Alicia thought, as if a bit of jealousy had popped up its ugly head. And then he wiped his mouth, following Jake's example again and looked hopefully at Alicia.

"Do you think you could come and cook in our kitchen once in a while?" he asked.

"Jason." The single word was a reprimand and Jake's lowered brows emphasized the rebuke.

"I just thought—"

"You're imposing on Miss Merriweather," Jake said firmly. "She was decent enough to bring us supper tonight. It would be rude to expect her to repeat the gesture."

No, Alicia thought grimly. *Rude* was a man who offered cutting remarks to the woman who'd carried a basket all the way across town to his house, a place where that man sat, totally lost in self-pity, brooding day in and day out.

"I'd be delighted to come and cook your supper once in a while," she said brightly, knowing that Jake was ready to burst with irritation at her high-handedness. "Shall we say once a week?" She smiled encouragingly at Jason.

"That would be..." Jason fumbled for a word to express his delight, and only grinned widely, including his father in the elation he made no attempt to hide.

"Will I be able to take Jason to the general store?" she asked Jake. "I am free tomorrow if that would be a good time for him."

Jake simmered, she could easily tell from the look he gave her. She had him neatly boxed in, and reveled in the fact. How she could find joy in making him fume was a question she wouldn't even attempt to answer. She had to admit, there was a certain sense of satisfaction that had accompanied this meal, eaten at his feet, so to speak, and obviously enjoyed by both father and son.

She decided to change the direction of their conversation, and pointed up at the two windows where late afternoon sunlight shone. "I see you decided to uncover your windows," she said. "It's an enormous improvement, Mr. McPherson." Tilting her head to one side, she made a sober observation.

"Perhaps I could bring over a bottle of vinegar and clean them for you tomorrow after Jason and I complete our shopping."

"I'm sure there's vinegar in the pantry," Jake said forcefully. "If you're of a mind to be our household help for the day, you just go right ahead."

"I'll help," Jason said quickly. "I can do all kinds of stuff to help."

She looked at the boy, her heart aching at his eagerness. "Perhaps we can repair the front step," she suggested. "You've a fine hand with a hammer and nails, Jason. We'll look for a board to use and make that second on our list."

"Yes, ma'am," he said quickly. Then he looked at his father. "Ain't that a good idea, Pa?"

"I'm sure your teacher has any number of talents that might come in handy around here," Jake told him, his gaze turning to Alicia as she got to her feet.

Never the most graceful of women, she came close to falling across his chair as she took note of his sarcastic observation. Her eyes burned as she turned aside and reached for her basket. "If you'll take the leftovers into the kitchen and put them away, I'll take the dirty dishes and go home, Jason. I think I've outstayed my welcome for today."

With a flourish of white tablecloth and the clatter of forks and plates, she packed up and headed for the parlor door.

Jake watched her leave, his eyes pinned to the straight line of her spine, noting the brown braids that circled her head, crossing over almost double. Her hair must be very long, he thought. Probably past her waist. Dark and thick, it was probably her best feature. Unless he counted the clear gaze she afforded him from blue eyes that did not waver or retreat from his own. Strangely enough, she seemed to fit the body she'd been given. In fact, she could almost be considered attractive, in a regal sort of way.

All that aside, she was definitely a woman to be reckoned with.

CHAPTER FOUR

JASON LOOKED ABOUT as uncomfortable as a boy could get, Alicia thought. She sat in a straight chair next to the door of the barbershop and tried unsuccessfully to pin a pleasant smile on her face. Jason slunk down in the black leather chair a bit farther, to no avail. Joe Hamlet, the barber, merely tucked his hands beneath the boy's armpits and boosted him higher.

It was an ordeal for both of them, Alicia decided. Jason, because he was the center of attention; herself, because the men who lined the wall on a row of chairs were offering her long looks of appraisal. She was unaccustomed to being the focus of male attention and found it disturbing. Not that the gentlemen who awaited their turn in the barber's chair were rude, only curious. Somehow that fact did not ease her discomfort.

The barber, mindful of the boy's wiggling, placed a firm hand atop the lad's head to hold him still. If it turned out to be a halfway decent haircut, Alicia would be most surprised.

"I think an ice cream is in order," she said to a very relieved young man as they exited the shop ten minutes later.

"I'm not goin' back there again," Jason said vehemently, totally ignoring her offer.

"I suspect I can do as well as Mr. Hamlet, myself," Alicia said. "Shall I give it a try when it's grown out enough to tackle?" She steered him into the doorway of the drugstore and approached the counter. "What flavor do you want, Jason?"

"Flavor?" He looked around, as if only just now aware of his surroundings. "Ice cream flavor?"

"How about chocolate?" she asked, and lifted a hand to Frank Gavey, the owner of the store.

They ate their ice cream slowly, savoring each lick, every bite of the sugared cone and finally the pointed end where the last drops had melted. The general store was behind them, their bottoms firmly parked on a bench just outside the establishment, and Alicia prepared herself for the next leg of this outing.

"Are you ready to pick out some clothing?" she asked Jason. She rose, leading the way to the double doors that opened into the store. Jason followed slowly, dragging his feet, as if the experience at the barbershop had made him leery.

Alicia waited inside the door for him, then placed her hand on his shoulder as they approached the long counter. A short, squat gentleman approached. Mr. Harris was a businessman. Perhaps he spotted Alicia's determined look, or else he saw a likely prospect for a complete wardrobe when he looked at Jason. Either way, he made it his business to be cordial.

"How can I help you, ma'am?" Mr. Harris greeted them jovially. "How about some new shirts for the lad? Looks to me he's been growing like a bad weed."

"We'd like some trousers and then Jason will choose some other things," she said crisply. "Is there somewhere he can try them on?"

"Naw. Just take them home, and if they don't fit he can bring 'em back."

"All right." One way or another, she'd see to it that the boy was outfitted with a new wardrobe today.

"May we see what you have in his size?" she asked.

The counter soon was literally covered with clothing. Trousers, shirts, drawers and stockings were stacked in separate piles, and Jason obligingly held them up before himself, testing them for size. As the pile grew, his eyes kept pace, growing wider with each item chosen.

Alicia nodded her approval. "Now, how about some new shoes?" she asked.

"Mine are good enough," the boy said quickly. "That's a lot of stuff for Pa to pay for, Miss Merriweather," he said beneath his breath, for Alicia's ears alone.

"He'll want you to be outfitted properly," she said firmly. "We'll look at shoes next," she told the store-keeper.

The man beamed. It was likely the best sale he'd had all week, Alicia thought. Well he might smile. Jacob McPherson's credit was as good as gold. The shoes were selected and tried on, then the items they'd decided on were wrapped in brown paper in two separate bundles and tied with string.

"There you go, ma'am," Mr. Harris said, pushing their purchases across the counter. "You're gonna clean up fine, young man," he announced to Jason.

"Ma'am?" Jason halted on the sidewalk and looked up at Alicia. "Don't you ever ask me to do that again. That fella was…" He groped for a word and Alicia filled the gap nicely.

"I believe *condescending* is the word you're searching for," she told him. "And I agree with you entirely. The gentleman needs to learn how to deal with the younger members of the public a bit better. 'Clean up fine,' indeed!"

If ever a youth needed some bolstering, it was Jason. Alicia could barely keep her arm from encircling his narrow shoulders, in fact had a hard time resisting the urge to drop a quick kiss on the top of his freshly barbered hair.

"Let's go and show your father the results of our

morning," she said briskly, leading the way, paper-wrapped bundle in one hand, her reticule swinging from the other. Jason followed, his package carried in front of him, like an offering. Several townsfolk nodded and eyed the two of them surreptitiously as they made their way home. Alicia breathed a sigh of relief when they turned the corner and walked along the line of picket fences that fronted the properties to the south of Main Street.

"Today was quite an ordeal for you, wasn't it?" she asked, slowing her pace a bit.

"I didn't have much fun, if that's what you mean." He kicked at a clod of dirt and frowned. "I won't have to do that again for a long time, will I?"

She thought his words were hopeful, and could not resist a smile. "I know how you feel," she said.

He looked up at her in surprise. "You do?"

"I dislike shopping for clothing myself," she confided. "In my case, it's because I'm not as small as most other women, and I feel uncomfortable choosing things that are the largest size the store has to offer."

"Being small isn't so great," he told her, as if to boost her confidence.

"It is if you're a woman," she said, wondering how she'd gotten into this conversation with a child.

"I think you're a nice lady," he told her staunchly. "I don't think you're too big at all."

They turned at the open gate and walked to the front steps. "When are we gonna fix this thing?" Jason asked as he stepped carefully on one side of the broken board.

"How about this afternoon?" She waited as he opened the door and then followed him inside the house.

"Pa?" Jason's voice echoed in the empty hallway, where no carpet muffled the sound. "We're back, Pa."

The wheelchair rolled from the back of the house toward them. He eyed their purchases and then waved toward the parlor door. "Let's go take a look," he said.

They spread out the clothing over the couch and Jason waited silently as his father inspected each item. "Is it okay, Pa?" he asked hesitantly. "I told Miss Merriweather it was a lot of stuff to get, and I really didn't need new shoes, but she said you wanted me to have it all."

Jake looked at Alicia. She sat on a chair, watching as he picked up the shoes they'd chosen. "I think Miss Merriweather did exactly right," he said finally. "I couldn't have done better myself." Then, as if the words he'd spoken registered with him anew, he looked away from her.

"I couldn't have done as well," he amended. "It would have been a day-long venture, just getting me to the store and back home. Thank you, ma'am, for helping Jason today."

She felt the flush of color rise to her cheeks as he

expressed his appreciation. It was the next best thing to a compliment, she decided, both his approval of her actions and his appreciation of her efforts. "I enjoyed it," she said. "Well—" she smiled at Jason as if they shared a secret "—all but the haircut part. That was an experience I'm not willing to repeat."

Jake frowned. "Did anyone give you a problem?" he asked harshly. "Did someone say something out of line?"

She shook her head. "No, I just felt uncomfortable in the barbershop with a whole row of men looking me over."

His eyes narrowed and then he made his own once-over of her appearance. "I don't see anything about you that would warrant undue interest," he said, his mouth twisting into a seldom seen smile.

"Well, that certainly put me in my place, didn't it!"

"You mistake my meaning," he told her. "You look like a decent, well-dressed woman to me."

She was silent. *Decent and well-dressed. The epitome of womanhood.* Somehow she would have preferred pretty, or elegant.

"I've hurt your feelings." It was a statement of fact. Jake rolled his chair closer to where she sat. For the second time in their brief acquaintance, he touched her. He reached out his hand and his long fingers grasped hers. Again she felt the warmth he exuded, and this time knew the strength of his grip.

Along with that sensation was a tension that seemed to travel from his hand to hers, a fact that surprised her, causing her to remove her palm from his grip. He looked up at her, eyes narrowed, unsmiling, and then glanced down at his own hand, clearing his throat.

She supposed he was strong, wheeling his chair around the house, lifting himself in and out of bed. She looked at him more fully. How did the man manage to tend to himself? It must be a major undertaking to get from his chair to his bed. She'd known him for almost two weeks—or at least been acquainted with him for that length of time, and was only now curious about the life he lived outside of the confines of that chair.

He reached for her hand again and held it firmly. She looked down at their joined fingers. "My feelings are not so easily hurt. I'm not so soft-skinned as all that."

"Perhaps your feelings are not especially tender," he told her. "But you are soft-skinned." His thumb rubbed over the back of her hand, and she felt the contact as if he'd dropped hot butter there and then rubbed it in. Silky smooth, his thumb massaged her flesh, and the gentle pressure sent heat shooting up her arm.

The man was only being polite. And she was behaving like a foolish female given her first bit of attention by a member of the opposite gender. Sadly, she'd had few encounters with men, and none of them had led to more than smiles and murmurs, and one never-to-be-forgotten kiss behind the lilac bush next to her parents' porch.

This time Jake was the one to break contact, dropping her hand as he backed his chair away and cleared his throat. "I repeat, Miss Merriweather. My thanks for your help." He looked over at Jason and raised his voice a bit. "How about taking your new things upstairs to your room? I expect you to put them away neatly."

As Jason gathered up his clothes and shoes and headed for the stairway, Jake turned back to Alicia. "The problem is that I have no idea how bad his room looks. I haven't been upstairs since we moved into this house. I thought of closing it off, but Jason wanted the bedroom next to the big maple tree and I couldn't refuse him."

"Are there bedrooms down here?" she asked, then recognized the foolishness of her query. There must be at least one, if Jake had a bed available to him.

"I sleep in the library," he told her. "The folks who lived here before called it their study, but I've filled it with books. If Jason slept downstairs, he'd have to use the dining room, and that would give him no privacy."

Alicia rose, smoothing down her skirts. "I think I'd better take my leave, Mr. McPherson."

"Alicia." He spoke her name softly and she turned toward him abruptly. "I think we might use our given names, don't you? I mean no disrespect, but *Miss Merriweather* is a pretty formal title for a woman who has made herself so important to my son." He smiled, and the effect was startling. The frown lines on his forehead disappeared and a small dimple appeared in his cheek, matching the one Jason owned.

"I think that would be permitted," she said. "Shall I call you Jake, or Jacob?"

"Better either one of those choices than the things you've been tempted to call me over the past couple of weeks," he said quietly. He watched her closely. "I'd like to ask a favor of you."

She stood stock-still, her gaze caught by the look of embarrassment he wore. "If I can do something to help, I'll be happy to accommodate," she replied.

"Do you think you could trim my hair?" he asked. "I know it's an imposition, and I have no right to expect such a thing from a lady, but I want Jason to—" He halted in the midst of his explanation and spread his hands wide. "I'm not much of an example for the boy. I've let myself become a recluse. I look like a hermit, and Jason deserves better than that from his father."

Alicia wanted to weep. It took all of her willpower to smile at Jake without allowing tears to well up. "I'd be happy to trim your hair…Jake. I watched Mr. Hamlet cut Jason's and I really think I could do as well."

"I wouldn't be a bit surprised." He rolled his chair

to the parlor door. "I have a pair of scissors in my room if you wouldn't mind doing it today."

The kitchen seemed to be the place best suited for the task, and Alicia found herself pinning a large towel around Jake's neck ten minutes later. She'd pushed the kitchen table against one wall, freeing up a large area in which to work. Jason sat wide-eyed on a chair and held the scissors. Jake's shaving mug and straight razor sat on the sink, in preparation for trimming his sideburns, and Alicia held a comb at the ready.

"Shall I wash it first?" she asked, for some reason breathless as she considered the deed she was about to embark upon.

"If you like," Jake said. "I washed it two days ago, though."

"It should be fine then," she said. Gathering her courage, she stepped closer to his chair and ran the comb hesitantly through the length of dark hair. Extending over his collar, it was raggedly trimmed. Obviously Jake had done it himself; the back looked as if it had been sawed at with a dull knife.

Beneath her fingers his hair was soft, silken to the touch, and she inhaled, aware that her breathing was a bit uneven. He glanced up at her, his eyes questioning, as if he sensed her apprehension. "All right?" he asked, then his mouth twitched and his eyes darkened as if he knew the extent of her unease, and was amused by her dithering.

Alicia only nodded and went to the sink for a cup of water. Dampening the comb, she drew it through his hair and then made her first cut. Uneven bits of hair fell to the kitchen floor and she blinked. Once she'd made the initial cut, she was committed.

Moving in a half circle, she trimmed and evened out the length of his hair, dampening as she went. And then she was faced with the front, where it hung over his forehead. "How do you want this part cut?" she asked.

"Your guess is as good as mine," he told her. "However it looks best to you."

She leaned from the side and gauged the first snip, only to have her wrist caught in his grip. "Step around in front of me," he told her. "I promise not to bite, Alicia."

Too close…she was too close to him. Too near the masculine scent of him, that musky blend she'd come to associate with this man, and the aroma of shaving soap that emanated from his skin. He'd shaved today, a fact she'd noted upon arrival. For her benefit? She smiled at the thought.

"What's so funny?" he asked, barely moving his lips as though he might disturb her concentration.

"Nothing. I was thinking of something else," she said hastily. Then she moved even nearer, her legs touching the front of his chair, the pressure of his right knee against her thigh. It was an intimate touch, his body heat radiating through her dress and petticoat. Beneath her fingertips, his face assumed a solemn look as she lifted the hair from his forehead and cut it in soft layers. The trembling she could not control threatened to botch her task before it was well under way.

He closed his eyes and she blew softly at the small clippings that fell on his cheeks. His nose wrinkled at that and she laughed, a soft sound that stilled his nose from wiggling and appeared to halt his breathing. Then his eyes opened—dark orbs that seemed to see beneath her skin, to the woman she kept concealed. She tensed, a shiver of anticipation traveling the length of her spine.

"You have lovely eyes," he said quietly. "I thought your hair was brown, but it isn't, is it? It's the color of chestnuts, sort of a ruddy hue."

She paused, holding the scissors upright. "Chestnuts?"

Again he smiled, and she stepped away from him, her fingers still tingling from the moments spent buried in his silken hair. He smiled at her, one corner of his mouth twitching. And yet, more than amusement lit his gaze as he searched her face and posed an idle query.

"Haven't you ever picked up horse chestnuts in the late summer and shucked them?"

She hesitated, not entirely trusting her voice to be steady. "No, I can't say I have," she replied, feeling she'd succeeded, her breathing steadier now that she was no longer held a willing captive by his warmth.

"I've done that, Miss Merriweather," Jason said eagerly, perching on the edge of his chair. "We play stuff with them. Kinda shoot them like marbles."

"I didn't do much playing when I was a child, Jason. You're a fortunate young man to have a father who allows you to play as a young boy should."

"All the boys play," Jason said, his brow furrowing as if he did not follow her line of thought.

"And so they should," she murmured, once more moving closer, the better to finish the task she'd begun. She lifted a lock of hair, drawing it to its full length, then trimmed the edges and allowed it to fall into place. The bits and pieces of shorn hair fell to Jake's shoulder and she reached automatically to brush them away.

"There," she announced briskly. "That should do it. I think you look fine, Mr. McPherson."

The word he murmured beneath his breath made her smile and she repeated it after him.

"*Jake.*"

THE HAMMER HIT THE BOARD and the nail went in true. "Bravo!" Alicia said, and offered Jason another nail. "We'll be hiring you out as a handyman before you know it," she told him.

"I suspect we can find enough for him to do right

here for a few days," Jake said from his place on the porch. He'd rolled out the door, stopping the chair a foot from the edge. Alicia had given the railing a dubious look, wondering if it was as sturdy as it should be, and felt a sense of relief when Jake moved no closer.

"I told Miss Merriweather I could do a lot of fixin' stuff around here." The boy was filled with his own importance this afternoon, and Alicia rejoiced in it. His eyes glowed, his cheeks were pink, and he smiled and joked without ceasing, it seemed.

"Maybe Miss Merriweather would let you call her Miss Alicia instead?" Jake suggested, aiming a questioning look in her direction as he spoke. "I think as long as you remember her proper name while you're at school, maybe she wouldn't mind if you break the rules just a bit after hours."

Jason's eyes widened as he considered the idea, then he looked at Alicia, his face earnest as he made his plea. "I'd like that if you don't think it would be disrespectful, ma'am."

She felt a churning in her breast and bent her attention fully on the boy. A wave of yearning almost swamped her, spilling over into two tears that made paths down her cheeks. "I think that would be fine," she said, her words clear and concise, her voice barely trembling. This boy had stolen a part of her heart.

Jake cleared his throat and issued a request. "Jason, do you think you could go out in the kitchen and get two glasses of that lemonade Miss Alicia made for us? My throat is drier than the Sahara Desert."

The boy grinned. "You're makin' jokes again, Pa." He placed the hammer on the step and sent a warning glance at Alicia. "Just leave it there, Miss Alicia, and I'll finish up the job when I get back."

The door closed behind him and Jake bent forward in his chair. "Can I say something to you, Alicia?"

She could only nod, acutely aware of her already teary state. She would not subject the two of them to such a display of sentiment.

"I've been thinking about something all day," Jake said. "I'd like you to be considering it, too."

She looked at him, frowning at the sober expression he wore. Only a moment ago he'd been smiling. Now he viewed her with a look akin to trepidation. "If you refuse, I'll understand," he said. "But at least think about it, will you?"

She was confused. "I don't think I know what you're talking about," she said finally.

"I'd like you to consider marriage, Alicia. To me." He sat upright again and his expression seemed remote, as if he were lost in a memory to which she would not be allowed access. "You said you did not plan on marriage, but I think you'd be a fine mother to my son. I'd ask nothing more of you than that you take him under your wing, be a mother to him and tend to his needs. On top of all that, I feel responsible for the damage done to your reputation over the past weeks."

She opened her mouth, then closed it again. Her words were slow, even though her mind was racing, repeating the phrases he'd used. "I don't hold you responsible for whatever gossip has been making the rounds, Jake. As to marriage, I'll admit that I hadn't thought of such a thing."

"I'll see to it you never want for anything," he told her, pressing on with determination. "I don't have a lot of money, but we're comfortable. I have an income from the ranch I own with my brother. He gives me one quarter of the profits, which is fair, since he does one hundred percent of the work. This house is free and clear and is well built."

She was swamped with myriad emotions. The unexpectedness of his offer—for it could hardly be called a proposal—was more than her mind could absorb. "I…I suppose I'll have to think about it," she said.

He nodded and his eyes clouded, as if she'd denied him already. "I understand that I'm no prize," he said quietly. "I'm hard to get along with, moody and temperamental. I've never been known as a nice man, Alicia. I'd probably be demanding, maybe even expect more from you than you'd be willing to give."

She managed a smile. "I'm sure you must have a few redeeming qualities. I can think of at least one, off-hand. You love your son, Jake. That you would consider taking on an old maid for Jason's benefit says a lot for you as a father."

"I haven't looked at you that way," he said. "I know you told me you're on the shelf, that you aren't the sort of woman to marry. But I find that I disagree with you." He raised his hand to halt her as she began to answer him. "Wait just a second, Alicia. Let me say this. I see you as a woman with a heart full of love for my son. I can ask no more of a wife. You have a beauty of your own." His eyes warmed as they met hers.

She shook her head. "Don't think you have to flatter me. I look in the mirror every morning. I know what I look like." She placed her hands on her hips and then hugged her waist. "I'm broad in the beam, my mama used to tell me. I have too much bosom—it makes me top-heavy." A flush touched her cheeks as she spoke. "I'm plain as dishwater, Jake. I don't consider myself a good-looking woman and that's all right. I'm a fine teacher, and that's what I've always wanted to be. I don't know if I could be a proper mother to Jason. That's something I'll have to think about."

"I won't push you for an answer. But there is one thing you need to consider. The damage to your reputation—" He broke off suddenly, turning to the door as Jason crossed the threshold with two glasses of lemonade held before him. The boy's tongue was caught between his teeth and a frown furrowed his brow.

"Let me take one of those," Alicia said, reaching for a glass. She tilted her head back and drank deeply. "I was so thirsty," she said brightly, thinking of Jake's unspoken warning, a warning she knew was valid. "Thank you for waiting on us, Jason," she said, flustered by Jake's offer. She looked down at the hammer the boy had left on the step. "You'll notice I didn't touch your tools while you were gone."

"Yes, ma'am," he said, carefully placing the other glass in his father's hand. He stepped carefully to the ground and lifted the hammer. Alicia handed him another nail and he placed it just so, then drove it home. His smile flashed and she returned it, nodding her approval.

Jake was watching her. She felt his gaze like a ray of sunshine, his eyes offering approval, his smile almost a duplicate of Jason's.

Jake McPherson was smiling at her, and he'd offered his approval. Indeed, for the second time today his mouth was curved in an unmistakable grin. *Glory be!*

CHAPTER FIVE

THE DECISION WAS NOT difficult to make. She'd already put an acceptance speech together by the time she walked back to her boarding house. Delivering her response might pose a problem, for Alicia feared she would become emotional. Perhaps writing a note would suffice.

No. Jake had made the offer face-to-face. She would do no less in return. The pros outweighed the cons, she'd already decided. Staying single meant being alone for the rest of her life. The likelihood of another man posing the question was unlikely. And Jake had twice spoken of her nicely, complimenting her appearance. *Hair the color of chestnuts.* Indeed.

Her age was a deterrent, for one thing. Then, too, her career as a teacher gave her no guarantee of an income for her old age. She would likely end up in poverty, for no matter how hard she scrimped and saved, her account at the bank showed a remarkably small balance.

The bottom line was that living in that big house would give new meaning to her life. Spending time with Jason would be a joy—although she was too wise not to acknowledge that he would offer her more challenges than you could shake a stick at.

Jake was truly the deciding factor. The man was alone, in every way. It was possible to live without the fellowship of another human being, but it was certainly not a pleasant way to spend your days. If she could find a way to reach him... She shook her head at the thought. Although, the idea of getting to know him better held appeal.

He had described himself well. Hard to get along with. Moody and temperamental. Demanding, and as he'd said, he would expect much from her. There would be no marriage relationship, of that she was certain, for Jake had long since placed a wall between himself and others. She stood no chance of surmounting the obstacles he'd set so firmly in place.

But for the first time in her life, she'd met her match. Another human being who could dish it out in abundance and not cringe when it was tossed back at him. He argued with her, said his piece with fervor and unless she missed her guess, he enjoyed their verbal sparring. Life would not be easy, but she'd find joy in that house with Jake and his son. And perhaps a friendship with the man that would fill her lonely hours.

She slowed her pace as she approached the porch to her boarding house and climbed the steps. The house was quiet, all but for little Catherine, who waved at her from her spot on the parlor couch, a book in her lap. What a contrast the girl was to Jason, who was as needy as a child could be. She looked forward to sorting him out and making a difference in his life.

Alicia sat on her bed after going to her room. She looked around at the small space, wondering what her future home would be like. She hoped for a bedroom with long windows reaching to the floor, with white curtains that might blow in the breeze at night. Perhaps a wardrobe to hold her clothing, not that she owned any great amount. But Jake had promised to provide her with all she needed.

I'll see to it you never want for anything. He'd made that promise right off. And if she were any judge of character, she'd put money on his ability to keep his word. Jake McPherson was a man of honor. That he should have given up on life, isolated himself in that big house and withdrawn from society for more than two years was a tragedy.

Alicia paced the floor, unable to sit still, aware that she would not be able to rest well until she'd given him her answer. And yet she must not appear too anxious. She bit her lip, wondering what a reasonable amount of time to consider the offer might be. Tomorrow? Would she be out of line if she walked back to visit on Sunday, after church perhaps?

When would he want to marry her? Next week? Next month? Or maybe by this time he'd reconsidered the whole idea and realized he'd been impetuous. She halted in the middle of the floor and raised a hand to cover her mouth. Surely not.

The door opened readily as she turned the knob and her feet barely touched the treads as she flew down the stairway. Catherine looked up from her book, eyes wide with alarm.

"Are you all right, Miss Merriweather?" The child had no doubt never seen her reserved teacher move so swiftly in the two years she'd known her.

"Fine, Catherine. I'll be gone out for a while."

The way to the McPherson home was becoming familiar to her, the path narrowing as she turned onto the side street.

She arrived, breathless and flustered, at Jake's front walk. The swinging gate caught her eye and she made a mental note to buy new hinges at the hardware. The clean finish of the new board drew her attention and she slowed to admire Jason's handiwork before she placed her foot in the center of it.

Then the front door was before her and she reached up with trembling fingers and removed the sign. *No*

Visitors. No Peddlers. No Admittance. Folding it neatly in half, she rapped sharply, then waited. From the length of the hallway, she heard the faint sound of rubber tires meeting the wooden surface of the floor, and then Jake's face appeared for a moment at the etched glass on the right side of the door.

He opened it, widely, she noticed, and waved her in. "Is something wrong?" he asked, his look one of apprehension. "Has something happened?"

She shook her head, feeling foolish now that she'd rushed over here and was making a spectacle of herself, after having left him only an hour ago. "No, I just thought we needed to talk a bit."

"I'm in the kitchen, helping Jason with supper." He turned his chair in a tight circle and nodded. "You're welcome to lend a hand."

He was attempting to be hospitable. Perhaps he was making an effort for her benefit.

She followed him, allowed him to push open the swinging door to the kitchen and then hold it for her to enter past him. Jason was at the stove, his back to her.

"Pa, I think I burned the eggs," he said regretfully. Indeed he had, for there was smoke and an overwhelming charred odor. He looked back over his shoulder, the skillet in his hand, and his mouth fell open. "Miss Merriweather...I mean, Miss Alicia." The skillet slipped in his pot holder and the dinner hit the floor, burnt eggs scattering across the wooden surface as if they'd developed a life of their own.

She took the situation in hand, her natural inclination to be helpful coming to the forefront. "Let me have that, Jason," she said briskly, reaching for the skillet. He obliged, obviously pleased with her interference, and backed away from the mess he'd made. "Find the broom," she told him, "and the dustpan, too."

The skillet was placed at the back of the stove and she bent to the task of cleaning the floor.

"You don't have to do that," Jake said flatly. "Jason can tend to it."

"I'm sure he can," she agreed. "But he could use a hand. And I'm available, after all."

"Are you?" The smile that touched Jake's lips asked more than his question suggested.

She stood, reaching for the broom. "About as available as a woman could possibly be, sir. I'm free to make my own choices, and I've made one over the past hour." She began to sweep the floor vigorously. "Would you like to hear my answer to the question you posed out on the front porch?" Her heart beat loudly in her ears as she avoided his gaze. Then she heard his soft chuckle, and looked at him quickly. "Are you laughing at me? Perhaps you've changed your mind?"

His eyes were sparkling, and she knew suddenly he'd been a scamp in his younger years. Were it not for the wheelchair and all it represented, he'd no doubt be popular with the ladies, even now. His mouth was full, his nose a sharp blade, his high cheekbones chiseled, and his hands well-formed.

He answered her questions succinctly. "No and no, Miss Alicia. I don't ask such an important thing lightly. I considered it long and hard before I made my proposal to you."

"Was that what it was? A proposal?"

"I didn't get down on bended knee, if that's what you're getting at," he said with a touch of sarcasm.

Ah, this was the man she knew. "I didn't expect you to," she snipped. "But then, I didn't really expect the question to be posed at all."

She finished sweeping up the remains and spoke to Jason, whose eyes were tracking the conversation and whose face was set in lines of confusion. "Please get a rag and wipe up the rest," she told him. "And toss this out into the yard. The birds will eat it. I believe I'll cook something else for the two of you for supper."

Jake cleared his throat. "I expected to live as a widower in this house for the rest of my days. But when you showed up at my door that first time, I knew I needed to do something different. For Jason's sake, if not my own."

"I gave you the impetus to change things?" she asked.

"That's a fancy way of saying it, but the answer is

still the same. You prodded me into thinking about the future. Not just my own, but my son's." He leaned back in his chair and folded his arms across his chest. "Now I'll have your answer, ma'am."

"I repeat, Mr. McPherson. I'm available, and I like the idea of having a house to run and a child to tend. Whether or not I'll be able to put up with your foolishness is another matter. But I won't know unless I give it a try, will I?"

He nodded in agreement. "Just one thing. My name is Jake. I've heard other women call their husbands by their formal address, but it doesn't work in my house. If you have to repeat it six or eight times an hour, do so. My name is Jake."

She took two steps to reach him and extended her right hand. "Shall we honor our bargain by shaking hands?" she asked.

"Yes, I believe we should," he answered. His wide palm made her strong, capable hand seem as that of a child, she thought. His hands were graceful, but large. As she'd noted earlier, his fingers were long and well formed. He'd been a concert pianist, she'd heard, but decided that was something they would not speak of now.

His eyes were dark with a look she could not decipher and she knew a moment of apprehension. She was committing herself to life with a man she hardly knew.

"Are you changing your mind?" he asked, his tone

mocking, as if he read her hesitant thoughts. He released her hand and watched as she shoved it in her pocket.

"No, not at all," she answered abruptly. "When I make a decision, I stick with it. You'll find me to be very predictable, Jake. I don't make promises lightly, nor do I accept those around me failing to keep theirs."

"Then I believe we understand each other." He looked up as Jason came back in the house.

"I did like you said, Miss Alicia."

"Then wash your hands and help me put a meal together," she told him. "What shall it be?"

They settled for a jar of beef Cord's wife had canned up and sent to Jake last fall. From the looks of the pantry shelf, Rachel McPherson took good care of her brother-in-law. At least so far as he allowed it. A jar of small new potatoes, canned with green beans mixed in, was opened and heated in a saucepan, and the beef placed in the skillet.

It was a simple meal, but one well appreciated, if Jason's and Jake's appetites were any indication. They ate silently, as if it had been a long time since food last appeared on this table, and Alicia almost feared taking a portion for herself when she noted their enjoyment of the food. Jake passed her the bowls though and nodded as she hesitated.

"The cook always eats at my house," he said. "Even

when we had a housekeeper, she ate what we ate. I figured it guaranteed us decent meals."

"Well, that's something I wouldn't have thought of," she said, smiling to herself. The man was canny, his thoughts a whirlwind, if she was any judge. And what he was thinking right now was something she'd give a whole lot to discover.

HE'D FELT A SENSE OF FEAR when she'd left earlier, had hoped against hope that he hadn't botched it with his offhand proposition. He'd certainly not offered her any hearts and flowers, but then he didn't think she'd have expected soft words and romance. If this arrangement was to work, it must begin on the right foot, so to speak.

Rena had been another story altogether. He'd been smitten with her from the time he was but a wet-behind-the-ears boy of sixteen. His childhood sweetheart had waited for him during the years of his training, then had waited some more while he went off to fight in that miserable war. He'd set her aside, ignored her, treated her unmercifully and still had not been able to put her out of his heart.

Rena had been persistent, and with Rachel as her ally, he hadn't stood a chance. The years spent with Rena had been a taste of heaven. And her death had plunged him into a torment surely not unlike what hell

must be. He'd thought never to find happiness again.
And perhaps he wouldn't discover any great degree of
it now.

But he had a suspicion that life with Alicia Merriweather might offer him some challenges, which
might be just what he needed. Not that she could do
much to change him. Never again would he leave himself open to the sort of pain he'd suffered when Rena
died. Loving a woman was a dicey situation. It offered
pleasure for today, but the knowledge that tragedy
could strike without warning was enough to make him
leery of ever giving that inner part of himself to another woman.

He regarded Alicia as she sat across the kitchen table
from him and ate sparingly. He knew she wanted him
and Jason to have their fill, so she would deny herself.

"Have some more meat, Alicia," he said, again offering her the bowl of beef and gravy. She shook her
head and smiled.

"I believe I've had enough," she said. "Perhaps
Jason would like more."

Jason would. Not even noticing the gravy that
spilled from the spoon, he helped himself to the savory
beef, and Jake winced. Alicia would have her work cut
out for her; Jason's manners were atrocious. Rena had
made a daily project of reminding the boy of good behavior. *Please* and *thank you* were important words to

learn, she'd said more than once. *A gentleman always holds the door open for a lady,* she'd told him. *Children must ask to be excused from the table.*

Jake smiled in remembrance, and for the first time the pain of loss was dulled by memory. Jason chewed and swallowed, then reached for the glass of milk Alicia had poured for him. It left a white moustache on his upper lip and he blithely ignored its presence. "Can I go?" he asked.

"Please may I be excused," Jake said, correcting him. "Yes, you may, and wipe your mouth, please."

Impatience ruled the boy's life, Jake thought, as Jason did as he was told and left the kitchen to go into the backyard. "He does have manners," he told Alicia. "It's just that sometimes he forgets."

"He's only a boy," she said, and he thought her eyes softened as she watched Jason's slight figure trot across the yard. "Will you tell him? Or shall I?"

"I'll tell him tonight," he said. "I doubt he'd protest, but I want to hear his opinion without you being there to blunt his response." He frowned. "I didn't mean that the way it sounded. It seems I must learn to watch my tongue with you."

"I wouldn't recognize you if you were unfailingly polite," she murmured, and he thought her eyes gleamed with mischief. She rose then and cleared the table, her movements womanly and sure as she handled the dishes and managed all the small tasks inherent in cleaning up after a meal.

Perhaps it would be difficult to adjust to a woman in the house. Sure, he'd suffered the presence of housekeepers over the past years; but this was entirely different. Once Alicia walked through that front door on their wedding day, she would not be leaving in a snit if things didn't go just the way she thought they should. Alicia Merriweather was not a woman to give her word and then go back on it. If she said she'd marry him and be a mother to his child, that's exactly what she'd do.

There might be some arguments, with sharp words spoken between them. But she wouldn't back away from a quarrel, if he knew the woman at all. And she wouldn't give in if she thought she was in the right.

He could deal with that.

"I DON'T WANT some other woman hanging around here!" Jake said harshly. "I told you I wanted you to be in charge of my household. Now you tell me you're going to hire a woman to clean for us. Why can't you do that? It's what wives do, as far as my memory serves me."

Alicia had known this would cause a problem, but it was an issue on which she decided to take a stand. "I can't take care of this big house and teach school, too," she said firmly.

"Then quit the damn school-teaching and stay home like other women do."

"I signed a contract for this year," she told him, aware that his anger was fast heading to the boiling point. "When I give my word, I keep it."

"When you marry me, you'll be giving your word, too. How do you plan to keep those vows if you're running off every morning to the schoolhouse?"

"I wasn't aware that you needed a woman around to wipe your nose all day, Jake," she said. "You're an adult male, fully capable of tending to yourself for six hours while I'm out of the house. And on two of those days, I'll have a capable woman here to do the heavy work and she can tote and carry for you if need be."

"I don't want a *capable* woman to look after me. I want you." Then he halted, his face ruddy with a combination of anger and, unless she missed her guess, a good bit of embarrassment. He ducked his head. "I didn't mean that the way it sounded."

"You have that line down pat," she returned. "I suspect I'll hear it repeated any number of times in the future."

"That may well be," he announced, spinning his chair in a half circle and rolling out of the kitchen. Her heart sang with the knowledge that the man enjoyed her presence. Perhaps not as a woman, but certainly as an adversary, one he respected.

She went back to her task, putting the finishing touches on Sunday dinner. Fried chicken to please Jason, mashed potatoes at Jake's request. She lifted her chin. He'd just have to get over his anger. A promise was a promise. Whether it was made to the school board or to a fiancé, it carried the same weight so far as she was concerned.

She whipped the potatoes with the masher, pouring in a dollop of cream and watching as a chunk of butter melted before her eyes. The chicken was in the warming oven and fresh corn on the cob sat in a small roaster on the back of the stove, staying hot. She'd found a pint jar of Rachel's applesauce in the pantry, and wished she might thank the woman in person for making things a little easier in this household.

Thanks in part to Rachel's stack of food, Alicia had not shopped for Jake's kitchen yet, and knew with certainty that the first time she did so she would be under the scrutiny of the townsfolk. Her name would be mud if anyone caught on to the fact that she was spending so much time here as it was. The wedding had better be planned quickly. She ceased her preparations and went off in search of the man who'd taken flight from her presence.

He wouldn't have gone far. The front porch was his boundary line, and she doubted he'd have gone out there without a good reason. The parlor seemed the most likely spot, and it was there she headed. The doors were open wide, but the room was empty. The dining room was dark and silent with no trace of Jake. That left the library, the room at the back of the house. His room—a room into which she had not ventured.

The door was closed and she rapped on it sharply. "Jake?"

Nothing stirred. No sound of wheels rolling across the floor. No protesting snarl from an angry man unwilling to be disturbed.

"Jake? I want to talk to you." Her voice grew firmer, her own irritation growing as he ignored her words. "If you don't come out here right now, I'm going to pitch this whole dinner out the back door and make such a fuss the neighbors will think you've taken leave of your senses." It was an idle threat, but perhaps he might believe her.

Ah! Now the wheels rolled across the floor, and now the handle turned and the door opened in front of her. "You know damn well you're too thrifty to toss food to the stray dogs of the neighborhood," he told her. "My money paid for that chicken and I plan on eating it whether you like it or not."

She suppressed a smile, difficult as it was. Jake was hungry, and willing to bluff his way back into her good graces. "Then get yourself back out in the kitchen," she said crisply. "I'll call Jason in."

They ate well, Jake enjoying the chicken as he had on the other occasion she'd cooked it for him. Jason was grinning from cheek to cheek, so delighted with the idea of Miss Alicia moving into his house he could barely restrain himself from spreading the news to the neighborhood. He'd been warned not to let the cat out of the bag until plans were made, but the effort was stretching his resolve to its limits.

"Are you gonna sleep in my Pa's room?" he asked, reaching for his third piece of chicken.

Alicia halted the movement of her fork, feeling a flush rise, knowing she looked the very picture of confusion. "I don't know. I hadn't thought about that."

"No, Alicia will have one of the rooms upstairs," Jake answered smoothly.

He'd apparently thought out this part of it, she decided, for his reply was quick and to the point. "You can help her choose which one she wants," he continued, never looking in her direction. "Maybe the one at the back of the house. Your mama always said it got the best breeze through the window."

"There ain't a big bed in there," Jason said. "Just that little, bitty thing. It's not any bigger than mine. I think Miss Alicia will need one like yours, Pa." The boy gave her a measuring glance and then he nodded. "Maybe we can move the one from the other bedroom back in there for her."

"I'm sure whatever is available will be just fine," she said, knowing discomfort such as she'd never felt in her life. The idea of her sleeping arrangement being discussed by father and son absolutely took the cake. "I'll go upstairs and figure something out." And as if that were the last word to be spoken on the subject, she shot a glare that included both of them.

She thought Jake looked relieved; Jason was oblivious to her mood and agreeable to whatever was decided.

The staircase was wide, with an oak banister and spindles that cried out for a dust cloth. The runner that fit the center of the steps was a nondescript color, no doubt due to the dirt Jason had ground into it over the past months. He had no interest in wiping his shoes at the door, and Alicia added it to her list of rules to be instigated.

The three rooms upstairs were spacious. The back bedroom had four windows looking out to the south and west. Alicia stood inside the door and surveyed the quarters. She slowly realized, as she looked down at the floorboards, that she was standing directly over Jake's room. Her bed would be almost atop his!

The idea of sleeping in the same house as Jake began to take on new meaning. He would note the sound of the mattress and springs squeaking every time she rolled over at night! Her footsteps would be discernible when she crossed the floor, and her every move would be open to his hearing.

On top of that, she would be obliged to dress as soon as she arose. No more lollygagging around in her wrapper while she fixed her breakfast. It would not be proper to appear in the kitchen without being fully clothed.

You're going to be his wife, and you can do whatever you please in this house. The words resounded in her head, as if they'd been spoken aloud. She looked behind her, but, of course, there was no one there. Jason was in the yard, Jake in the parlor, and she was alone.

From outdoors the birds sang and children's laughter rang out. Here in this room, there was only the peace of acceptance. How or why it should be, Alicia didn't know. Only that it was true. Tears streaked her cheeks as she stood stock-still in the middle of the room; her hands were folded before her, almost as if she had paused to pray.

She shook her head. Such foolishness. Her handkerchief was large, white and handy in her pocket. Mopping her tears with brisk movements, she walked to the nearest window, bent and lifted it, opening it wide to the breeze Jake had promised would be hers. He'd been right, she thought. The wind from the west blew stronger the higher from the ground you climbed, and the open window on the second floor seemed to beckon it within.

There was a dresser, a large wardrobe and a night-stand. All anyone could need for comfort. A rocking chair sat by the window, and she wondered if some mother, sometime or another had sat there in the middle of the night, holding a nursing infant to her breast. Shaking herself from the meanderings of her mind, she opened dresser drawers, finding them empty. Jake said the house had come to them furnished, and they'd only ever used Jason's room and the airing cupboard for storage.

Her feet were light on the stairs as she made her way back down. "The back bedroom will do nicely," she told Jake. "It's large and well lit, and a nice breeze blows through. You were right."

"Well, mark that one down," he said with a lifted eyebrow. "Jake was right once today, at least." He cast her a measuring look.

"You're being sarcastic at my expense," she admonished him. And then she sobered. "Will we be able to get along? Neither of us is a simple soul, Jake. We're both headstrong, I fear. You more than I, probably, but I'm afraid we'll bump heads often."

"It'll do you good to have someone disagree with you on occasion," he said. "I think you're used to having your own way, Miss Schoolteacher."

"Aren't you one to talk," she answered. "Mr. Agreeable, himself."

He laughed aloud. Jake McPherson laughed at himself and by his amusement invited her to join him. And she did.

CHAPTER SIX

"WHAT THE HELL BROUGHT all this on?" Cord McPherson's voice boomed from the parlor, and in the kitchen Rachel and Alicia halted supper preparations to listen.

"He's angry," Rachel said, to which Alicia nodded agreeably.

"I'd say he's related to Jake. Sounds just like him."

"What do you suppose he's hollering about?" Rachel frowned. "He's usually pretty laid-back when it comes to Jake." She smiled. "As a matter of fact, he's generally pretty easy to get along with."

"You wouldn't be prejudiced, would you?" Alicia asked.

Rachel had arrived half an hour previously, her youngsters in tow. Melody and Matthew were eleven and nine, as different as any brother and sister could be, but both well liked by Alicia and the roomful of students she taught. Rachel had pitched right in, joining forces to finish preparing the meal Alicia had begun. It was an auspicious occasion, one Jake had planned over the past two days, once he'd decided it was time to announce his wedding plans.

"Should we do this together?" Alicia had asked, and been promptly given a firm shake of Jake's head.

"I think I need to be alone with him. Cord's going to think it's a spur-of-the-moment idea, and I'll probably catch hell from him. You'd think he was nursemaid or something, the way he tries to look after me. I can almost guarantee he'll be upset because I didn't discuss this whole thing with him first."

"I think he wants to protect you, Jake. Maybe he thinks I'm after your money and looking for a soft place to land. And so far as this being a spur-of-the-moment idea...well, it is, you know," she'd conceded.

"There are many reasons why I might consider you as a wife, Alicia," he'd said tartly. "I think you're intelligent, quite attractive and certainly you'll be a good mother to Jason."

"I'm attractive?"

He'd grinned. "Yeah, sometimes you're downright pretty, in fact."

"Well, that's a switch," she'd said curtly.

"I'm serious," he'd said quietly. "You have lovely skin, beautiful eyes and we've talked before about your hair." She felt his scrutiny warm her through her clothing. She drew in a quick breath when he touched her hand. "I find you an attractive woman, Alicia."

She'd felt the heat of his body, knew a moment of confusion as his hand lent the warmth of his body to hers. She'd tried to shake off the sudden attraction she felt for him.

"What are they talking about?" Rachel asked, bringing Alicia back to the present. "Do you know?"

Alicia nodded, then pointed to a chair. "You might want to sit down while you hear this," she said with a wry grin. Rachel did as she was bid, and Alicia drew in a deep breath. "Jake and I are going to be married next Saturday. We've already asked the minister to have the ceremony here, and Jake wants you and Cord to join us."

"Married." The single word fell from Rachel's lips like a stone. She sat up straighter. "You're going to be married? When did you decide this? I wasn't even aware that you and Jake were acquainted until yesterday when we got the invitation to come to town today for supper." She looked askance at Alicia. "Are you really sure this is a good idea? Jake is a wonderful man, of course, but he's awfully temperamental, you know."

"I know," Alicia said serenely. "I've felt the full force of his temper more than once. He's also moody and stubborn."

"Well, it *sounds* as if we're talking about the same man," Rachel said agreeably.

A rumble of voices came from behind the closed

parlor doors. It seemed the two men were at least holding things down to a dull roar, Alicia thought with a smile. That Jake would triumph in this was not in doubt. If he couldn't persuade Cord to accept his marriage, he'd just go on without the other man's approval.

"You're sure?" Rachel asked quietly.

Alicia allowed her feelings to show, not entirely, but she knew her smile gave a clue to the other woman that this was a choice she had made gladly. "I have the chance to raise Jason as my own," she said. "I'd thought never to be married, Rachel. I'm outspoken and independent and...different than most of the other ladies in town. I'm far from you, as well."

"Well, you've certainly figured it all out, haven't you?" Rachel said sharply. "In the first place, you have lovely eyes, beautiful hair, smooth skin and a smile that would make any man sit up and take notice. I'd say you have all the right parts. In fact, you have a bosom many women would die to own. You're not what I'd call petite, but you're tall, so you carry your weight well."

Alicia laughed with delight. "You're a cheering section all by yourself, Rachel. I think I'm going to enjoy having you around."

"Well, let's just hope those two in there settle their fuss before they come out here and spoil this celebration we're about to put on the table," Rachel said. She tilted her head to one side. "Are you sure you don't want to use the dining room? There's going to be a bunch of us around this table."

Alicia shook her head. "You obviously haven't taken a good look at the dining room for a while. It's full of cobwebs and dust, and dark as a tomb. Once I get the parlor in hand, the dining room will be my next project."

"And this plan goes into effect on Saturday? That's not long to get a new dress made."

"A new dress? Do you suppose I'd better be thinking along those lines, too?" Alicia felt panic strike. "I hate to go shopping. Nothing ever fits."

"You won't need to go shopping. I can sew up a storm," Rachel told her. "We'll buy some pretty yard goods and I'll measure you, then you can decide how you want your dress made. It won't take any time at all to have it ready."

"You're sure?" Alicia felt a bit dubious about taking advantage of the other woman, but the offer was too good to refuse.

"It's decided already," Rachel said firmly.

"What's decided?" Cord asked from the doorway. His eyes pinned Alicia where she stood, and she thought his mouth was a bit too firm for friendly conversation. "Jake tells me the two of you are getting married," he said.

Rachel moved to his side, her hand clutching his

forearm. "Isn't it wonderful?" Her smile was directed at his face, and for a moment Cord's expression faltered, softening at his wife's query. As Alicia watched, Rachel's fingers gripped Cord's flesh tightly, and he grinned suddenly.

"All right, sweetheart," he said agreeably. "I'll back off."

She leaned upward, standing on tiptoes to press a kiss against his cheek.

"Is that the best you can do?" he asked beneath his breath. Alicia heard the note in his voice that promised retribution at a future time, and then Rachel laughed.

"You'll find out," she said glibly. "Now, the two of you come in here. We've got supper about ready to put on the table. Call the children in, Cord. I think Matthew and Jason are teaching Melody the fine art of playing mumblety-peg."

Cord muttered a word Alicia pretended she hadn't heard and then looked at Rachel. "His language leaves a lot to be desired some days," Rachel admitted with a shrug.

"If Melody gets cut, you get to take care of it," Cord told his wife, and then as his half-grown daughter approached, his eyes lit with pride.

"She's got him wrapped around her little finger," Rachel whispered.

"Has not," Cord responded automatically, and Alicia suspected this was an ongoing conversation. For just a moment she envied the love these two obviously shared.

"Everything all right?" Jake was at her elbow and he touched her hand, drawing her attention. Sober as a judge, he was, she thought, and in an attempt to relieve his concern, she bent to him, aware of the unique scent of the man she'd promised to wed.

"Fine," she whispered, her mouth close to his ear. "I like Rachel."

His fingers clasped her hand and he squeezed it gently. "Good girl."

She preened. There was no other word for it. Her mouth curved in a smile, her chin lifted proudly, and she returned the pressure of his fingers.

The children storming through the back door caught her attention then, and she moved away from Jake's chair. "Wipe your feet," she said, the words automatic as Jason crossed the threshold.

"Yes, ma'am," he answered, and shot a look that reeked of pride at his cousins. *See? What did I tell you?* The words might as well have been spoken aloud, so obvious was the boy's message.

"This is your aunt Alicia," Rachel told her children quietly, drawing them within her arms, one on either side of her. "She and your uncle Jake are to be married."

"No, Mama," Matthew said stoutly, ignoring the

second part of his mother's announcement. "That's Miss Merriweather. You know that. She's our teacher."

Melody looked long and hard at her uncle Jake, then back at Alicia. Her smile was subtle, her expression more adult than child as she nodded her acceptance. "Shall we call you Miss Merriweather in school?" she asked.

"There are only a few days left to worry about it, but I think that might be wise," Alicia answered. "You don't mind, do you?"

Melody's expressive face held a touch of sorrow. "No. Aunt Rena wouldn't, either. She always wanted everybody she loved to be happy." As if that solved the whole thing, she turned to the sink to wash her hands for supper.

Cord set aside his disapproval with a wave of his hand as Jake murmured something for his brother's ears alone. "I know. It's all right," he answered, and then held out his hand. Jake took it, and then was obviously stunned when his brother bent low and hugged him instead. "It's all right," Cord repeated aloud.

"RACHEL IS GOING to make me a dress," Alicia said. They were at the front door, watching as Cord's surrey moved from in front of the house. Jason leaned on the fence, watching them head out of sight.

"I'll give you money for the material," Jake told her

quickly. "Or else just put it on my credit at the general store."

"No." One word sliced between them, and Jake jerked his head back to look up at her.

"Why the hell not?"

"Please don't curse at me," she said stiffly. "I was taught not to use such language. And my reasons for buying my own wedding dress should be obvious, even to you."

"Well, *obviously* they aren't. I have a running bill at the store, and you have the right to use my credit."

"I'm not your wife yet, Jake. And until I am, I'll provide for my own needs. No one will say I've married you for what you can give me."

He was silent, and then he nodded. "All right. I can understand your thinking. As to the other, I'm sorry I insulted you with my language. I'll try to clean it up."

She looked down at him in surprise. "Is this Jake McPherson I'm talking to? Where did all this sweetness and light come from?"

"Maybe I'm pleased that my brother will stand up for me at our wedding, and I'll be just one less responsibility for him to worry about. You may not be marrying me for what I can give you, Alicia, but I fear my motives are not altogether pure."

She frowned. "And what does that mean?"

"Having you in my life will free Cord up from the

visits he's felt obliged to make, checking up on me and seeing to things I haven't been able to take care of."

"Are you sure he feels an obligation to look after you, Jake?" she asked. "Did you ever consider that maybe he loves you and enjoys spending time with you?"

Jake shrugged diffidently. "Maybe, to a point. Nonetheless, having you here to do the shopping and banking, and just dealing with the everyday household business will make my life a hell—" He stopped suddenly and grinned.

"See there? I'll have to work hard at the language thing, Alicia. Anyway, you know what I mean, I hope. I'm planning on taking shameful advantage of you…and your good nature." The last was spoken with a touch of sarcasm.

"I'm nice every once in a while," she told him, pleased that he was becoming comfortable with their decision. That was the bottom line, she thought. They should enter this marriage with the right attitude, knowing and understanding what each stood to gain.

She moved into the parlor and heard Jake's chair following her. Choosing a seat on the couch, she waited until he drew near and then spoke quietly.

"I want to ask you about something," she said, having decided on the spur of the moment that she'd put this encounter off long enough. "I don't know much about your life before three years ago, but I've heard talk in town. I'd rather hear the details from you, Jake."

"Like what?" He bristled. There was no other word for it. Had he been a dog, his hackles would have been standing on end.

"I was afraid you'd take offense, but I think I need to know about your life before Rena died. More to the point, I think I deserve to know. I'll feel as if I'm in the dark if folks begin to speak to me about it, and I haven't an idea what they're talking about."

"That's easily solved. Just tell anyone who quizzes you that it's none of their damn business. And that's one cuss word I'll not apologize for," he said forcefully. "My life before you met me is the past. We won't dwell on it, and I don't want to discuss it."

"Is that your final word on the subject?" she asked, rising from the couch and smoothing her skirt. "If so, I think we have a problem. We'll discuss it another time, when I've had a chance to make up my mind about this."

"Wait, Alicia," he called as she headed for the parlor door. He reached out and snagged her skirt, holding fast to the material he grasped. "I won't let you walk out on me this way. You seem to think I'll give in if you make threats, and trust me, sweetheart, I won't."

She stiffened. "Don't call me that. I'm not your

sweetheart. You had one of those in your life already. I've accepted the fact that I'll be a poor substitute for Rena. Don't insult me by using that term so loosely and with such sarcasm."

He released her, carefully brushing her skirt as if to remove the wrinkles he'd put there. "For that you have my abject apology, Alicia. Go on home. We'll talk later."

She left then, waving a farewell at Jason as he played hopscotch with a neighbor girl in front of the house. "I'll see you in the morning, Miss Alicia," he called out, and then, in a softer voice, he said to his friend, "Miss Alicia and my pa are gonna get married next Saturday. She's gonna live in our house from now on."

"Don't count on that too much," Alicia murmured under her breath as she stepped up her pace. One good thing about being tall was that she marched along rapidly when the spirit moved her. This evening she felt the need for action. If she were a child she'd be running right now, away from her angry exchange with Jake. If she exerted herself with a brisk walk, maybe she'd be tired enough so that she might actually sleep tonight.

Somehow that prospect didn't seem likely, she thought. Jake McPherson was a stubborn man, she'd known that from the beginning. If he wouldn't talk to her, she'd go over his head. One way or another, she'd find out what she needed to know.

In one corner of his parlor sat a grand piano, covered with dusty sheets and taking up a large part of the room. Unless she missed her guess, Jake was determined never to touch the keys again. A tragedy in itself, if what she'd heard about him was true. Catherine's mother had shown her a poster advertising Jacob McPherson's debut concert in Green Rapids eleven years ago.

Any man who played well enough to perform in front of the whole town must be talented, she'd decided. Somehow, his love for music must be regenerated. How it was to come about, she had no idea, but she hadn't been called obstinate and bullheaded by her father for nothing. If Jake married her, he might as well know right off that she planned to bring some purpose to his life.

"I'M GOING TO ASK YOU for your help, Rachel." She'd thought it over, and approaching her would-be sister-in-law seemed like the best path to take. Rachel looked up from her sewing machine and arched an eyebrow at Alicia, nodding serenely.

"What do you want to know?" she asked. "Let me tell you right off that I've been waiting for you to begin asking questions. And I don't mind providing answers. I wouldn't do anything in the world to hurt Cord's brother. He's been my brother, too, for a long time now, and I love him dearly. But the man is like a wounded bear, and he's needed somebody to pull the thorn out of his paw for a long time."

"That story was about a lion, not a bear," Alicia said with droll humor. "Since you've managed to read my mind, I'll only ask one thing of you. Tell me about the piano in the parlor and about his training. What he's capable of."

"That would take a while," Rachel said, lifting the skirt of Alicia's dress to check the stitches. She held it before her, shaking it and then turning it so that the sleeves were before her. "I just have to hem these by hand and we'll be done," she said. "You're going to look lovely, Alicia."

"Pretty is as pretty does, my mama used to say. What do you suppose that means?"

Rachel shrugged. "Probably not much. We've already had this discussion, anyway. Jake likes the way you look, and that's all that matters."

"You think so?" She cleared her throat, hoping to disguise the wistful note she'd inadvertently allowed to creep into her voice. "He thinks I'm efficient and capable and will make a good mother for Jason. Let's not pretend this is a love match, Rachel."

"I didn't mean that it was. I don't think anyone falls in love that quickly. But I do think that, given time, you're going to be very happy with Jake. I'll remind you of this conversation one day," she said with a smile. Leaning forward, she touched Alicia's hand. "I like you, my friend, more than I'd thought possible. I'm hoping we'll be sisters in every way there is."

"Oh, please, don't make me blubber," Alicia said, feeling tears of gratitude well up. "I'm not a sentimental woman, but that sort of talk will turn on the waterworks if you're not careful."

"A few tears never hurt anybody," Rachel said, threading her needle with care. She looked over at the kitchen range. "Why don't you put my irons on the front of the stove, and you can press this when I'm finished."

"All right." Alicia rose and did as she was asked. The dress was beautiful, rose-colored and nicely fitted across the bodice. Her waist was defined by the lines of the pattern Rachel had used, and at first Alicia had felt uncomfortable at the accentuated display of her womanly shape.

"You have good lines," Rachel had said firmly. "I believe in showing off your good points."

Alicia had given in to Rachel's superior knowledge as far as fashion was concerned. If the woman said the dress was becoming to her, she'd just have to take her word for it. Alicia's own sense of style was sadly lacking, a fact she had admitted to herself years ago.

She set up the ironing board, and was soon at work pressing the dress. Rachel sat watching, chatting quietly. "Jake spent years at the conservatory in New York City, played in concert halls and was an acclaimed success," she said. "Then the war came along. His father had a fit when he put on a uniform and picked up a gun. He'd already bought the piano for Jake's use and had it installed in the parlor here."

"But Jake couldn't play it afterward, could he?" Alicia asked. "Not without having a foot to touch the pedals."

"That's the wonderful part of this story," Rachel said. "A piano tuner came one day, a blind fellow, old and wise. He told the blacksmith how to fit the piano with wires that connected with the pedal. Then they built a pedal that could be used by Jake's right knee. It wasn't perfect, but it worked.

"I'll never forget the morning he first sat down and played." She shivered as if the memory was one that brought a thrill to her very being. "After his marriage to Lorena he worked for the opera company, making arrangements for touring companies to visit Green Rapids, setting up concerts for various artists. It brought some culture to this town, something we've lacked ever since Rena died."

"Then Jake withdrew," Alicia murmured, holding her iron in the air as she whispered the words.

"Yes." Rachel's eyes filled with tears. "Rena would hate it if she knew that Jake buried his music in the grave that day in the cemetery. I think he was so angry, he just determined never again to gain any pleasure from the instrument he loved. And he hasn't. He just sat and brooded. Until you came along."

"He still broods a bit," Alicia said. "He's a difficult man."

"But you love him, don't you?" Rachel asked softly.

Alicia shot her a surprised look. "I hope it doesn't show. I'll never tell him. I wouldn't put him under that sort of obligation."

"I'll never tell," Rachel said firmly, lifting her hand to make an X over her breast. "Hope to die if I tell a lie," she intoned with a smile.

"I haven't allowed myself to even think about it, not till this minute," Alicia said. "I know what I'm risking in this marriage, Rachel, but I know it's the right thing for all of us. Especially Jason. He needs a mother as much as any little boy I've ever seen in my life. I think I can fill the bill."

"I know you can," Rachel told her. "Your presence in that house will work a miracle. Maybe not this week or even this year, but someday, down the line, things will do a complete turnaround for you and Jake. You'll be glad you took the chance."

"I'm getting a little nervous," Alicia said. "The big day is only forty-eight hours away. I know there isn't much preparation to do, just final cleaning in the parlor, and a meal to put together. I've hired a lady in town to help me. She's cleaned floors, and together we washed every window in the house. I found some pretty new curtains for the parlor. They let in all the light, and Jake hasn't complained about them."

"I doubt he will," Rachel said bluntly. "He's appreciative of everything you've done. He may not say so, but I can't even begin to describe to you the difference in the man. It's almost like he has a new lease on life."

"Well, he's not very happy with me right now," Alicia said. "We aren't talking, to tell you the truth. I asked him about the past, about what he was like before Rena died, and he threw a fit."

"That sounds like Jake," Rachel said, laughing and shaking her head. "The first time I ever saw him he scared me half to death. He was wild and woolly and ranted at me like a madman."

"That sounds familiar. You must be acquainted with the sign on his door that dared anyone to rap on it?"

"It was effective, you have to admit that. How did you have the nerve to get past it?"

"I've always had more guts than brains, my mama used to say. In fact, I took it down one day and put it in the trash bin, and he hasn't mentioned it. I suspect he thought he'd do well to pretend he didn't notice it was missing."

Alicia looked down at the watch she wore pinned

to her dress front and sighed. "It's past time for me to leave. It'll be dark by the time I get back to town as it is."

"Well, get going, then. I'll have Sam bring your buggy up to the house for you."

"It's Jake's buggy, you know," Alicia told her. "He'd had it stored at the livery stable and told me I might as well use it. He sent Jason to the livery and gave orders that he wanted to buy a new mare to pull it. Then gave me the whole kit and caboodle. He said it was a wedding present."

"What did you get for him?" Rachel asked, rising and going toward the back door.

"I'll decide that tomorrow. I don't know what to choose. I'm going to the general store in the morning."

"Did he get you a ring?"

Alicia nodded. "He sent a note to the jewelry store— you know, that new little place by the bank. Directed the man come to the house with a whole assortment of rings, and he chose one for me." She blushed and smiled, remembering. "Actually he had me pick it out. Said I'd be the one wearing it, and I'd better find one I liked, since I'd have it on my finger for a long time."

"Sounds like a man with a plan," Rachel said.

The buggy was brought from the barn, and once Alicia had folded her dress with care and placed it beside her on the seat, she was ready to leave. Impetuously, she hugged Rachel and listened to her voice whisper words Alicia had never thought to hear from another woman.

"I love you, sister of mine." Rachel reached to brush back a wisp of hair that had fallen against Alicia's cheek. "Be happy."

Her natural reserve almost kept her from replying, but she'd learned over the past weeks to let down her guard, and now she did so, gladly and freely.

"I love you, too, Rachel. Thank you."

CHAPTER SEVEN

"WHAT'S THIS I HEAR about a wedding?" Mr. Harris leaned over the counter toward Alicia, his voice booming. "Minister's wife said tomorrow's the big day."

The eyes of several women turned in her direction and Alicia froze where she stood. After a moment she gathered her nerve to speak. "That's right, Mr. Harris. I'll be the new Mrs. Jacob McPherson by this time on Saturday."

That was enough to set tongues into action all over the store, and the ensuing flurry of conversation brought a smile to Alicia's lips. From behind her, one of her students tugged at her skirt. "Ma'am?" the child said, gaining her teacher's attention. "Ain't you gonna be our teacher anymore?"

The murmurs of the store patrons stopped dead as Alicia bent to answer the little girl. "Of course I'm going to be your teacher, Beatrice. Did you think I could just leave all my children to fend for themselves? I'll be your teacher for the rest of the school year."

The girl hugged Alicia impetuously. "My mama said you was gonna have your hands full just keepin' Jason in line, without taking care of a whole schoolhouse full of children."

Alicia laughed, wondering if the "mama" in question was the lady with crimson cheeks, standing just to her right. "Jason and I get along very well," she assured the child.

"It'll be the boy's pa she'll have to contend with," another lady offered, shooting a pitying glance at Alicia, who had now become the center of attention.

"I get along nicely with Mr. McPherson, too," Alicia said sharply in her best schoolteacher voice. She surreptitiously crossed her fingers at the gravity of her fib. Although she supposed it could be said that getting along didn't always mean agreeing on every subject.

"You got a new dress for the big day?" Mr. Harris asked. "If not, I'll warrant I can help you find something."

Alicia shook her head. "Rachel McPherson made me a dress this week. It's really quite lovely."

"How about a new pair of shoes? Maybe a pretty nightgown?" Mr. Harris was persistent, and his questions made Alicia blush furiously.

"I have shoes enough," she said. "And—" she glanced around at the women who were now actually circling her "—I don't think I need another nightgown. I already own several."

Enough was enough, Alicia decided firmly. "Actually, I'm here to find something appropriate for Mr. McPherson—for a wedding gift." She looked at all the ladies in turn. "Perhaps one of you ladies has a suggestions for me?" she asked smiling sweetly.

As do all women when asked for their advice, the ladies warmed to the subject and, in turn, to Alicia. "How about a pocket watch?" one asked.

"Maybe a book of poetry?" said another, to which Alicia almost laughed aloud. Visualizing Jake reading a book of poetry was an exercise in disbelief.

"A pair of cuff links? Or maybe—" the lady paused "—maybe a ring?"

Another woman spoke up. "I've heard that men are wearing wedding rings these days. My sister's husband has one. Says it keeps the women at arm's length."

What would Jake say to that? Alicia wondered, then decided she'd be better off to settle for the cuff links. Although where he would wear them, she had no idea. The man hadn't darkened a church door in almost three years, and didn't seem likely to make a habit of it in the future.

"What is he giving you?" one of the ladies asked, her eyes bright with curiosity. Leaning toward Alicia, she seemed almost to be holding her breath.

"Actually," Alicia said with satisfaction, "he gave me a buggy and a new mare to pull it. He wants to make certain I have transport when I want to go somewhere. He's kept it at the livery stable up until now, but he's having a shed built for it right soon."

"A horse and buggy? He hasn't gotten you a ring?" another woman asked, disappointment edging the words.

"Yes, he bought me a ring. In fact, he had me make the selection myself. The new jeweler in town came out to Mr. McPherson's home and offered us a nice selection to choose from."

"Well, I have a real dandy pearl-handled penknife in this glass cabinet I'll warrant any fella would like," Mr. Harris said, pointing at a shallow case where several knives were displayed. He opened the lid and drew forth a specimen that brought a sigh from a young boy who watched from down the counter.

"This'n is made from German silver, with a genuine pearl handle and four blades. You won't find a better knife anywhere. Any man would be proud to own it." He leaned closer and the boy, who had pressed his way nearer, edged forward, the better to inspect Mr. Harris's offering.

"It's only two dollars," the storekeeper said, intoning the price with awe, as though his product was of much greater value than that paltry sum.

Two dollars was a lot of money in any man's language, Alicia thought privately, but if Jake would like the knife, she was willing to raid her bank account for it.

"That's a dandy," the young boy said, now standing beside her. "If I ever get married when I get old, I'd like to have one just like it."

To Alicia's ears, the boy's reverence signified approval, and she turned the knife over in her hand, admiring the pearl finish. "Lined with solid brass, too," Mr. Harris added eagerly.

"I believe I'll purchase it," Alicia said. "Does it come with a case?"

"That's ten cents extra," he told her. "For another nickle, I'll put it in a nice box, too, and you can wrap it up when you get it home."

"That sounds like a deal to me," she told him, relieved that the decision had been made. Around her the ladies were conferring; one of them spoke up to ask if Alicia would like to join them at a quilting bee the following Tuesday. She offered a regretful smile.

"I'm sorry, but I'm going to have my hands full, just moving my belongings and settling in at Mr. McPherson's home this week. Perhaps another time, thank you."

She paid Mr. Harris, then watched as he fit the knife into an appropriate case and searched for a suitable box. Finally, the deed was done and Alicia counted out the money for her purchase. It left her exactly forty cents in her reticule, but since there didn't seem to be anything else she needed, she was satisfied.

And then she spied the jar of candy sticks. "I believe I'll take a half dozen of those for Jason," she said. "Various flavors, please."

As Alicia left the store, she once again felt all eyes focused on her, and knew the women were bursting with questions, none of which they had the courage to ask.

She was just as glad. Her arrangements with Jake were personal and private, and sharing any of their bargain with an outsider was unthinkable. Her steps were brisk as she marched down the sidewalk and headed for her rooming house. The carpetbag she'd already packed was waiting inside her bedroom and her trunk was open, almost filled to the brim, just a few items left to be added.

With only her wedding dress hung on the wall, the room seemed empty as if she'd already taken her leave. Alicia stood inside the door and leaned against it. She would sleep in that bed tonight for the last time.

She thought of the large room she would have as her own in Jake's house. There would be a place to put her beloved books, drawers for her small things and a wardrobe in which to organize her dresses and shoes. The larger bed from the other room was yet to be moved in, but Cord had said he would come into town this afternoon and do that for her. He'd promised to pick her up and carry her things to his surrey and transport them.

She would leave behind only a few things for now, all of them a part of her wedding apparel—the dress Rachel had made and the petticoats she'd purchased to wear beneath it. Her best shoes sat near the window and her nightgown lay across the bed. An assortment of personal items sat on the dry sink.

She went to the window as the sound of voices caught her ear and she saw the surrey at the front gate. Cord was speaking with Catherine's father and then the two men walked toward the house, Cord looking up as though he felt her gaze upon him. He raised his hand in greeting and she waved back, then picked up her carpetbag and placed it outside her room in the hallway.

With a flurry of movement, she tossed her slippers and wrapper into her trunk and closed the lid—then awaited Jake's brother. He was there in moments, peering in the open door and grinning in her direction. "You all ready?" he asked.

At her nod, he bent and picked up the heavy wooden trunk, placing it on his shoulder and making his way toward the staircase. "I'll get the carpetbag," she said, coming behind him, but Catherine's father was there beside her and beat her to it.

She felt cosseted, a rather pleasant experience, she thought. She was used to fending for herself, as she had for her whole life. Now it seemed she had two gentle-men toting and carrying for her. She followed Catherine's father down the stairs and out the front door. Cord was already stowing the trunk in the backseat of the surrey and her carpetbag was placed beside it.

"Let's get going," he said, offering his hand so she could climb up on the seat. She accepted it readily, and her thoughts immediately flashed to the touch of Jake's hand on the occasions when it had brushed against her own. There was no flare of heat, no tingle of awareness to be gained from Cord's callused palm against hers.

It was just a hand…whereas Jake's strong fingers and wide palm seemed imbued with the ability to make her aware of each muscle and sinew that covered the bones beneath his skin.

Cord picked up the reins, urging his horse to a trot, and headed for the big house just a quarter mile away. The man was strong, tall and capable, but she felt no shivering response to his smile, knew no aching need for his approval. Rachel had been right. Love had entered the picture.

The surrey drew to a halt before the sagging gate and Cord murmured disapproving words under his breath. "I've already bought new hinges," Alicia said, aware of his irritation at the sight.

He shot her a look of surprise. "*You're* going to fix it?"

"Jason will help me," she told him. "We worked on

the porch step a while back and Jason has learned some skills over the past weeks." Then she smiled.

"Jake is going to have a shed and lean-to put up out back so we can keep the horse and buggy he gave me for a wedding gift, handy for me when I want to go out."

"I heard Jason helped board up the schoolhouse windows with you," Cord said, his eyes crinkling at the corners. "He bragged to Matthew that he could handle a hammer better than Miss Merriweather."

She shrugged. "He's learning. He'll be helping supervise the shed building."

The trunk was carried upstairs and Jason lugged the carpetbag, eschewing her offer to take it herself. "Pa says I'm to help you with whatever you need," he told her earnestly. "He told me I'm old enough to pitch in with whatever needs doin'."

"Shall we tackle the gate this afternoon?" she asked in a low voice. "After your uncle Cord leaves, we should have time to work on it before supper."

The beds were exchanged quickly. Clean sheets that had not seen the light of day in years were in the airing cupboard and smelled of lavender.

"Mama always liked to have her sheets smell nice," Jason said, sniffing the fabric as he carried them into Alicia's new bedroom.

"You miss your mama, don't you?" Alicia asked.

She snapped the first sheet and watched as it drifted down to cover the mattress.

"Yeah, I guess. But not so much lately," he admitted. "It's nice having you around to do stuff for us."

"I hope you won't change your mind about that," she said, holding the first of her pillows beneath her chin in order to slide the embroidered pillowcase into place.

"Why should I?" Jason asked, rocking in the chair by the window.

"There are some new rules I think we should put in place," she said quietly. The second sheet went on and was tucked in at the bottom, the corners neatly squared. She tossed a quilt over the top and propped the set of pillows against the counterpane.

Jason had watched her, his eyes narrowed. "What kind of rules?" he asked.

"We'll work that out one evening next week, I think," she told him. "Your father will want to be included in the list-making."

Cord stuck his head in the doorway. "I'm leaving now," he said. "We'll be here right after noontime tomorrow for the ceremony. Rachel's cookin' up a storm out at the ranch. She said not to worry about the food. She's handling everything."

"I feel like I should be doing something," Alicia protested.

Cord looked around the room and then stepped

back, motioning toward the wide staircase. "I'd say you've already worked a miracle on this place. That parlor hasn't looked so spiffy in years. I like the new curtains you hung." He grinned. "Jake looks better in broad daylight, don't you think? I thought for sure we'd never get him out of the dark, Alicia."

His grin faded and he stepped a bit closer. "You've been good for him. I hope he'll give you a decent life here."

"I'm planning on it," she said, reaching to tug at a lock of Jason's hair. "We're going to be a family."

"Why don't you run on down and give my mare a drink from a bucket, Jason?" Cord asked. Jason nodded and clattered down the stairs.

"I want to tell you something, Alicia," Cord began, his face a bit flushed as if he were embarrassed by the words he would speak. "I wasn't in favor of this wedding when Jake told me what he was planning, and I know you heard me carrying on in the parlor. But I need to let you know I've changed my mind. If ever a man needed a woman to look after him, it's my brother. I hope he'll give it his best shot, really try to make you happy here."

"I'm of the firm belief that we all make our own happiness, Cord," she said. "I've never looked to another person to make my days happy or my life complete. I'm simply hoping Jake and I will get along well and give Jason the sort of home he needs."

Cord's voice lowered as he looked intently at her, as if he could read the meaning behind her words. "I hope for more than that. My brother is capable of loving deeply. He's been hurt, but the man has much to offer, if he'll just give you room in his life. You're a woman who deserves to be loved. I'd like to think that Jake will realize that one day."

"Thank you," she said. There were no other words to express her appreciation for his good wishes, and for the courage it took to speak so honestly about his brother. "I think I'm going to like having a brother, Cord." She stepped closer to him and grasped his hand. "Rachel has already named me as her sister. I'd like to think I can be a sister to you, too."

He reached for her, his arm circling her shoulders, and dipped his head to press a kiss against her cheek. "I'd like that," She thought his voice sounded deeper, choked up even, and then he cleared his throat. "As a matter of fact, I'm planning on it."

JAKE SAT ON THE PORCH as Alicia and Jason worked on the gate. Shiny new brass screws held the hinges in place. The gate was heavy and Alicia stood by, holding it at the right height until the boy properly tightened the screws. The job completed, Jason reached out, pushing the gate to and fro as he laughed aloud in triumph.

"Did'ja see what we did, Pa?" he called out to where Jake sat watching. His pride was almost palpable, Alicia thought.

"Why don't you take care of the tools while I pick up the old hinges and make sure we didn't leave any screws lying around," she told Jason.

Agreeably, he did as she asked, then paused to speak to his father for a moment. The boy's delight was almost enough in itself to make this marriage worthwhile, Alicia thought. Cord might have high expectations from their arrangement, but Alicia would be content to see Jason blossom, would be happy to watch Jake perhaps regain the sort of life he'd once had.

But change would come slowly, she reminded herself. Jake was not a man to be rushed, and he would not think twice about thwarting her plans should he not agree with them. She would be dealing with a man not easily managed.

"Are you going to stay for supper?" Jake called. He watched her as she approached the porch, his gaze touching her from head to toe, a realization that made her uncomfortable in the extreme. Did he see a woman too old, too tall and too plain to find a husband?

"Thank you, I think I might," she said decisively. "What can I fix? Do you have any ideas?"

"Rachel sent us some fish she canned last summer. How about some fried fish cakes?"

"I can do that," Alicia said. "I'll just bone it first. Nothing worse than biting into a piece of fish and finding a bone stabbing you."

"I believe you'll come in right handy, ma'am," Jake said, exaggerating the droll words he spoke. He rolled to the door and opened it wide, allowing her to walk past him into the house. She went directly to the kitchen, where she deposited the old hinges and screws in the trash bin, then washed up at the sink.

He watched her intently as she moved about, his fingers steepled against his mouth, elbows propped on the chair arms. "What?" She stopped abruptly halfway to the pantry and turned to face him. "What on earth do you find so fascinating about me, Jake? I feel like you're trying to dissect me, piece by piece."

He shook his head. "Not at all," he said, denying her claim. "I merely find you graceful in whatever you do. You move so smoothly, especially—" He broke off and frowned, and she completed his sentence for him.

"Especially for such a big woman?" Her smile was strained and she felt discomfort sweep through her at the knowledge that she was not what he would have chosen for a wife, if circumstances had been different.

Jake grinned then. "You are not a petite woman, Alicia. There's no getting around that. But you are far from plain. What matters is that you make me feel at ease with you. I don't have to fear that my opinions will offend you. You're not afraid of me, and I like that.

"Besides, believe me or not, I find you feminine in the extreme." His gaze moved to her bosom and she felt heat rise to her flesh at the realization that he inspected her so blatantly.

She turned away and he called her name. "Alicia. Please look at me. I want you to know that I admire you for taking on such a task. Facing the future with Jason and me will not be easy for you. I'm not a simple man. You know that already. I'm blunt and I'm sure you'll think more than once that I'm downright obnoxious."

She turned her head and nodded. "Well, you've got that right."

"I have no legs, Alicia. That makes me about half a man. If you can accept the fact that your husband is a man who will never walk under his own power, ever again, then I can accept gladly the fact that my wife is a woman of great strength and stamina, a woman with a sense of honor that will make me proud to claim her as my wife.

"I won't mention this again since it makes you uncomfortable, but I think you need to know my feelings. If I wish to look at you and admire the woman you are, please don't take offense."

She turned and bustled off to the pantry without a word. Hot tears burned behind her eyelids but she refused to shed them. Not for the world would she make Jake think he'd hurt her feelings, for the opposite was true. He'd made her proud of who she was, made her realize that she had something to offer him that he was pleased to accept.

Hiding in the pantry was not the thing to do, she decided. Locating the jar of fish on the shelf, she returned to the kitchen and placed the Mason jar on the counter. Then she turned to where he waited, his expression anxious, which struck her as unusual for Jake. He was a man who spoke his mind without fear or favor.

"I need to say thank-you, Jake," she told him, hoping against hope that the tears would not escape. "I think we'll get along one way or another. I'll try not to invade your privacy too much, but I expect one thing from you that might not be to your liking."

He lifted an eyebrow in question.

"I want you to stand behind me when I make attempts to change Jason's habits. I'm going to set some rules in place and he needs to know that his father will not side against me in this."

"What sort of rules? Rules of behavior? I told you his manners were atrocious already. I won't argue with that."

"I want to sit down with the both of you one evening next week and compile a list. I want your word that you'll back me in this."

"May I see your list first?" he asked, and she thought she noted a gleam of leashed anger in his eyes.

Perhaps she'd run roughshod over his pride in his son, she thought. Jake was a good father, but had neglected the boy's behavior. It was time to call a halt.

"Yes," she said. "Of course you can. I'll show it to you before we call Jason in on the discussion."

Jake nodded. "All right. That sounds fair." His eyes narrowed a bit and he tapped the arm of his chair with his index finger. "I hope you aren't planning on coming up with a list for my benefit, Alicia. I'm not sure I'm in the mood for being changed to your way of thinking."

"Of course not," she said vehemently, and behind her back she crossed her fingers.

THE WEDDING was short and to the point. The minister spoke briefly about the sanctity of marriage and Alicia felt like squirming where she stood. That she and Jake would have no problem with the vow of purity was a given. He wasn't about to trot off to the saloon to take up with one of the girls who plied their trade in the rooms over the bar. And heaven knew that she had no inclination even to flirt with any of the men of her acquaintance.

Jake would be enough for her to handle. But intimacy between them would only confuse the matter.

"With this ring I thee wed." The words were familiar, but never had they applied to her, and Alicia felt a thrill that made her shiver as Jake took her hand and placed the ring they had chosen onto her left hand. He looked into her eyes as he spoke the vow, holding her hand even after the ring was in place. Her fingers trembled in his grasp, and he clasped them more securely.

Then the minister spoke the final phrases that would make their marriage legal. "Since Jacob and Alicia have repeated their vows…" His voice intoned the solemn words and Alicia knew a moment of panic.

In her innermost being she recognized the wisdom of this union. And yet, she felt she was walking into a chasm, feeling her way, without a light to guide her and no path marked for her journey.

"I now pronounce that they are man and wife…" Jake's fingers tightened again and she returned the pressure, her other hand occupied with holding the small bouquet of wildflowers Rachel and Cord had brought to her for this occasion.

The young minister smiled at Jake. "You may kiss your bride, Mr. McPherson."

Surely not. She looked down into Jake's gaze, her panic sending color to her cheeks. But it seemed that he felt no such trepidation for he tugged her closer, and his other arm reached up to draw her down within reach of his lips.

She obeyed his unspoken command, for surely it was more than a request. He was leaving her no choice, she thought, and closed her eyes. He obviously had more experience in this endeavor than she, and so she allowed him to take the lead.

His lips were warm against hers, his mouth open just a bit, so that she knew the scent of his breath. She thought a small trace of spirits clung to it, and wondered if he'd had to fortify himself for the ceremony. His lips moved against hers, brushing gently in a warm, welcoming gesture, and then he released her and she stood erect once more.

Cord was reaching for Jake's hand, even as Rachel hugged Alicia tightly. Tears were flowing in abundance and Rachel wiped her eyes even as she smiled. "I always cry at weddings," she explained. "And this one is special. Welcome to the family, Alicia. I'm so glad my brother-in-law had the good sense to marry you."

"That was going to be my line," Cord said with a laugh. He released Jake's hand and turned to Alicia. "Hello there, sister," he said quietly, his gaze warm as he met hers. He bent to her, kissing her forehead, then her cheek, and his arms enclosed her in a gentle embrace.

With that Melody, Matthew and Jason descended on them and Alicia was greeted by Melody, who announced that she was going to be the most envied girl in school. Jason grinned, his eyes sparkling with delight, then stood as close to Alicia as he could get, as if he staked a claim on her. "I've got a new mother," he said proudly. And then frowned.

"What am I supposed to call you?" he asked her.

"Whatever you like," she said warmly. She glanced at Jake and, taking note of the tightening of his mouth at Jason's words, she backtracked. "Maybe Miss Alicia would be best until you decide that for yourself."

Jason's smile broadened. "All right. I can do that."

The dining room table was opened to its fullest length. With the addition of two leaves it held the entire group, including the minister and his wife. Rachel would not hear of Alicia helping to serve and Melody lent a hand instead. The room was clean, aired only yesterday, with the draperies tied back and the sashes open to the fresh air.

Alicia had found tablecloths in the buffet drawer and had pressed one for the occasion. Fold lines had almost seemed permanent, but she used a damp cloth and managed to leave them without wrinkles. Now she looked down the length of the table and knew a moment of happiness so sharp it almost took her breath.

To think that only a month ago she had not known Jake McPherson, had only heard bits and pieces about him from the town gossips, and had grieved over the child who so obviously needed a parent's love and guidance. Now she had taken her place in this home and was partially responsible for the boy.

Cord lifted his glass filled with lemonade and offered a toast to the couple. His words were few, his message clear. "Joy and long life to you both, and happiness within the walls of your home." With a grin in Jake's direction, he added a final thought. "You have a wonderful bride, brother. I'm not sure you're good enough for her, but she seems to think you are, and that's all that matters."

Jake raised his glass and bowed his head a bit, as if he received the toast with pleasure. "I agree, totally," he said, and took a long swallow. He was handsome, Alicia thought, in a white shirt that had been starched and ironed. His suit fit him well, with no need of padding over his wide shoulders, and he'd left the lap robe in his room, eschewing it for the trousers that were pinned in place beneath the remaining lengths of his lower limbs.

He'd made special note of her new dress and his gaze had been admiring as she told him the particulars of Rachel's work. "She did a nice job," he'd said. "You look just like a bride should."

They went to the dining room and gathered around the long table. The meal was tasty, and yet Alicia barely noted the food that went into her mouth. The three children ate quickly, anxious to be excused from the table. They left to go off and play with admonitions from Rachel to keep their clothes clean for church on Sunday.

"You're no fun," Cord told her in an undertone. "How are two boys supposed to have a good time and stay clean while they're doing it?"

She shot him a long glance. "You aren't the one who had to iron Matthew's white shirt and scrub the grime out of his trousers."

"Enough said," Cord murmured, capitulating without an argument.

Within an hour the minister and his wife were gone, Rachel and Alicia were cleaning up in the kitchen, and the brothers were tugging at the dining room table, Jake in his chair at the far end, so that Cord could remove the leaves. "You want this table-cloth out here?" he asked, carrying it into the kitchen.

"Put it in the pantry," Alicia told him. "I'll send it to be washed tomorrow with the rest of the laundry."

"You know, I could almost envy you," Rachel said, her mouth turning down. "Imagine the luxury of having someone else scrubbing out your clothes."

"It's either that or I'll have to do it in the evenings and hang them before I go to school the next morning," Alicia said with a shrug. "Jake said that since his wash lady has been doing it for three years, it wouldn't be fair to remove her source of income just because he'd gained a wife."

"That makes sense to me," Rachel agreed.

Alicia leaned closer. "I've never been fond of a scrub board, anyway."

"Are you about ready to get these young'uns home?" Cord asked, looking out into the yard where the two boys were kneeling in the dirt, shooting marbles. He winced. "You'll be grumbling tomorrow, Rae, when you get a look at Matthew's trousers."

They gathered up their children and Cord harnessed his mare, leading her from the side yard where she'd been cropping the grass. Rachel stacked her dishes in the basket she'd brought along and looked around the kitchen, then cast a sidelong glance at Alicia.

"Are you all right?" she asked. "You're quiet all of a sudden."

Alicia pinned a bright smile in place. "Of course. I'm fine. Just tired, and maybe a little let down after all the excitement."

"Will you be in church in the morning?" Rachel asked.

Alicia nodded and then had another thought. "Jake doesn't go, does he?"

"No," Rachel said quietly. "Not since Rena…" She paused for a long moment. "Neither does Jason. I've hoped you might be able to change that."

"Don't count on it. Not right away, anyway." *Maybe*

not ever. If Jake balked at the idea, she would have no comeback. And getting him beyond the front porch seemed an insurmountable obstacle right now.

"I'll be there, anyway," Alicia said. She hugged Rachel, holding her close for a few seconds. "Thank you," she whispered, kissing the other woman's cheek.

Rachel looked deeply into Alicia's eyes. "It will be fine. Just wait and see."

"I know," Alicia answered staunchly. "I'm sure it will." But the thought of climbing the stairs to a lonely bed on the only wedding night she would ever have made her heart wrench with sadness.

She smiled, hoping that her lips did not tremble as she repeated Rachel's words. "It will be fine."

CHAPTER EIGHT

JAKE HAD REMOVED HIS TIE by the time the surrey rolled away. "Never did like getting all gussied up," he muttered, stretching his neck and loosening the collar of his shirt.

"Well, you clean up pretty good," Alicia said, straightening a lamp on the library table and then plumping the pillows on the couch. Unable to look him full in the face, she busied herself with meaningless chores, aware that he watched her closely.

"One thing I'll never have to worry about with you is getting a big head," he told her.

She glanced at him quickly, aware that her words might have caused him to bristle, but his smile reassured her. And then the smile faded and he seemed to be considering what he would say next.

"What is it?" she asked, already pretty sure of the topic he was about to open. It had stuck in his craw since right before the wedding ceremony, and she'd been relieved that he'd let it ride until now. "If we're going to talk about the piano, get it said, Jake."

He waved a hand at the instrument, although his eyes did not follow the gesture. "You know how I feel about the thing," he said gruffly. "It was not pleasant to see it taking over the whole room again."

"It's always taken up the same amount of space," she told him.

"Don't be dense. You know what I mean. You took the sheets off of it and got it all dusted up, even put those dratted flowers on it."

His words stung, but she did her best to shrug them off. "I thought it looked odd to have it all draped and hidden from sight. If you like, I'll take the sheets out of the laundry basket and put them back." She waited for his snarl, certain he would let her know, in no uncertain terms, that he was upset with her.

"I'd rather never see the thing again," he said harshly. "If there was an easy way to get it out of here, I'd already have done it."

"It's a beautiful instrument," she said quietly. "I would give much to be able to play it myself. I fear my childhood lessons left me with little knowledge. Although, I suspect my lack of talent was the real problem."

"I'd rather you didn't open the lid," he said. "Music is no longer a part of my life."

"How sad." She turned from him and walked out of

the room, aware that she'd riled him enormously. That he hadn't made an issue of the matter while Cord and Rachel were present was a small miracle, she decided.

Don't be dense. He had the ability to come directly to the point, and she had been the target once again.

The stairs were beneath her feet and she climbed to the second floor silently. The sound of Jake's chair against the floor caught her ear and she knew he watched her as she reached the top of the staircase. "Are you going to bed?" he asked.

"I thought I might. Why, did you need something from me?" And wasn't that a foolish question. The man was self-sufficient, at least insofar as tending to his lying down at night and rising in the morning. He had no need of her.

"No. As you may have noticed, I prefer to be alone a good share of the time. It was a polite question, Alicia. Appreciate it. I'm not often polite."

She bit her tongue. She would not add to the flame of his anger. The sun was low in the sky, would have sunk below the horizon by the time she donned her nightgown and took care of the new dress. There didn't seem to be much else to do, anyway. The rules of their association had been put in place and she must abide by them.

It was fully dark when she heard Jason coming in the back door. It slammed behind him and then Jake's low tones could be heard from the kitchen, his words indecipherable. Probably telling the boy to go to bed, she thought. In a few minutes, the stairs were attacked by Jason's boots, his feet thumping on every step.

She'd lay odds he'd not wiped them on the rug by the kitchen door and had no doubt left his mark behind him all the way to his room. She could tell when he paused outside her door, and she thought she could almost hear him breathing, just the other side of the wooden barrier.

"Miss Alicia? Are you sleeping?" he asked, his voice soft, as if he feared it would carry to the rooms below.

She came near the door and answered, equally as restrained. "No, I'm awake, Jason. You may come in if you like."

He opened the door, sticking his head inside the room, as if he would not unduly invade her privacy. "I just wanted to tell you good-night," he said. He looked across the room toward the bed, and she was aware that he could not see her clearly in the deeply shadowed room. "I'm glad you're here," he said. And then the door shut with a click.

"WILL YOU GO TO CHURCH with me?" she asked Jason at the breakfast table. Already dressed for Sunday morning service, she'd tied a large apron around her middle to protect her clothing. The meal was simple—

eggs and pancakes, along with a pan of fried potatoes. She'd used up yesterday's leftovers, and found a jar of applesauce in the pantry to add to the meal.

"Do I hafta?" the boy asked plaintively. "I'd rather go fishin' in the creek."

"I'm sure the fish would wait until this afternoon to be caught," she said, trying her best to lighten the rebuke. As his mouth drooped, she forced a smile. "You may make your own choice, Jason. I'm going, anyway, with or without you. I just thought it might be nice to have a handsome gentleman escort me down the aisle."

He squirmed in his chair and shot his father a pleading look. "As Alicia said, it's your choice," Jake told him.

"*You* never go anymore," Jason said defensively. "I don't know why I should have to."

She rose from the table and gathered up the dishes, then checked the time on her watch. She had only a few minutes until she must leave if she planned on being there early. And since she tried to avoid bringing attention to herself by arriving late, she'd made it a practice to be among the first arrivals.

"We'll have our Sunday dinner about two o'clock, Jason," she said. "When you hear the church bells ring for the second time, you'll know you have two hours before you must be here."

"Yes, ma'am." He looked relieved that she did not pursue the matter further, and rose from his chair.

"Please, may I be excused," she said, prompting him.

He wrinkled his nose but dutifully repeated the phrase, and at her nod left the room.

"What are you fixing for dinner?" Jake asked, pushing his chair from the table.

"I have a pot roast on the back burner," she said. "I'll let it cook during church service and finish the rest of the meal when I get home." The reservoir on the side of the iron cookstove held hot water, and she scooped out a panful and carried it to the sink, pouring it over the dirty dishes in the basin. Bubbles foamed from the soap she'd poured in, and steam rose hot against her hand.

"Don't burn yourself," Jake admonished her, as if he felt obliged to make conversation of a sort. The meal had been eaten in silence, as she'd decided it would be up to him to speak first after their unpleasant exchange the night before. Now he'd made two attempts to draw her into some sort of dialogue, to no avail.

To be fair, she knew she must accept his feeble attempt as a peace offering. At least as much of a peace offering as she was ever likely to get from the man. Another panful of water was splashed on the dishes, then she pumped cold water to fill the wash basin. In minutes she'd washed and dried the dishes and put them away in the kitchen cupboard. Words were hard to come by, she decided. For everything she could lay her tongue to held more than a touch of sarcasm.

"Well," she said, untying the apron and hanging it on a hook, "I'll be leaving in a few minutes for church. As soon as I get my hat and gloves."

"You look nice this morning," he said, his appraising glance touching upon her second-best dress and rising to her hair. "You don't usually wear combs. Those look pretty against your dark hair."

"Thank you," she said politely, aware how suddenly ill at ease she felt with him. If this was what being married had done to her, she didn't like it one little bit. She'd have to get over her snit from last evening and put it aside. Either that, or spend the rest of the day searching for something to talk about.

He rolled from the kitchen and she watched the door swing shut behind him. Her hands were trembling and she forced them into fists, then rubbed at her eyes with her knuckles. Using one of his cuss words was a temptation she almost succumbed to, the single harsh syllable ringing in her mind.

And then her head rose and she marched from the kitchen and up the stairs to her bedroom. Her hat was pinned in place in moments and her gloves smoothed over her fingers. The stairs needed a new piece of carpet laid, she thought as her boots thudded softly on each step. She'd talk to Jake later today—it would give them something to converse about. He sat in the parlor and she paused in the doorway.

"I'll be back right after twelve," she said, and he nodded morosely.

"Is something wrong?" she asked, hesitating just a bit.

"I'd thought once we got married you'd quit the coming and going and be here on Saturday and Sunday."

"You can solve that problem by going to church with me," she said with a shrug. "I wouldn't mind figuring out a way to accomplish that."

"I know how to get to church," he told her harshly. Then he waved his hand, dismissing her from his presence.

She turned toward the front door and headed down the walk, aware of him watching her from the parlor window.

"DID YOU CATCH any fish?" It seemed like a good opening, she thought, as she watched Jason wash his hands at the sink. Dinner was on the table, the savory aroma of pot roast filling the room. The potatoes were whipped into a steamy white cloud, and green beans flavored with onions and bacon swam in the broth she'd cooked them in. A pie, offered by one of the ladies of the congregation as a small token to celebrate the wedding, would serve as dessert.

Brought to the front door right after the morning service, the pie had been accepted by Jake, as Alicia was busy in the kitchen. He'd carried it on his lap and offered it to her just inside the kitchen doorway. "Mr. Robbins said his wife baked this for us," he told her gruffly.

"I hope you were gracious to the gentleman," she said, doubt lacing her words.

"About as nice as I could possibly be," he retorted, and she thought she caught a glimpse of humor in his eyes. He leaned back and watched her as she went about the work of putting a meal together.

When Jason came in to wash, his father greeted him. With a quick look at Alicia, the boy had turned to the sink, and at her query, he grinned. "Got three nice ones!" he said quickly as he dried his hands on a handy towel. Apparently pleased that she held no grudge, he opened the back door. "They're in the bucket out here. You wanta take a look?"

She shuddered just enough to make him grin and then shook her head. "No, I'm sure they're lovely fish. I just hope you know how to clean them. Personally, I think there's nothing quite so off-putting as fish scales."

"If I clean them real good, can we have them for supper?" he asked, closing the door and hurrying to slide into his seat.

"I suspect so," she told him, and felt Jake's look of appreciation touch her from across the table.

They ate in silence, Jason obviously hungry, Jake

relishing each bite as if the meal was well worth waiting for. When he was done he pushed his plate back and brought his coffee cup to sit before him, offering her a nod of approval. "You're a top-notch cook," he said. "I haven't eaten so well in a long time."

"I'm hoping your dinner put you in a good mood," she told him, knowing that the subject she would mention now was not to his liking. "I was approached by two of the ladies in church, making inquiries about you, Jake."

"Me?" His brows rose, his surprise authentic. "Why on earth would anyone ask about me?"

"They weren't asking about your health, but about your activities," she said, wary of continuing, knowing she'd opened Pandora's box and now must face his frown.

"What activities? Surely the things I do can't possibly interest the ladies of this town."

"Catherine's mother wanted to know if there was a possibility of you teaching piano to her daughter. And then Toby Bennett's mama chimed in. I think they'd decided to approach me together, hoping I would be more likely to concede to their joined forces."

"I hope you set them straight," he said emphatically.

"Actually, I told them I'd ask you about it." Her jaw set firmly as she spoke. "It would be a way for you to become a part of the town again, Jake. And those children are in need of your talent."

"I have no interest in becoming 'a part of the town,'" he said mockingly. "You can just go and tell your lady friends that I'm not interested."

She lowered her gaze to her plate and found herself straightening her silverware with trembling fingers.

"Alicia?" He spoke her name in low, terse syllables. "Look at me," he said.

Jason rose quickly. "I'm gonna go and clean my fish," he told them, and hurried to leave. He opened the door, then turned back. "Please, may I be excused?"

She nodded and he cast her a relieved look as he hastened out the door.

"You had no right," Jake said. "No right at all to offer my time to those women."

"Not to the mothers, actually," she said. "To their children." She bit at her lip. "I said that Catherine and Toby could come by tomorrow after school and see your piano." She met his gaze and realized that she was pleading for his cooperation. "They were thrilled, Jake. Neither of them has ever seen a grand piano like the one you have hidden in the parlor. They've only heard about your work, and they're both—"

"No. A thousand times no Alicia," he said sharply. "I can't make it any more clear to you without raising the roof and having a battle royal. I'd like to avoid that."

She shrugged, as if it was of little matter to her. The dishes kept her occupied, and she used the diversion to its fullest extent, her thoughts filled with guilt. She'd tried to manipulate him, and it was too soon. Yet, she couldn't begin any other way. It just wasn't in her to dissemble.

IF HE'D BEEN ABLE TO LAY his hands on her, he'd have shaken the stuffing out of her. Jake sat in the parlor and glared at the piano in the far corner. It loomed there like a great black beast, a presence he could not escape. He'd managed to ignore it for almost three years, once he'd been able to toss the sheets over it and hide it from sight.

It wasn't bad enough the woman had uncovered it before the wedding and left it in plain sight afterward. Now she'd offered it as a bribe to the children of the town to invade his privacy and tramp their way into his parlor. There was no way in heaven he was about to allow such a thing to take place.

There wasn't a smidgen of guilt to be found in his contemplation of the whole situation. Except perhaps for the way he'd allowed her to walk away last evening. He'd watched her retreat to her room, noted each step she took on the wide staircase, and felt uneasy at his own rude behavior.

Don't be dense. He couldn't believe he'd said such a thing to her. Once more, he'd spoken words he'd give a whole lot to eat.

As it was, he merely wished he could retract the statement with polite words and genteel phrasing. How did one go about telling an intelligent woman that she was far from dense, that, in fact, she probably was equipped with the sharpest mind he'd ever made acquaintance with?

The fact remained that he had no desire to cope with children who were wanting to put their grubby hands on his piano. Where had that come from? *His piano.* The instrument he'd relegated to an imaginary trash heap. He had no interest in ever touching those keys again. Music was gone from his soul, as was the woman who'd made his life a living melody.

You were born to make music.

He looked up uneasily, certain for just a moment that he'd heard a woman's voice whisper in his ear. His eyes were drawn to the piano and he blinked in surprise. The lid was pushed back, the keys uncovered, the ivory gleaming richly in the sunlight from the open window.

When had Alicia opened the lid? Surely not since church was over. She'd gone right to the kitchen upon returning, leaving her hat and gloves on the staircase to be taken up to her room later on. Jake shook his head; his memory must be dulled. And yet, he would have sworn that the keys had not been exposed earlier today.

It was past time for him to make amends, he decided. He rolled from the room and out onto the porch. Alicia knelt beside the steps on a fold towel pulling weeds. "You'll get your dress dirty that way," he said quietly.

She looked up and brushed a lock of hair from her forehead. Her hand left a smudge of dirt behind and he smiled at the effect, which made her seem more vulnerable, he decided. "It needs washing, anyway," she told him, then bent to her chore.

"You'll get in trouble with the ladies, working on Sunday," he said.

"And you think I care?" she asked. "That's the least of my worries."

"What's the greatest of them?"

She gave him a sharp look. "Trying to learn how to be a wife to you, Jake McPherson. I fear I'm not doing a very good job of it."

"You'll do," he said. His mouth twitched, the words he felt compelled to speak burning his tongue. "I owe you an apology, Alicia. You're probably one of the most intelligent persons I've ever known. You're far from dense, and I had no right to speak to you the way I did."

She settled back on her heels and wiped her face again, this time leaving dirt on her right cheek. "Well, well," she intoned. "How do I rate such kind words?"

He felt like squirming. The schoolteacher in her

was obvious in the arch look she shot in his direction, its effect spoiled just a bit by the smudges on her face. "Take it or leave it," he said. "It's the best apology you'll get from me."

She smiled, her face coming alive as her lips curved. "I'll take it," she said. "I fear I may never get another. Apologies are pretty scarce around here."

"Did anyone ever tell you that you have a smart mouth, Mrs. McPherson?"

"Yes, now that you mention it." She bent to her weeding. "I find it a good method by which to protect myself from hurt."

"Have you been hurt often?" He really wanted to know, he discovered. That Alicia was so vulnerable was a surprise to him. She'd seemed capable, sure of herself, and certainly efficient in all she did.

She looked up at him and her eyes were dark with pain. "More than you can imagine." Her mouth tightened. "And that's all I have to say on the subject."

MONDAY MORNING DAWNED early, with Alicia in the kitchen at daybreak. Jake heard the skillet scrape across the range top and then smelled bacon frying, the scent filtering through to his bedroom. By the time he'd managed to get himself decently clean and into his clothing, he heard her call Jason from the foot of the stairs. By the time the sun was crowning the eastern horizon, he smelled the bracing aroma of coffee.

This having a wife was going to come in handy, he thought, rolling across his room to open the door. Alicia was in the hallway, and looked up at him in surprise from her spot on the floor.

"What are you doing?" he asked. "I thought you'd hired a housekeeper to keep the floors clean."

"I did," she answered, "but it looks like Jason tracked dirt all the way across the hall yesterday. I'm just wiping it up."

"If he made the mess, let him take care of it," Jake said. "It'll make him think twice before he does it again."

She grinned at him. "Now, that's the sort of thing I like to hear."

"What is?" Jason came down the stairs, his boots clattering on each step.

"Do you see what Alicia is doing?" Jake asked him.

Jason peered over the banister. "Looks like she's washin' up stuff."

"Your stuff," Jake said sternly. "This is the last time she'll be cleaning up behind you, young man. If you can't remember to wipe your feet at the door, you can just plan on taking care of your own messes."

Jason lifted one boot and peered at the bottom, then the other. "They're clean now," he said.

"And well they should be," Jake told him. "The dirt is scattered from the back door to the stairway. We won't talk about this again, son. You'll not make extra work for Alicia. She has enough to do just cooking and making things nice for us. Not to mention going out to teach school all day."

"Yes, sir," Jason said sheepishly. "I won't forget again."

"I suppose you think that's going to mend all your fences," Alicia said quietly as she smiled up at Jake. She tilted her head to one side as if she considered the idea. "You know, it might very well go a long way toward doing just that very thing." And then her smile broadened and she laughed aloud.

It was strange, he thought, how laughter could change a woman's appearance. It made her eyes sparkle and put color in her cheeks, and Alicia's smiling face was no exception.

THE DAY SEEMED LONG with both Alicia and Jason gone. He'd not noticed the slow passage of time before, but on this Monday, he thought the clock would never move its hands at more than a snail's crawl. School was out at three-thirty, and by three-thirty-five, he was watching the front walk, waiting for Alicia's now-familiar figure to come through the gate. He'd be glad to see the last day of the school year arrive on Friday.

Jason appeared first, two children accompanying him, and he burst through the front door with a clatter of boots against the wooden floor. Then he skidded to a stop and returned to the rug Alicia had placed on the threshold for his convenience. "I'm wiping my feet, Pa," he called out.

Jake was torn. A smile was twitching at his lips at Jason's words, but his spine was stiff with irritation as he heard the voices of all three children just outside the parlor door. And then a small girl poked her head into the room.

Her eyes were wide with apprehension, and she hesitated as if unsure of her welcome. "Mr. McPherson?"

"That's my name," he returned gruffly.

She stood straighter in the doorway. "My teacher said if we came by you'd let us see your piano."

"Did she, now?" *Damn Alicia,* anyway! She had no right.

The little girl—had Alicia said her name was Catherine?—backed away tentatively. "Maybe we shouldn't have come," she whispered, and Jake was struck by shame.

"It's all right," he said quickly. "Come on in." Even an old grouch such as he had no excuse to frighten off a little girl.

Catherine stepped closer. "You don't look like a hermit to me," she said candidly. "I think you look like a nice man."

"Do you?" Probably his recent haircut and the shave he'd indulged in this morning might have something to do with that, he thought. "So, you want to see my piano, do you?"

"Yes, sir," she said politely, peering beyond him to where the black monster sat.

"Can Toby come in, too?" she asked.

"I suppose he'll have to," Jake conceded, and then watched as the boy appeared from around the corner, where he'd obviously been hiding. "I guess you want to see the piano, too," Jake said to him.

"Yes, sir." Toby was of an age with Jason, Jake thought. The boy approached the piano, his footsteps soft on the wooden floor, as if he approached a sacred shrine. His eyes shone with anticipation and he tucked his hands in his pockets, as though he feared they might betray him by reaching to touch the ivory keys.

"Have you ever played on a piano?" Jake asked, recognizing the boy's yearning.

"Yes, sir. The one at church. Mrs. Howard gave me some lessons, but I didn't do very good at it. She only knows the stuff in the hymnal. She said we couldn't play anything else in the church."

"What do you want to play?" Jake asked reluctantly.

"Real music. Not just songs that people sing words to." Jake only nodded.

"Can I touch the keys?" Toby asked softly.

Could he allow it? Could he bear the sound of hammer striking string? Would he be able to contain his anger if those keys should once more resound with the clear, pure tones he'd once cherished?

He'd put Rena and all she represented into storage when she'd been carried from this house for the last time. She'd been the inspiration for the music he wrote, the melodies he'd played. Once that dear, beloved spirit had left him bereft, he'd shut out all the joy she'd brought to his life.

Now this child stood before him and asked him to allow those keys to respond to the touch of his fingers. Jake found that he had no defense against the boy's beseeching look.

"Go ahead, Toby," he said, gritting his teeth against the pain to come.

The boy walked slowly toward the piano, lifting the bench to pull it from beneath the keyboard, and then settled himself on the shiny surface. He looked quickly at Jake, as if asking final permission, and Jake found himself nodding acquiescence.

The boy's right hand lifted and his fingers touched the keys, one at a time. He tried out a simple melody, and his head tilted to one side as if he heard a whole orchestra providing accompaniment to the simple tune he played. His left hand lifted to touch the lower octaves and he added harmony to the mix, his right hand moving now more rapidly, his fingers agile as they skimmed over the keyboard.

Then he stopped, placing his hands in his lap and turning his head in Jake's direction, as though offering an apology for taking liberties with the instrument.

"Thank you, sir," he said, and walked past Jake to the doorway, his eyes wide, his expression stunned as though he had experienced some wondrous thing.

"Toby." Jake spoke the name softly, unaware of the other two children who stood silently by. "Tell your mother I'll give you lessons."

"Me, too?" Catherine asked eagerly, stepping closer to Jake's chair, her gaze moving uneasily to the empty spaces where his legs should be.

Could he do this thing? And then he looked again at the boy who lingered in the doorway, hope alive on his narrow face, joy flooding his countenance. How could he not?

"Yes, you, too," he told Catherine. "Now, off with both of you. I'll have Mrs. McPherson tell you when you may come again."

Alicia appeared behind the children, her eyes meeting his anxiously. She touched Catherine's head briefly, brushed her hand across Toby's shoulder and smiled at Jason. For Jake, she reserved a look of restraint. He could not bear that she allowed him to intimidate her in this way.

"Come in, Alicia," he said, offering her his hand. She approached and he tugged at her, nudging her toward the couch. "Sit down. We need to talk about this."

CHAPTER NINE

"I WAS OUT OF LINE, JAKE. I'm sorry." He thought for a moment that a tear glittered against her cheek, but she turned her head away. "I thought about this at school today, and realized I had no right to interfere the way I did. It was too late to stop Catherine and Toby from coming over, but it's not too late to put a halt to the whole lesson notion."

He nodded an agreement as she glanced his way. "You're right about one thing," he told her. "To my way of thinking you were interfering in something you didn't understand."

She frowned. "Maybe."

Making Alicia understand his feelings suddenly seemed important. "I don't know if this will make sense to you," he said. "In fact, I'm not sure anyone but Rena had any concept of what music meant in my life. When Rena married me she should have been the prime focus of my life. I should have set aside all else for her sake. But the music always came first when things were rolling with my job."

"You blame yourself for not paying enough attention to her, don't you?" she asked.

Jake shook his head. "I'm not sure that's all of it. For some reason her death and the grief I felt turned me away from music. I'd been so wrapped up in my work I hadn't been aware of how sick she really was at the end. If I hadn't devoted myself to the schedule I was setting up for the coming year, if I'd been more available to Rena, things might have been different."

"Did she feel neglected?"

"I don't know. She didn't seem to, but Rena had taken second place her whole life. Even as a child, she was not the favored one. Then she devoted herself to me and I took advantage of her."

"So you punished yourself by turning away from music."

"I don't think that's altogether true. I just lost interest in it."

She pressed her lips together, refusing to offer a rebuttal.

He spun his chair from her and approached the piano. His hands were not gentle as he closed the lid over the keys. "I can't play. No matter what, I can't put my fingers on those keys, ever again."

"No one has asked you to, have they?"

You were born to make music. The words rang again in his mind. "I'm not sure," he said quietly, dropping his head, feeling the pain of loss. Not so much for the woman he'd loved and then lost, although she had lent beauty to his work by her presence in his life. But for the threads of melody that wove his days and nights into a tapestry of brilliant hues—the music that spoke to his soul. The two were so closely interwoven it was difficult to separate them.

He only knew that yesterday, in this room, he'd heard Rena speak to him. Alicia would surely think him mad if he told her. A thought struck him and he looked up at her. "Did you open the lid over the keys?"

She shook her head. "I dusted the piano Saturday morning and wiped the keys with a damp cloth, but I haven't touched it since."

"Not today, but yesterday," he persisted.

"No, Jake. I haven't touched it. Did you ask Jason?"

"He wouldn't go near it. He knows better." There was no getting around it. He'd have to tell her what happened and leave himself open to her scorn. "When I came back in here on Sunday, the lid was open. It hadn't been lifted since I closed it after Rena's funeral." He hesitated and continued. She might as well know the whole foolish story.

"I heard a voice, Alicia. I'd have sworn that someone was in the room with me."

She turned pale and bit at her lip, and he hesitated before he continued. "The voice said, 'You were born to make music.'" He sighed, shaking his head at his own foolishness. "You'll think I've lost my mind."

"No," she said quietly. "I don't believe in spirits haunting those they've left behind, but I wonder if some part of Rena isn't still alive in your mind, Jake, and that part of her is able to communicate with you."

"Thank you," he said. "I feared telling you, lest you laugh."

"I wouldn't do that. And if you'll listen, I'd like to say something to you."

"Anything."

"When I went upstairs, to choose my bedroom…do you remember that day?"

He nodded and she continued. "I heard a voice. Not an audible voice, but a whispering sound that I understood as well as if you had been standing there speaking to me."

"What did it say?" He felt his heart pump.

"'You're going to be his wife, and you can do whatever you please in this house.'" She swallowed as if a lump threatened to choke her as she said the words aloud. "I swear to you, Jake. It happened."

He was silent, attempting to absorb her words. Then he nodded. "I believe you, Alicia. I don't have the answers, but I think Rena would have wanted me to marry you. I also know she would never have wanted me to close up that piano the way I did. I can't do the rest," he said. "I don't want to play, and I don't have the heart to work with the opera house, but perhaps I can work with those two children."

She closed her eyes and he watched as tears spilled from beneath her lids and made silver trails down her cheeks. "Don't cry, please," he whispered. "I don't want to make you unhappy."

"You haven't!" she said. "I'm just so relieved to know that I didn't botch things with my meddling."

"Don't ask any more of me than this, Alicia," he warned her. "I'll do as you asked in this one thing. But don't push me."

"All right," she said, wiping her eyes with her fingertips.

"Where's your hankie?" he asked, then watched as she groped in her pocket for the white square of linen. "Shall I give you a hand with supper?"

"I thought we'd make stew out of the leftover beef roast," she said. "It won't take long to prepare. I'll just mix up biscuits and put them on top and then bake it while I set the table and—"

He held up his hand. "Whoa," he said with a laugh. "I'll be thinking you're entirely self-sufficient. I'm probably going to be organized to death. I don't think you leave anything to chance, do you?"

She blushed and shook her head. "I try not to, Jake. I'm used to a schedule. If I don't stay up-to-date I lose track of my students. My life is too full not to be organized."

"I suspect I'll get used to it," he said, shaking his head. "Now, before you begin, why don't you go up and change your clothes and get comfortable. I'll cut up the meat for you and get things started best I can. Will that help?"

She shot him a grateful look. "More than you know. I do like a man who's at home in the kitchen."

"How many men have you liked, ma'am?" he asked smartly, and was gratified when she blushed anew.

"None, to be honest," she said. And then she left the room and he heard her feet touching the stairs as she climbed to the second floor.

NONE, TO BE HONEST. Far from the truth, Alicia thought as she entered her bedroom. Indeed, up to this time she'd not felt desire for any particular man; but Jake was different. She'd felt drawn to him from the start, had known for the first time in her life the thrill of touching a man, even though that touch had not even been under romantic circumstances.

Then, on their wedding day, his hands had been warm against her own, his lips had kissed her with tenderness, as though he had recognized her reticence.

Little did Jake know how many times she'd replayed that kiss in her mind.

He would never know, she determined. For she would lose his respect if he knew of her yearning to discover the textures of his skin, to feel his whiskers against her cheek, to hold his dark head against her breast.

She changed her clothes, pulling an old housedress over her head, one that hung in a shapeless drape about her body. The mirror reflected her image and she frowned. There wasn't much to work with, but she ought to at least make the most of what was available. With that thought in mind, she pulled off the dress and sought out another, a wrapper she'd first thought might be too intimate a piece of apparel to wear in Jake's presence.

Brightly colored flowers dotted the fabric and tucks defined the bosom, and a sash fitted neatly around her middle. She looked again into the mirror; it would do. At least the colors brought new life to her skin, and for that she was grateful.

He was in the kitchen when she went back downstairs, and she set to with a will, taking over the chore of putting a stew into the oven. It would be a simple meal, but Jake seemed happy with whatever she put before him. The man was easy to please…in some areas, at least.

"When can I tell Toby and Catherine to return for lessons?" she asked lightly.

"You kinda snuck that in, didn't you?" he asked, and she turned her head to catch a grin on his face.

"I'm not sneaky," she protested. "I only want to know what to tell them."

His grin faded. "Have you any idea of the talent that boy holds in his hands?"

She thought for a moment. "I know he seems to have perfect pitch. Sings like an angel, in fact. And his sense of rhythm is superb."

Jake nodded. "All of that is good to know. What I'm referring to is his gifted playing. He said he'd taken lessons from Mrs. Howard, but she was only willing to teach him hymns."

Real music, Toby had answered the question of what he preferred to play. As if Jake would surely understand his meaning, the boy had spoken the words with reverence. In so doing, little did Toby know he had won a place in Jake's heart.

"Hymns are fine," Alicia said, interrupting Jake's reflection.

"Yes, they are," Jake agreed. "I'm sure that Catherine will do well one day as a church pianist. She seems like a competent enough child. I'm sure she can learn to read notes without too much trouble."

"Your prejudice is showing," Alicia said quietly as

she stood at the table and prepared the dough for the biscuits.

"Would you like some coffee?" she asked Jake, when she was finished at the stovetop, leaving the stew to simmer.

"If you'll have some with me."

He was almost too agreeable, she decided, as if he wanted to keep this day on an even keel, as though he actually desired her company. For a man who'd said only yesterday that he needed his privacy, he was being downright gracious.

"Have you made your list of rules for Jason yet?" he asked, and when she nodded, he went on. "Why don't you tell me about it? We can talk to him after supper."

She sat across from him and folded her hands on the table. "First off, I think he needs to spend a little more time on his schoolwork. Jason is a very bright boy, but he tends to be lazy when it comes to learning. He doesn't like the chore of writing out problems and solving them. He thinks if he knows the answer in his head, it's a waste of time to work it out the long way."

Jake nodded. "Well, I think I tend to agree with him on that. I always found schoolwork to be tedious."

She frowned. "I can see that you're not going to be much help."

"What else?" he asked, urging her on to the next issue.

"You've already addressed the point of his messy behavior, tracking in dirt and such. I think he's well aware that it will not be tolerated, especially since you spoke to him."

"Don't tell me that's the whole of it? I find it hard to believe that a list-maker like you will call it quits after two items."

"No," she said. "Third is his religious education." She raised a hand in protest to halt his automatic response. "Just listen to me, Jake. I understand that you won't go with me to church, but I think Jason needs some background in that area." Then she drove her message home. "I think his mother would agree if she could express an opinion."

It left him without a rebuttal, and that was what she had intended.

"I'm not sure I'm ready for the rest of your list," he said, his expression sour as if he'd eaten an unripe persimmon.

"Well, you're going to hear it, anyway," she said, gaining confidence. "I want him to have daily chores, instead of running wild."

"He does chores," Jake said defensively.

"He does what needs to be done, only when the need becomes critical."

"He cleans his room."

She raised her brow in a cynical expression. "I know

An Important Message
from the Editors

Dear Reader,

Because you've chosen to read one of our fine romance novels, we'd like to say "thank you!" And, as a **special** way to thank you, we've selected <u>two more</u> of the books you love so well **plus** an exciting Mystery Gift to send you — absolutely <u>FREE</u>!

Please enjoy them with our compliments...

Pam Powers

Lift here

Peel off seal and place inside...

How to validate your Editor's *"Thank You"* FREE GIFT

1. Peel off gift seal from front cover. Place it in space provided at right. This automatically entitles you to receive 2 FREE BOOKS and a fabulous mystery gift.

2. Send back this card and you'll get 2 brand-new *Romance* novels. These books have a cover price of $5.99 or more each in the U.S. and $6.99 or more each in Canada, but they are yours to keep absolutely free.

3. There's no catch. You're under no obligation to buy anything. We charge nothing—ZERO—for your first shipment. And you don't have to make any minimum number of purchases— not even one!

4. The fact is, thousands of readers enjoy receiving their books by mail from The Reader Service. They enjoy the convenience of home delivery...they like getting the best new novels at discount prices BEFORE they're available in stores... and they love their Heart to Heart subscriber newsletter featuring author news, horoscopes, recipes, book reviews and much more!

5. We hope that after receiving your free books you'll want to remain a subscriber. But the choice is yours— to continue or cancel, any time at all! So why not take us up on our invitation, with no risk of any kind. You'll be glad you did!

GET A *Free* MYSTERY GIFT...

SURPRISE MYSTERY GIFT COULD BE YOURS **FREE** AS A SPECIAL "THANK YOU" FROM THE EDITORS

The Editor's "Thank You" Free Gifts Include:

- *Two BRAND-NEW Romance novels!*
- *An exciting mystery gift!*

Yes! I have placed my
Editor's "Thank You" seal in the
space provided above. Please
send me 2 free books and a
fabulous mystery gift. I
understand I am under no
obligation to purchase any
books, as explained on the
back and on the opposite page.

PLACE
FREE GIFT
SEAL
HERE

393 MDL DVFG   193 MDL DVFF

FIRST NAME   LAST NAME

ADDRESS

APT.#   CITY

STATE/PROV.   ZIP/POSTAL CODE

(PR-R-04)

Thank You!

Offer limited to one per household and not valid to current MIRA,
The Best of The Best, Romance or Suspense subscribers. All orders
subject to approval. Credit or debit balances in a customer's account(s)
may be offset by any other outstanding balance owed by or to the
customer.

© 2003 HARLEQUIN ENTERPRISES LTD.
® and ™ are trademarks owned by Harlequin Enterprises Ltd. ▼ **DETACH AND MAIL CARD TODAY!** ▼

The Reader Service — Here's How It Works:

Accepting your 2 free books and gift places you under no obligation to buy anything. You may keep the books and gift and return the shipping statement marked "cancel." If you do not cancel, about a month later we'll send you 3 additional books and bill you just $4.74 each in the U.S., or $5.24 each in Canada, plus 25¢ shipping & handling per book and applicable taxes if any.* That's the complete price and — compared to cover prices starting from $5.99 each in the U.S. and $6.99 each in Canada — it's quite a bargain! You may cancel at any time, but if you choose to continue, every month we'll send you 3 more books, which you may either purchase at the discount price or return to us and cancel your subscription.

*Terms and prices subject to change without notice. Sales tax applicable in N.Y. Canadian residents will be charged applicable provincial taxes and GST.

If offer card is missing write to: The Reader Service, 3010 Walden Ave., P.O. Box 1867, Buffalo, NY 14240-1867

BUSINESS REPLY MAIL

FIRST-CLASS MAIL   PERMIT NO. 717-003   BUFFALO, NY

POSTAGE WILL BE PAID BY ADDRESSEE

THE READER SERVICE
3010 WALDEN AVE
PO BOX 1341
BUFFALO NY 14240-8571

NO POSTAGE
NECESSARY
IF MAILED
IN THE
UNITED STATES

you haven't had occasion to see his bedroom or you'd realize the humor of that remark."

"Boys aren't much for housework."

"Neither are women who work at a profession for seven hours a day and then go home to a family that demands she tend to them."

He glared at her. "I didn't realize we were so *demanding* of you."

Her shrug was a statement in itself. "*You* are. And that's fine. I married you knowing that I would be called upon to do the very things I'm doing right now. I don't mind cooking for you and cleaning up behind myself. I enjoy spending time with you and Jason, and I plan on keeping the yard and the house in order."

"That's what a wife is expected to do," he said sharply. "I thought it was understood between us that you were going to be a real wife."

She was silent, looking into his eyes with an unspoken message she feared he might decipher. "A *real* wife, Jake? Is that what I am?"

His jaw set firmly and his gaze hardened. "Probably as real as it's gonna get."

He spun his chair and went through the kitchen door.

Her heart yearned for him, for the pain he felt and for her own aching need to be loved. She rose to the stove and checked the coffee. It was strong enough to suit her and she poured a cup and settled back at the table with it. She'd only taken one sip when he rolled through the door and faced her, a belligerent frown furrowing his brow.

"You promised me a cup of coffee."

"So I did." Retrieving a second cup from the buffet, she filled it and placed it before him. He'd made an effort, had done a turnabout, and she would not push him further today. It was apparent, however, that he was determined to have the last word, which gave her warning that he was willing to do battle if need be.

TOBY APPEARED at the front door on Wednesday, and knocked with a subdued rapping sound. Jason swung the door wide and cheerfully invited the boy inside. "Is your pa in the parlor?" Toby asked, and Jake could not mistake the note of anticipation in his tone.

"Yeah, he knows you're comin'," Jason replied. "Go on in."

Jake spoke up then. "Jason? I want you to do those problems Alicia gave you. Work at the kitchen table, if you please." He'd determined to back her in this, even though he winced at Jason's pain. But Alicia had specified a half hour a day must be spent on schoolwork. He owed it to her, had vowed to honor his commitment to keep Jason on the straight and narrow.

Toby walked into the parlor, Jason standing behind

him, wearing a frown. "Pa?" the boy asked. "Will you tell me when the half hour is over?"

"I'll send Toby to tell you," Jake said agreeably, aware now only of the lad who watched him, whose eyes held a reverence he did not deserve.

"Sir?" Toby said. "My mama said to give you this. She said it's what Mrs. Howard charges, and if it's more she'd make it up next time." He held out a quarter in his hand, a princely sum for a half hour of Jake's time. Then Jake thought of the money he'd earned by playing in concert halls in New York.

Quite a comedown, one that left a bitter taste in his mouth.

"That's for a half hour," Toby added. He waited for Jake to take the coin from his hand and his lip trembled. "If it isn't enough I'll go back home and she'll give me some more."

Jake touched the boy's hand quickly, picking up the coin with thumb and forefinger. "That's exactly right," he said quietly. "Let's see what we can do for you," he said, rolling his chair toward the piano.

He lifted the lid gently, careful not to touch the keys. "Pull out the bench and sit down," he told Toby, and waited until the boy did as he was told.

"Now, tell me what you know about the notes," he said. "Show me where middle C is, Toby."

The boy pointed immediately to the correct key.

"That's easy," he said, and released a sigh. "Mr. McPherson? Don't you feel lucky to have this piano right here where you can see it all the time and play it whenever you want to?"

"Lucky?" Jake repeated the word. "Maybe that's a good word for it, Toby. In many ways I've been a lucky man." *Alicia.* The first good thing that had come into his life in three years. "Lately I've been lucky," he amended.

The piano bench held music—sonatas, études, simple tunes he'd written for his own enjoyment—and he had a ream of paper with music staffs printed on it, ready to be filled with notes from his pen. He selected one of his own easily played melodies for Toby's use today.

"Let's see how much you know," he said, placing the sheet on the rack. "Can you read those notes?"

Toby nodded. "I think so." He played the melody readily with his right hand.

"Now add the bass notes," Jake told him. He leaned back in his chair as Toby followed his instructions.

The boy looked at him. "I never heard that before. Does it have a name?"

"No one but you and I have heard it, son. I wrote it."

Toby looked stunned, glancing back at the music, then again at Jake. "You can write real music?"

"Is that what you call it?" Jake asked, amusement lightening the words.

Toby nodded; his eyes lit with eagerness. "Will you play for me sometime?"

"I don't play anymore." The words fell like rocks between them, heavy with the weight of Jake's determination.

"Never?" The boy looked down at the piano keys and touched one reverently. "How can you not want to make music?"

"I DON'T KNOW IF I CAN do this." Jake sat across the parlor from Alicia, the lamplight reflecting off her hair, lending it a richer chestnut hue than ever before.

She looked up from her mending. Jason had torn out the knee in another pair of trousers and she was patching it neatly. Her fingers were agile as they plied the needle and he watched her, admiring the graceful movement of her hands.

"Do what? Teach Toby? Or is it Catherine you aren't pleased with?"

He glared at her. "The girl is amazingly inept," he said. "But she can't help what she is. With an enormous amount of practice she'll be a run-of-the-mill pianist. She's a nice enough child, with a mother who wants her to have some social skills."

"And Toby?" she asked, her fingers halting as she spoke, the needle shining in the light. When he was silent, she continued.

"You see yourself in Toby, Jake. You recognize his talent, and it hurts to imagine him going where you can no longer go, to know he dreams of doing things you may never accomplish again."

"You know how to get to the heart of the matter, don't you?" he said gruffly. "Am I so obvious, Alicia? Are you saying I'm jealous of the boy?"

She dropped her sewing beside her on the couch and rose to come to him. Kneeling beside his chair, she touched his hand, and he felt the warmth of her fingertips, knew the comfort that hand could bring him. Her eyes were soft, tender with caring, and he thought of how undeserving he was of her concern, how needy he was of her warmth.

"No, you're not jealous, just grieving for what might have been in your life," she said quietly. "But you won't turn your back on him, of that I'm certain. You'll give him the chance he needs to fulfill his destiny, Jake. Because you're a man of honor and you cannot look upon talent without wanting to encourage it."

"I'm all of that?" he asked, his mouth twisting in the semblance of a smile. "You think too highly of me, Alicia."

She shook her head. "No, I only speak the truth. You're a man who's been robbed of a career. A man who settled for second best, because he had no choice. Toby is giving you a chance to use your gift in another person's behalf. If you succeed at this one thing, it will have made your existence worthwhile."

He bent to her and his lips touched her forehead. "How did you get so wise?"

She tilted her head back and her eyes were filled with a sheen of unshed tears. "Jake? Will you do something for me?" she asked.

"Yes, if I can." He turned his hand to grasp her fingers, knew a moment of pleasure as her hand conformed to fit against his palm. He noticed a faint scent of flowers from her hair, and the fragrance drifted up to him and lured him closer, made him recognize the feminine grace she carried with her. If she were willing, he'd—

Her next words threw him for a loss, almost as if her mind had followed his down the road to intimacy, a road he yearned suddenly to travel.

"Will you kiss me, Jake?" She bit at her lip, as if she felt she'd been presumptuous, and moved his thumb to brush the place where her teeth had left their mark. "I know we don't have a real marriage. I know what I am," she added with a smile. "But I feel the need of knowing the touch of a man's lips against mine."

"I kissed you on our wedding day," he reminded her. "Not good enough?" His brow twitched upward as she smiled again.

"I want to be kissed as if you really care about me."

"I do care about you," he said softly. "You are a very appealing woman, Alicia. It's only a lack in myself that keeps us from having what you call a real marriage."

He released her hand and cupped her face between his palms, then bent to her again, this time taking her mouth in a kiss that began as a tentative brush of lips, only to turn into a blending of mouths that startled him. She tasted good, sweet and yet not cloying. Her mouth was firm beneath his, softening as he touched her bottom lip with his tongue.

She opened to him at his silent bidding, allowing him to explore the heat of her mouth, the ridges, the edges of her teeth and the rasping surface of her tongue. He suckled there, carefully, gently lest he startle her. But it seemed she was not fearful of him, for she clasped his wrists firmly and leaned into the caress.

Too long, he thought. He'd kissed her for too long, and had gone far beyond what she'd asked for. Her lips were full and pink, her mouth tempting him to remain there where he'd taken his pleasure for those few moments. His body was reacting to her in a way he remembered from his marriage. He wanted her, and yet…he did not feel right to offer himself to her as a man.

With a sigh, he released her, raising his head, looking down into lovely eyes that shone with an emotion he could not accept from her.

"Is that what you wanted?" he asked, deliberately

injecting a teasing note into his words. "Did I meet your expectations?"

She stilled beneath his hands, her face flushing, the fine texture of her skin turning rosy with embarrassment. "Yes, to both your questions," she said. And then she drew away from him and rose swiftly. She was graceful, he thought, regardless of her statuesque form, and he admired her elegant demeanor.

Now she looked down at him and her eyes misted over again. "I think I need to go up to bed," she said. "I have a few papers to grade, and I want to look at Jason's work."

He nodded. "Whatever you say."

"Do you need anything?" she asked.

Your warmth. He winced, fearful for a moment that he'd spoken the words aloud. He shook his head. "No, nothing. I'm about ready for bed myself."

"Shall I blow out the lamp then?" She bent to the flickering light and looked his way again.

The glow turned her eyes to liquid, her skin to porcelain, stained by the flush she wore, and her hair gleamed as if fire dwelt within its depths.

"Yes. I'll follow you," he said. He watched as she climbed the stairs and heard her door close before he rolled to the back of the house to enter his lonely room.

CHAPTER TEN

IT HAD BEEN MORE THAN a month since school let out. Alicia had been living the life of a full-time housewife for four weeks, the last day of classes freeing her from teaching with the prospect of a permanent vacation from the schoolhouse. Though she loved her students, it was a relief to set aside that part of her life for the days and years she would spend in Jake's company.

Other summers had found her seeking out employment at various places. This year was different, with her contract to teach null and void. Her skin was turning golden from the time she spent outdoors. A garden was flourishing behind the house, Rachel pronouncing her thumb to be green as grass. The garden had been late going in, but the growing season was long, and the vegetable seeds she'd chosen to sow were rapidly turning into recognizable plants.

Jake sat in the shade and watched as she weeded, offering comments that amused her. He'd sent her to the store for a hat in the midst of her initial planting spree. "You don't need to get sunstroke," he'd said sternly. "Who will fix my dinner if you get sick?"

"I never get sick," she'd told him arrogantly. "You obviously wouldn't know a healthy woman if you saw one." And then at the stricken look on his face, she touched his hand. "I'm sorry. I speak before I think sometimes. I didn't mean to make you…"

"It's all right," he said. "I'm too easily reminded sometimes, but I'm getting better."

"Yes, you are," she'd said, agreeing without hesitation, bending to press her lips against his cheek, a deed he seemed to enjoy, if his smile was any indication.

Now she watched him from beneath her hat brim. He held a book on his lap, and she knew for a fact he'd turned nary a page in the hour he'd sat there. "Enjoying your novel?" she asked brightly, catching his attention.

He looked up at her, as if pulled from some deep contemplation. "Yes. It's a good story."

She denied herself the pleasure of teasing him, of asking him about the plot line, and instead rose and carried her basket of weeds to the compost pile at the back of the yard. "We need a goat to keep the grass down," she said. "Poor Jason is tired of whacking away at it."

"You wanted him to have chores," Jake reminded her mildly. "I've been trying to cooperate with your list."

"Well, at least he doesn't have to do arithmetic problems until school starts again. He was thoroughly sick of that ordeal." She paused halfway across the yard and looked around her at the work yet to be done.

"But you let him go fishing," Jake said. "Did he work on his bedroom?"

She sighed and reflected for a moment on the perpetual degree of disorder in Jason's room. "He tried this morning. The dirty clothes are gathered up and he made his bed. I thought about going in there and dusting, and then letting him sweep the floor." She made a face signifying distaste.

"Then I thought it might be better left for another day. I'm not any more fond of housework than he. I'm so glad we have Mrs. Bates coming every week."

"You have enough to do," Jake told her. "Just keeping the garden and cooking and looking after Jason and me is a full-time job."

She looked dubious. "You think so?"

He leaned forward in his chair, and she thought his face took on an admiring look. "I think you're doing well at the task you've taken on, Mrs. McPherson. I asked you to marry me with one thing in mind. I wanted someone to take care of Jason and get him turned around. You've done that and more." He thought her smile trembled at that remark and for a moment rued his own honesty. In fact, he wasn't certain how honest his words had been. He'd married Alicia for more than practicality. He'd found her to be a woman he could admire, perhaps even love one day. It was for certain he'd like to have her in his bed. But he was wary of that sort of intimacy between them, and he would not embarrass her by suggesting it. Not yet, anyway.

"I've done that and more? Are you sure?" Her left eyebrow twitched as she urged him to continue. Jake's assessment was good for her soul, and heaven knew she could use a boost for her sagging ego.

Jake grinned. This was the Alicia he'd wanted in his home, this woman who taunted him, teased him and cajoled him out of his isolation.

"We haven't eaten so well in years, as you very well know. And my evenings are spent in pleasant company these days. Jason has learned new games, and I've enjoyed hearing you read to him. He was in desperate need of a mothering influence, Alicia. You've filled the bill abundantly."

"Well, it's good to know I'm considered pleasant company," she said lightly. "I thought for a while you were going to toss me out on my ear, when we first began."

"I was tempted a couple of times," he admitted, "but I recognized that I was better off with you than without you." *And wasn't that the truth?*

"That makes me feel appreciated," she said, returning to her garden and digging around the plants with a small tool. She looked up at the sky. "I hope we have rain soon. The ground is so dry."

"Should be coming on by tonight," he said.

"How can you tell?" She looked up at the clear sky, wondering what he saw that escaped her notice.

"I was raised on a ranch, remember? It was our business to know the weather." He pointed to the west. "See the clouds just above the horizon? Those are rain clouds. Should be dumping on us by early evening."

She shot him a dubious look. "All right, Mr. Know-it-all. We'll see."

He was right, she conceded hours later. The sky opened up just after sunset, a particularly beautiful sight with heavy clouds silvered by the fast-falling sun in the west. Red-and-pink hues painted the underside of the rain clouds, and when the heavy drops began falling Jake and she rushed in from the porch.

They'd taken to sitting out there of an evening, and neighbors had at first looked surprised, then pleased to see them. Townsfolk raised their hands in greeting when they strolled by or buggies and wagons made their way up the road. She felt more a part of the community, Alicia decided; marriage to Jake had given her that.

The weeks seemed to pass swiftly, the calendar leaves turning, the garden coming in well. She learned from Rachel how to can tomatoes, when her sister-in-law came to visit in early September. They spent hours in the kitchen, laughter resounding from the walls, Rachel teasing her, Alicia responding in kind.

"You're happy, aren't you?" Rachel asked, regarding with satisfaction the rows of jars filled with tomatoes ready to store in the pantry.

"I've never been so contented." Alicia spoke with emphasis, needing to convey the full extent of her feeling.

Rachel shifted uncomfortably, and then leaned closer to Alicia. "I'm going to ask you something, and you needn't answer if you don't want to." As if she gathered her courage, she met Alicia's gaze head-on. "Are you still sleeping upstairs?"

Alicia frowned. "Of course. Where else would I sleep?"

Rachel made a face. "How foolish. I can't believe that two reasonably intelligent people like you and Jake would not take advantage of being married, and spend your nights together."

Alicia blushed, felt the crimson staining her cheeks and waved a hand as if to dismiss Rachel's words as folly.

"Ours isn't that sort of a marriage," she said. "We both knew what we were agreeing to when we spoke our vows."

"Are you telling me you have no interest in Jake as a husband?"

"I didn't say that," Alicia said quickly. "I just said ours is not that sort of a relationship. We spend a lot of time together and we get along reasonably well. We just don't share a bed."

"Well," Rachel said bluntly. "You're missing a good bet, Alicia. Good loving is the glue that holds a halfway decent marriage together. It also makes a really good marriage seem like a slice of heaven."

Alicia sat down heavily in a chair. "You're probably right. I'd move into his bedroom if he asked me, but he won't. Then, too, I'd have to take off my clothes in front of him and I don't think I could do that."

"For heaven's sake, why not?" Rachel seemed totally flabbergasted by Alicia's words. "None of us are perfect. I've been as close as a woman can be to a man right up until I had my two children, and Cord never seemed to mind. He just worked around things." Her grin spoke of good memories, and Alicia felt a pang of envy that she would never know such intimacy.

"On top of that," Rachel said, "Jake has flaws, too, you know. It would no doubt be difficult for him to be exposed to you. He's a proud man, Alicia, but I'll warrant you'd love him in spite of his physical limitations, wouldn't you?"

"I already do." It was an admission she'd made before, but now it was even more valid, Alicia realized. Jake had come to be the focal point of her existence over the past weeks. Her days began with fixing his breakfast and lingering over coffee as they planned their hours together. They also fought, sharp words flying between them, arguing over bits and pieces of their lives.

Yet, she knew that Jake derived great enjoyment from their verbal sparring, as did she. They never deliberately caused pain. Not since the day Jake had called her *dense*. She had been very wounded by the insult, until Jake admitted his wrongdoing.

She'd give him credit for that much. He'd owned up to his mistakes, more than once. The man she'd married had changed: a gradual softening of his moodiness, a slow acceptance of her in his home, and an appreciation of what she did to make his life easier.

From the parlor she heard Toby begin to play the piano. Beside her, Rachel stilled, her eyes widening as she listened.

"Who?" she asked. "Not Jake, surely."

"No. Toby is his student. A talented boy Jake has taken under his wing."

They listened together for long moments, and Rachel smiled. "It's good for him, isn't it? Do you think he'll ever play again?"

"He says not," Alicia said. "I yearn for the day when I see him at the keyboard and hear the music he's capable of coaxing from that piano. But he says it'll never happen."

Rachel's eyes seemed to look far into the past as she listened, and then she shared her thoughts. "The first time I saw him he almost blasted me from the piano bench, told me his piano wasn't to be touched by anyone. And then he called me Cord's *play toy.*"

Alicia gasped in horror. "What a horrible slur on your reputation!"

"Well," Rachel said with a smile, "it wasn't long before I actually was his prized possession. Though whether or not he considered me a play toy might be another story."

The music stopped, and Alicia heard the low rumble of Jake's voice and the answering tones of Toby's, the boy's excitement apparent even though she could not make out his words.

"What does Jake say about the boy?" Rachel asked.

"He says he's very talented, and probably has a great future if he gets the right training. But he's well aware that the sort of training Toby will need might not be what his parents can afford. He tries hard not to show his feelings. But I know he cares."

Rachel looked out the back door to where Jason and Matthew played in the yard. "Are you getting along all right with Jason? Has he called a halt to his reign of terror?"

"Well, that's one way of describing his stunts," Alicia agreed. "He's been much better, but some days I think he resents me being in authority over him." She hesitated a moment before sharing what had been in the back of her mind for several weeks.

"I think Jason is jealous of Toby." She lifted a hand to halt Rachel's response and continued. "He knows that his father is pleased with Toby's progress and Jason needs that same kind of approval from Jake. He has my approbation, but it's not nearly as important to him as that of his father." She made a wry face. "After all, I'm only a woman."

"I'm glad he thinks of Jake that way, but I hate that he makes you out to be the bad guy."

Alicia laughed softly. "I'm a teacher, remember? I'm used to the image. I've had to cope with worse than Jason in my years of working with children. It's just that he pushes me to the limit sometimes. Things like taking a bath twice a week don't go down well with him. Jake made him clean up behind himself when he tracked dirt in, and that had more influence on him than all my yattering."

"I still think you're the best thing that's happened here since Rena died," Rachel said stoutly. "You've been married four months now, Alicia. Do you think things have improved a lot since May?"

"Maybe."

From the front of the house a door closed, and the sound of Jake's chair could be heard rolling on the bare wooden floor of the hallway. He pushed open the kitchen door and looked at the two women sitting amid the clutter of canning jars, cooking kettles and empty bushel baskets.

"About done for the day?" he asked, his hair ruffled, his eyes dark with anger.

"What's wrong?" Alicia asked, crossing the room to the kitchen doorway. He sat just the other side of the threshold, and the look he shot in her direction was dour, as if he resented her very presence there.

"What should be wrong?" he asked harshly. "I'm just wondering if we'll have supper tonight, or if this infernal canning project is going to go on for the whole evening."

"I believe I'll be on my way," Rachel said brightly. "Let me help you clean up this mess and I'll take my leave, Alicia. I fear your husband is feeling neglected."

"Go on," Alicia said quickly. "I'll take care of it. You don't need to be included in Jake's little tantrum."

"Ouch." Rachel ducked her shoulders and gathered her things together. "I'm leaving before the fur starts to fly. See you in church on Sunday, Alicia. Bye, Jake." With a wave of her hand she was gone, out the back door and across the yard, calling to Matthew as she went. The horse was beneath a shade tree in the side yard, and she slipped the bit into the mare's mouth before she led her to the front of the house where the buggy waited.

"Tantrum?" Jake asked. "I'd think you could show a little more respect to the man you call your husband, madam."

"Do you?" Alicia turned to face him, her anger in hand. "The day you begin to offer me that same sort of respect is the day I'll reciprocate, *sir.*"

"At least I haven't accused you of throwing a tantrum," he said.

"That's because I haven't managed to commit that particular sin."

"Sin?" He laughed harshly. "You don't know what sin is, Alicia. Sin is resenting a nine-year-old boy who will one day be on the concert stage while I'll still be sitting here in this house, mourning the loss of my career."

"No, Jake," she said, correcting him quietly. "Sin is a man hiding his talent from the community around him and the world at large because he's suffered a tremendous loss in his life. It's my understanding that you can still play that piano, that only your stubborn pride keeps you from the keyboard."

"Do you think I'd get up on stage again and feel like an exhibit in a circus? Let folks cluck their tongues at the poor legless man who can't use the pedals but must make do with an assortment of wires and levers?"

"Don't you consider yourself fortunate that such an invention was perfected for your use? Or hasn't that fact occurred to you?" she asked.

"What has *occurred* to me is that it was a mistake to take on the task of giving piano lessons to those two children. Catherine will never be more than competent. Toby will be past the need for my limited help within two years. He should go to a conservatory, and I doubt if his parents will send him. They have no concept of his talent. If the boy makes it to a concert stage, it will be because of his own ambition."

"Don't you think your influence might be the deciding factor at the end of two more years of lessons? Don't you think his folks would listen to you? In fact, did you realize that his mother is scrimping and saving her pennies to pay for his lessons? Does that sound like a woman who has no concept of her son's talent?"

Jake looked at her in silence, his face set in hard lines, his jaw thrust forward. "It's easy for you to come up with these pat phrases, isn't it? You don't know what you're talking about."

She shrugged. "Maybe not. Maybe I'm ignorant about such things, but I do know that we're each put on this earth for a purpose. You could have just as easily died the night you were wounded. Instead you came home with a long life ahead of you."

"You call this living?" he asked, looking down at his

lap. "I call it merely existing, getting up and going to bed, providing a subject of gossip for the townspeople, and allowing you to vent your spleen on me."

She laughed aloud, his words so patently ridiculous she could barely give them credence. "'Vent my spleen'? What a thing to say." She picked up the freshly washed kettles and carried them to the pantry and then reentered the kitchen to face him.

"You'll have your supper in thirty minutes, Mr. McPherson. Now, get out of my sight while I cook. I can't abide looking at you."

HE'D NEVER SEEN HER so upset. In all the months they'd shared, she'd never lost her temper as she had during the past few minutes. Jake rolled backward from the kitchen door and let it close behind him. Spinning the chair in a half circle, he went back to the parlor. The late afternoon sun shone in the windows, the lacy curtains creating a pattern on the floor. The windows gleamed with the application of vinegar and water Alicia used on their surface every couple of weeks; fly specks were a thing of the past.

He'd been nasty. Downright rotten, taking out his mood on the one person who had put up with him without complaint for the whole livelong summer. She seemed, sometimes, to bring out the worst in him, and he had a sneaking suspicion that his own foul mood was due in good part to one thing.

The fear that she might not see him as a man.

True, he was not physically fit, but Rena had thought him worthy of her love. His arms and chest were muscular, his body not gone to fat. Yet Alicia looked at him as though he were a neutral being, neither male nor female.

He wanted her to see him as a man, needed to know that she felt some spark of desire in his direction. Since the night she'd asked him to kiss her, and he'd so readily obliged, she'd backed away. She seldom touched him, only when she trimmed his hair or helped him wash it in the kitchen basin. Except for the tender touch of her lips against his cheek, once. A touch he'd cherished.

She carried hot water to his room in the evening, waited on him at the table, took care to keep his clothing in order, putting it away in his dresser drawers when the washer lady brought it back in the big basket. As far as her duties were concerned, Alicia had done all she'd bargained for, and more, too, he admitted to himself.

They sat on the porch of an evening, speaking of various topics. She kept him on his toes, gave him food for thought. First and foremost, she did her best to keep Jason in line. That the boy refused to cooperate at times was frustrating, but it would all work out eventually.

The only thing she didn't do was look at him as Rena had, with soft smiles and warm glances. He hadn't asked for that. To be honest, he'd told her there would be no intimacy in this relationship. So why was he critical now because she was living up to the rules he'd set in place?

He rolled to the piano. The lid was still up, neither he nor Toby thinking to close it down. He reached for it and his hand slipped, one finger brushing a key. The hammer touched the string and the single tone resounded in the room. D above middle C.

He forced down the lid with a thud and he glared at the inanimate object. To be angry at a piano was an exercise in futility indeed. The piano couldn't even give him a good argument in return. As had Alicia. As she'd done for the past months of their marriage. His anger vanished as quickly at it had sprung into being.

Again, he owed her an apology, though his frown belied his willingness to perform the task. He rolled from the parlor and found Jason sitting on the bottom step of the long staircase.

"Are you done fightin' with Miss Alicia?" the boy asked. "She sure was mad at you, wasn't she?"

"She had good reason," Jake told him. "If you want to hear me make amends, come along to the kitchen. I might need some moral support."

Jason rose from his spot and meandered ahead of

the rolling chair. "What's moral support?" he asked, pushing open the kitchen door for his father to pass through.

"It's you standing next to me and smiling a lot when I tell her what an idiot I was a few minutes ago."

Jason looked at him and whispered words of rebuke. "Pa, you're not ever supposed to call anybody an idiot. Miss Alicia told us in school that it was the height of ignorance to belittle another person's shortcomings." He spit the words out as if he had memorized them and stored them in his mind for just this moment.

"She was right, Jason," Jake said quietly, watching Alicia across the room, her back stiff, her head held high as she stirred something in a kettle on the stove. "But in this case, *I'm* the idiot, and I don't think that rule applies.

"I need to talk to you," he said, raising his voice to get Alicia's attention.

"Go ahead," she said. "I can hear you from here."

"I think I could do this more easily if you'd look at me."

"Then you'll have to wait until I dish up your supper."

The woman was still fuming. Even though she'd laughed aloud at his remark about her venting her spleen, it had not been the sound of merriment, but rather bitter sarcasm.

"All right. I'll wait." He rolled to the table and motioned toward the sink. "Wash up, Jason, and get out the plates and silverware."

"Yes, sir," the boy answered, doing as he was bid. He slanted a long look at Alicia as he sorted through the forks and knives, found three napkins in the drawer, and placed them on top of the plates before he carried the stack to the table.

"Fork on the left," Alicia said automatically.

"What's the difference?" Jason asked with a sigh of patience gone awry. "Who cares where the fork is?"

"I care," Alicia said from the stove. "If you're going to do a job, do it right."

Jason rolled his eyes, and Alicia turned to him. "You will not be disrespectful to me, young man. I will not tolerate it."

As if inviting Jake to step in and soothe Alicia's ruffled feathers, Jason sent him a pleading look. His father only shook his head and lifted an eyebrow in response.

Alicia dished up the food—an assortment of leftover chicken from the night before, with noodles and broth added to make a thick stew of sorts. Carrots and fresh peas from the garden were in another bowl, and small whole potatoes were buttered and sprinkled with parsley in a third. Rather a sumptuous feast for a woman to put together in thirty minutes' time, Jake thought. No one had ever said Alicia was not efficient in the kitchen.

She put the food on the table and sat down, placing her napkin on her lap. Jake waited, as she bowed her head and gave thanks. "I'll fix your plate, Jason," his father said, and noted that the boy was agreeable in the extreme.

"Yes, sir," he said politely. "May I get some bread, ma'am?" he asked Alicia, and at her nod, he went to the buffet and brought back the loaf and a knife to slice it with.

Alicia made short work of the task, and Jason carried the wrapped bread back to where it was kept.

"I have an apology to make," Jake said quietly. He heard Jason's indrawn breath at his words and shot the boy a silencing look.

"Really?" She was not going to make this easy, and he couldn't blame her, he decided.

"Yes. I was rude and nasty, and I said some foul things to you. And I'm truly sorry."

"Which things exactly are you apologizing for?"

"Well—" Jake began spooning the stew onto his plate and then serving some to Jason "—probably we should start with the 'venting your spleen' remark. That was pretty harsh. Then I said you didn't know what you were talking about. I'll have to admit, ma'am, that you generally don't speak your mind until you've got things all sorted out."

He reached for the bowl of vegetables. Jason made

a face, but his father ladled a heaping spoonful onto his plate. "If there's anything else I'm forgetting, I guess I'll have to include it in a general blanket apology." He looked up at Alicia and took note of the pain she didn't bother to conceal from him.

"All around, I've been a first-class grouch today. You were handy, so I took it out on you." His words were softly spoken and he watched her closely for a reaction of some sort. She only nodded and bent her head to the food on her plate.

Jake ate silently, making quick work of the meal Alicia had prepared, then he looked at Jason and pointed at the back door. "Out with you, son. You're excused from the table."

"I didn't finish my peas, Pa," Jason said.

"You can eat twice as many next time," Jake said briskly. "You're excused."

"Yes, sir." With an agile movement, Jason slid from his chair and placed his napkin beside his plate. Shooting a glance at Alicia, he ducked and headed for the back door.

"Now, let's talk." Jake leaned his elbows on the table, aware that he was breaking one of Alicia's cardinal rules of table manners. In response to her disapproving look, he leaned his chin on his folded hands and frowned.

"I'm not sure what you want from me, Alicia. Whatever it is, I'm apparently not capable of giving it. I have a nasty temper. I warned you before you married me that I was hard to live with, but you assured me you could handle it. Some days I feel like a man on a treadmill, the only difference being that I couldn't walk on a treadmill if I wanted to. My days begin and end with a struggle to get in and out of bed, and in between times I work to keep my body clean and presentable.

"I know I'm not easy to live with, but I'm trying. You have to believe that."

"I'd be happy to help you get in and out of bed, if you'd just ask me," she said, biting at her lower lip after the offer had left her lips. "I can help you wash every morning if you like. I'm willing to do whatever it takes to make your life easier, Jake."

"You're too damn good to me, and I feel guilty and then I act like a bas—"

She held up a hand and halted him midway through the word. "Don't say it," she said. "You're not a child born out of wedlock. It's my understanding that your parents were married before your birth. As to my being 'too damn good' to you, I hardly think that's reason enough for you to be ornery with me. If you like, I can start behaving like a shrew and see if that will help things."

He laughed aloud. Alicia knew exactly how to put him in his place, and moreover knew how to keep him there.

"If you won't accept my apology, I'll just have to repeat it in the morning, I suppose," he said, his humor greatly restored. "As to helping me in and out of bed, I won't ask that of you, Alicia. I won't subject you to the sight of my body."

She shrugged. "That's fine with me. I won't have to let you laugh at mine, then."

I wouldn't laugh, he wanted to say aloud. The words stuck in his throat, and he swallowed them whole. Right now, he'd give just about anything to have Alicia in his bed.

Just when he had become so fixed on the woman was beyond him.

CHAPTER ELEVEN

THERE WAS DELAY in school starting. The harvest was late and the children from the surrounding farms and ranches were needed to help in the fields. Older boys from town were in demand and most of them were willing to pitch in, especially when it would pay them so well.

But September was school time and she chafed at having to put all her plans in abeyance. Still, there was certainly enough to do around the big house to keep her busy. She arose on a Monday, looked out the window and noted the last of her crop of red tomatoes still hanging on the vines. Enough to make chili sauce, she decided. She had onions aplenty and green peppers in abundance.

The thought of the aroma of spices and vinegar turning the tomatoes into a savory mix made her hurry into her clothing, preparing for the day. Coffee was the first order of business and she put it on the stove. By the time she had the oatmeal cooked and the sausage fried, she knew Jake would be enticed and heading toward the kitchen.

My days begin and end with a struggle to get in and out of bed. He had sounded so bitter when he'd made the statement. Now she stood at the stove and wondered if he were grasping at the trapeze that hung over his bed, aiming for the rolling chair, or if he were already sitting at his dry sink, washing in fits and starts in the basin. He was making do with cold water this morning. But she was comforted by the fact that she'd provided him with a hot pitcherful last evening.

She'd empty his slop pail later on, when he was elsewhere in the house. It bothered him that she waited on him in that way, but his waste water and the rest of the contents of the covered bucket were simple enough to carry out back to the outhouse and dispose of.

She poured a cup of coffee for herself after ten minutes, keeping an ear out for his chair. In another ten minutes the food was on the back of the stove, keeping warm, and she began to worry. He'd never been this late rising. The door to his room was closed and she rapped on it twice.

"Jake? Are you up yet?"

There was no answer and she frowned, rapping again; surely he could hear her.

"Jake? Can you hear me? Are you awake?" She waited another few seconds and turned the handle. It opened readily and she looked into the room. The curtains were drawn, a new practice, Jason had told her, since Jake had lived day and night in the gloom before Alicia's arrival.

Now the sunlight shone across the floor and she scanned the room quickly. His chair sat beside the bed, empty. Jake was still beneath the sheet and she called his name again, then walked toward the bed. As she approached, he stirred, mumbled under his breath and rolled to face her. His face was flushed, his hair matted and the sheet was tangled around him as if he'd fought with it all night. Her palm on his forehead proved her to be on target, for his skin radiated heat.

"What's wrong?" she asked, aware even as she spoke that he did not hear her. Jake was sick, feverish it seemed, and she was hard put to know what to do about it. He would resent it if she took charge the way she was prone to do in every circumstance.

Yet, she really had no choice. First, though, the doctor must be called. Backing from the room, she went to the staircase and called for Jason. He appeared in moments, rubbing his eyes, his hair sticking up at all angles, looking so much like his father, it took her breath.

"What's the matter?" he asked, peering down at her.

"I need you to get dressed and go for the doctor, Jason. Your father is sick, I'm afraid. He seems to be running a fever and I'm not certain what to do."

The boy's face turned pale, his freckles standing out like so many specks of paint. "I'll hurry, Miss Alicia," he said, moving back into his room. Within a few seconds he was on his way down the stairs, buttoning his shirt and tucking it into his trousers. "I'll run real fast," he told her, and as he got to the front door, he turned and asked a question that sent chills down her spine.

"Is he gonna die? Like my mom?"

Alicia stiffened her spine and cast the boy a severe look, intent on making light of his fears, lest he panic. "Of course not, Jason. He's just caught a chill. He'll be fine in a day or so."

He slipped out the door and was gone. The doctor lived in the center of town and, with any luck, Jason should be back with him inside half an hour. In the meantime she needed to be busy trying to get Jake's fever under control.

The basin of cool water was simple enough to carry to the bedside. She dipped a towel in the water, then wrung it out and placed it on his head. She placed a second towel on his chest. Jake's undershirt opened up with pearl buttons all the way down the front and Alicia had no qualms about opening it wide to apply the cool wet cloth to his chest.

She lifted the towel from his forehead and felt the heat it had collected. A quick rinsing and wringing out made it ready for another application, and by the time

Doc Hayes had arrived, she had managed a system that kept her changing towels at a regular pace.

"What seems to be wrong, Mrs. McPherson?" the doctor asked. He approached the bed, bent over Jake and gently raised one of his eyelids to take a look. "He's got quite a fever, hasn't he?"

Since he didn't seem to expect a reply, Alicia didn't bother offering one, but kept on with the task she'd set for herself. The doctor opened his bag and took his stethoscope from its depths and positioned it on Jake's chest to listen to his heart.

"His heart's beating like a trip-hammer," he said quietly. "We need to get that fever under control." He rolled Jake to his side and pulled the shirt from his back. "Wonder what in the world brought it on." He looked up at Alicia. "I surely hope you're not excessively bashful, ma'am. We're going to have to strip him down for this."

"That's fine," Alicia said quietly.

"Lend a hand here," the doctor said, stripping the sheet back and bending to remove the drawers that were buttoned at Jake's waist. He moved them quickly down the muscular thighs and then took up a towel and placed it in a strategic spot to protect the unconscious man's modesty.

Careful to keep her gaze from Jake's legs, Alicia picked up the drawers and placed them with the pile of clothing Jake had removed last evening. It seemed an intrusion to gape at his scars, when he couldn't deny her the sight of his wounded legs. "What can I do?" she asked, anxious to help.

Doc Hayes rummaged in his bag and drew forth a bottle. "Make him some tea with this. Six drops in a cup of hot water and add some sugar. It doesn't taste like anything you'd want to guzzle down, but he won't care at this stage. We'll give it to him in sips with a spoon."

Alicia hurried to the kitchen, where Jason sat at the table, trying valiantly to eat a bowl of oatmeal. "Is he gonna be all right?" he asked, clearly worried. He was a child, Alicia reminded herself. Only a boy. And so she knelt beside him and put her arms around the narrow shoulders and drew him against her.

"Of course he's going to be all right," she said, wishing she could cross her fingers to take away the lie. She didn't know that Jake would be all right. In fact, right now he didn't look anything like the man she'd fought with just two days since.

"I have to make some tea for your father," she told Jason. "Would you clear up the kitchen as best you can while I help the doctor?"

"Yes, ma'am," Jason said obediently, the most docile she'd seen him in the months since school let out.

The tea was ready in moments, the big kettle holding hot water at the ready, the six drops measured carefully. Carrying the cup back into the bedroom, she stirred the sugar in and prepared to dose him.

"Try to get a few drops down him," the doctor said. "Sit down right there beside him and talk to him. See if you can persuade him to open his mouth."

"Jake?" She leaned over him, her hand against his forehead, then bent to whisper in his ear. "Jake? Can you hear me? I need you to take some of this tea. Open your mouth for me, will you?"

His eyes opened, shiny with fever, his pupils shrinking to pinpoints as he looked toward the sunlight pouring in the window. "Rena?" he asked, his voice hoarse as he spoke the name.

"Yes, Jake. Just open your mouth and take some of this tea."

Alicia felt the doctor's gaze touch her as she coaxed the sick man to respond, knew his eyes held pity for the hurt she must feel. That Jake should call Rena's name was enough to make her howl with anguish.

The teaspoon trembled in her hand and half the tea dribbled down his chin. "Open your mouth," she repeated, attempting to pour a scant teaspoonful at a time between his lips. She feared him choking on the liquid, yet he seemed to swallow automatically.

"We need to keep that up," the doctor said. "I'll work at the towels if you'll keep up with the tea."

"Whatever it takes," she told him, concentrating on

Jake. His big body radiated heat, and it seemed the towels were having little effect on him.

"Let's try some rubbing alcohol," the doctor murmured. "Dilute it half-and-half with water, ma'am, and we'll douse him good with it."

Alicia rose and did as she was bidden, then settled back down to bathe Jake with the alcohol mix. The moisture lay against his skin and evaporated quickly. Then his eyes opened, and he looked up at her, his expression dazed, his brow furrowed.

"Alicia? What's wrong?" he asked hoarsely. He tossed his head from one side to the other. "I'm hot. Can you open the window?"

"You have a fever, Jake. Just lie still and let me bathe you."

His mouth twitched and he laughed, a rusty sound that held not a shred of genuine humor. "I didn't think to get you in my bedroom this way."

"Pardon?" The word slid from her lips automatically as she bent closer. Fortunately the doctor was busy digging in his bag and missed the byplay, but it mattered little, for Alicia felt a blush creep over her cheeks at Jake's words.

His eyes closed again and he groaned as a chill gripped him and his body shuddered. "Cold," he whispered, his arms crossing over his chest as if he tried to preserve body heat.

"Doc?" Alicia raised her voice and the doctor looked in her direction. "He's taken a chill," she said.

"Not surprising. When a man runs so high a fever, it sometimes goes in the other direction, kind of a re-action to the strain on his body." He looked toward the wardrobe. "Any quilts in there?"

Alicia rose from the bed. "I'll get one." She opened the wooden door and reached for a thickly quilted cov-erlet, opening it and spreading it over Jake's body. He was trembling in earnest now, and she felt the urge to hold him against her in order to lend him her own heat.

For almost an hour, they fought the shivers, tried to stem the trembling with a second quilt and a hot water bottle Alicia found in the airing cupboard upstairs. They rolled Jake onto his side, then placed the warmth against his back and held it there with a pillow, doing their best to offset the effect of chills.

"I think he's taken with a fever of some sort," Doc Hayes said. "Probably something he picked up in the war. Sometimes these things hibernate and then show up years later. If that's what it is, it shouldn't last more than a day or two." He sorted through his bag and brought forth another small bottle.

"Once he comes to, you'll need to dose him with this, Mrs. McPherson. Just the same way you made the tea. Six drops or so in a cup of hot water. It'll help with the fever. A high temperature is more dangerous to him than the chills." He picked up his bag and approached the bed again.

"Just do the best you can. I'll stop by this afternoon when I've returned from seeing a couple of sick folks outside of town. I think you can handle it all right."

The thought of being left with the sick man was frightening. But, unwilling to admit her fears, Alicia nodded agreeably and followed the doctor to the bedroom door.

"I can find my way out," he said, and shot her a penetrating glance. "You seem like a capable woman, ma'am. But if you want me to, I'll send a message out to Cord and let him know you're needing help."

She shook her head. "I think we'll be fine. If Jake doesn't perk up by evening, I'll think about letting Cord know."

Doc Hayes nodded and walked quickly toward the front of the house. Jason came from the kitchen and watched the man leave, then looked to Alicia, his eyes shiny with tears he refused to shed.

"Will my pa be all right?" he asked. "Can I go look at him?"

"Yes, to both questions," Alicia said briskly. "You keep an eye on him while I fix myself a piece of bread. I'll need something in my stomach to keep me going. Just sit beside him and call me if he stirs."

Jason nodded and Alicia went on into the kitchen.

She'd purposely kept her gaze averted from Jake's legs, but the sight of scarred stumps had touched her peripheral vision and she swallowed hard as she thought of the pain he must have endured while his wounds healed. It was no wonder the man was grouchy sometimes, bitter most of the time and a recluse without a desire to associate with his fellow man.

One leg was indeed longer than the other, his right knee still intact, and she closed her eyes as she recognized the cruel results of war. He had a right to be ornery, surely must be filled with anger at the limitations he lived under. She'd been able to overlook his injuries so long as she did not actually see the tortured limbs. Now they loomed before her, making her aware of the pride that had kept her from viewing the damage.

She might never be allowed admittance to his bed, although his remark had startled her into wondering just what his thoughts had been on the matter. *I didn't think to get you in my bedroom this way.*

Well, like it or not, she was situated there now. At least for the next day or so. Long enough, anyway, to get him past the sudden illness that had struck him during the night. Maybe Cord would know if Jake had been prone to a recurring fever. It might be worthwhile to send someone out to the ranch to let him know about the situation.

She took her cup of coffee with her, carrying a plate with a slice of bread on it, and returned to the bedroom. Jason sat still beside his father, only turning his head to regard her beseechingly as she approached the bed.

"He's going to be fine," she whispered, hoping to comfort the boy. But his eyes grew shiny once again, and he rose hurriedly and went to the window, as if he would not allow her to be an audience to his tears. "I'm sure of it, Jason," she said more firmly. "I wouldn't lie to you. I think you know that. Besides, the doctor wouldn't have left if he weren't sure that your father was going to be all right."

Those words seemed to reach him, for he turned to face her. "I suspect you're right," he said. "I think I'll just stay here, though, if it's all right with you." At her nod, he settled in a chair near the window and watched as she adjusted the quilts over Jake.

He'd ceased trembling now and had tossed the quilt aside, though he shifted restlessly beneath the sheets. "Hot…" he muttered beneath his breath.

Alicia went to the basin and dampened the towels again, placing one on his forehead, the second on his chest. She spoke soothingly, calming words that seemed to settle him. His hand reached for her, groping against her dress, restless fingers tugging at her. Setting aside the cup she held, she lifted his hand and cradled it between her palms.

"I'm here, Jake," she said quietly. "You're going to be fine."

"Hot." He repeated the word, moving restlessly against the sheet. The bowl of rubbing alcohol and water was nearby and Alicia began smoothing the cooling liquid over his skin, leaving it to evaporate and dry.

She lost track of time, knowing only that Jason came and went, bringing her more coffee, carrying in a cup of hot water for her to use in making the tea required. She spent long minutes coaxing Jake to swallow, watching carefully to gauge his reaction to the medicine. It helped, she decided, soothing him, taking the edge off his fever.

When the doctor returned late in the afternoon, she was still beside Jake and waited anxiously as he was examined. "I think he's doing well," Doc Hayes said finally. "He'll no doubt be restless tonight. Fever always seems to rise around midnight. Never could figure out why it's thataway, but I know it's true."

He gathered his things, closed his bag and readied for his departure. "I'll drop by in the morning, ma'am," he said. "If you need me through the night, send the boy."

Jason elected to sleep on the couch in the parlor, as if he would not rest being farther from his father. Alicia prepared for the long night, putting on her nightgown and wrapper, then settling into a rocking chair she brought from the parlor, in order to gain some small amount of comfort during the dark hours.

She dozed off and on, rousing when Jake complained of discomfort, bathing him and then covering him when he became chilled. The night was long and she rested little, her eyes closing when it seemed she could no longer hold them open.

Late morning found Cord at the back door, and he came to Jake's room without delay. "What's going on?" he asked gruffly, his gaze falling on the man who did not respond to his voice. "Doc Hayes went past early on and let me know Jake was down with the fever again."

"He's had this before?" Alicia asked, feeling relief that Cord recognized an ongoing condition.

"Something he brought home with him years back," Cord said. "This happens once in a great while, but it lasts for a couple of days usually. Makes him miserable while it keeps a grip on him. But if you'll just keep him cool when the fever hits and warm when he takes a chill, he should get over it without any trouble."

He looked at Alicia, his gaze measuring. "I want you to go up to bed. I'll stay with him while you sleep. I'm afraid you'll be up all night again tonight, so you'd better rest while you can."

She didn't argue with him, but gratefully trudged up the stairs and sought her bed, only rising late in the afternoon when Rachel came to her door. "Alicia? Are you all right?" she asked. "Cord is about ready to go home, but I can stay if you need me to."

Alicia sat up, then scooted to the edge of the bed, her toes seeking out the carpet slippers she'd left on the rug earlier. "No. You both go on home. I'm awake now, and I'll be fine through the night." She yawned widely and smiled.

"I didn't think I'd sleep so long." She rose and picked up her wrapper, donning it quickly, then reaching for her brush. "Is Jake still the same?" she asked, gathering her hair together in her palm in readiness to braiding it.

"Just about," Rachel said. "I've seen this before, and it's frightening, but he usually comes out of it in a day or two. It just takes a lot out of whoever has to tend him. Cord is wiping him down again right now. The fever returned a while ago."

"I'm coming," Alicia said, braiding her hair with haste and preparing to return to the sickroom. "Can you see to it that Jason gets something to eat?"

"I'm going to try persuading him to go home with me," Rachel said quietly. "He's worried about Jake, but you don't need the distraction of him being here, and he'll do better if he's somewhere else with something to occupy his mind."

Alicia was grateful for the suggestion. The boy had fears enough without watching his father in the throes of illness. Perhaps Cord could be the deciding factor.

She went downstairs and headed directly for Jake's

room. Cord was bent over the bed, drawing the cloth over Jake's body, the scent of alcohol in the air. He looked up as Alicia neared.

"I think it's working," he said, standing erect and rubbing at his back. "I hate to run off and leave you, but I've got a horse down with colic, Alicia, and I need to be back at the ranch. Will you be all right till morning with him? Did you get a good sleep?"

"I'll be fine," she assured him, then sat down beside her patient. Jake's eyes opened and his hand reached for hers.

"Alicia." His voice sounded rusty as he spoke her name and she was grateful he'd managed to recognize her. Had he called for Rena, she'd have been mortified. It was bad enough that the doctor had been privy to that bit of delirium, let alone having Cord know that Alicia was definitely in second place in Jake's thoughts.

By late evening the house was in darkness, only a candle on the bedside table lighting the sickroom. Jason had been persuaded to go home with Cord and Rachel, and Alicia was fortified with a cold meal of cheese and bread. She'd managed to get three cups of tea down Jake's throat and sensed that he was feeling better.

He slept for several hours and she leaned back in the rocking chair, closing her eyes and relaxing. Then, with a start, she was awakened by his voice, muttering and then rising as he called out with harsh tones.

The words were unintelligible, but the terror in his eyes as they opened wide spoke of some remembered horror in his past.

She moved quickly to sit beside him and he reached for her, his hands gripping her tightly, her arms almost numb from the hold he maintained on them. "Don't let them—" he said harshly. "Don't let them do it!"

And then his eyes closed and he groaned, a sound that reflected an agony she could only wonder at. "Jake," she whispered, leaning over him, thankful that his fingers had loosened their grip on her. He did not hear her, but muttered under his breath. Then he reached for her again, this time drawing her over him, his arms enclosing her as she leaned awkwardly against his chest.

As if he could not release her, could not bear to be alone where he lay, he drew her to his side, his hands strong, his arms capturing her, and she found herself lying beside him, held against his warm body. She shifted a bit and he tightened his hold.

"Don't go," he said. "Lie with me. I need you." He opened his eyes and slurred the syllables of her name. "Alicia." He spoke it softly, pleadingly, and she responded in the only way she could. She reached her arm across his chest, rested her head against his rib cage, and heard the reassuring thudding of his heart as he inhaled deeply and then released a shuddering breath.

He was quiet then, neither hot nor cold, and she determined to be thankful for this respite from the ordeal he'd suffered. She closed her eyes and slept.

THE WOMAN IN HIS ARMS was soft, curving against his side, and Jake felt a satisfied grin curve his lips. He was exhausted, still feverish, but knew that the worst of his attack was a thing of the past. The fever had come on suddenly, before he could call out for Alicia to help him.

Alicia. The woman he held was Alicia. He'd thought… For a moment, he'd thought it was Rena, had thrilled to the joy of holding her close. But Rena was gone. She would ever be beloved to him, but Alicia had somehow moved in to fill that hollow place in his life where Rena had once reigned.

Alicia. He opened his eyes and saw her lashes against her cheek. Dark and sweeping, they touched the rosy skin, concealing her blue eyes from his sight. She must be worn out with nursing him, he thought, and felt a moment's tenderness for the woman he'd married. He'd expected much, and received abundantly from her hands.

Now she opened her eyes, as if she sensed his regard and blinked up at him. "Jake?" she asked. The dawn was breaking, the window becoming filled with the glow of radiance that preceded the rising of the sun. "I must have slept," she whispered. Then, as if she became aware of her position, she jerked from him, rising in a quick movement to stand, swaying, beside the bed.

"Don't fall," he said, reaching to steady her.

"I won't." She was embarrassed, her face flushing as he watched. Looking around her as if she sought some distraction to turn his attention from her, she raised her hands to her hair, smoothing back the waves and loose tendrils that had come free from her braid. "I'm sorry, Jake. I didn't mean to intrude."

He uttered a sound of protest. "You haven't done any such thing," he told her. "You only stayed with me and took care of me." And then he recognized that he lay naked beneath the quilt that covered him. The woman had seen him, had no doubt gotten an eyeful of his maimed body. He felt a rush of shame that she should have been forced by the weakness of his condition into this situation.

"I'm sorry to have put you through this," he said roughly. "I'll be fine now. Go on up and get some rest, Alicia. I'm all right to be alone. The worst of it is over."

She stepped back from him as if he'd struck her, and indeed he had, in a figurative manner. She'd only done what any considerate, concerned person would do. Had no doubt spent long hours tending him, and all he could think of was the shame he felt at her viewing his body, with its scars and the stumps he called legs.

Before he could speak words of apology, she was

gone, turning with an awkward movement and heading for the door. He heard her go into the kitchen, knew when she put wood into the stove, then heard the coffeepot scrape across the iron surface.

As if his senses were refined, and his hearing attuned to each movement she made, he listened for her. Her footsteps were light as she left the kitchen, approaching his doorway. And then she watched him from the threshold. "I'll fix you something to eat," she offered. "How about some toast, maybe a scrambled egg or two?"

He shook his head. "I don't think I can swallow anything yet. I still feel a little feverish."

"You are," she agreed. "Perhaps I should make another cup of the tea the doctor said you should drink."

He shivered, an automatic reaction as he recalled the vile taste of the stuff she'd poured down his throat during the long hours. Most of his illness was a blur, as it usually was when he had these episodes, but he distinctly recalled her sitting beside him, spooning the tea past his lips and into his mouth. "I'll be fine without any more of it," he said firmly. "I'll settle for some ordinary, everyday tea, instead, if you don't mind."

"Certainly." She spoke the word with formality, as if a barrier had been set between them. And then she was gone.

CHAPTER TWELVE

NO MATTER THAT HE HAD been abrupt, Alicia could not turn away from Jake, recognizing that his pride was involved, that his disability would perhaps forever be a barrier between them. Whether he liked it or not, he still needed her, required care that she alone could give for now. And so she went to her room and dressed for the day, returning to him as soon as she had fixed his tea. Her own cup sat on the kitchen table, for she would not presume to join him, leaving him to the privacy of his bedroom.

His bedroom. She'd been in his bed. That fact was enough to make her want to sink through the floorboards. She'd been in his arms, no matter that he'd pulled her down against him. She could have left his side. He wouldn't have clung to her, especially once he'd recognized that it wasn't his beloved Rena he held.

The cup trembled in her hand as she carried it to him, the tea threatening to slosh over the side. He watched her, raising himself on one elbow, and she thought that his face looked drawn, his skin waxen. His bout with fever had not left him unscathed, for there was an air of fragility about him that reminded her of how very ill he had been only hours before.

"Is that for me?" he wanted to know, and at her nod he scooted up in bed to rest against the headboard. "Will you prop my pillows behind me?" he asked, taking the cup from her hand. Leaning forward, he waited until she did as he'd bid her and then leaned back, his breath leaving him with a shudder.

"I'm worn out," he admitted, lifting the cup to sip with appreciation.

"I can believe that," she replied, feeling uncomfortable, smothering her natural inclination to pass the time of day with him. She felt strange, almost like a trespasser in his room, and yet there was no need. She'd been here for a purpose, and her presence had been of necessity.

"You look like you'd rather be somewhere else, Alicia." He regarded her from beneath his brows as he raised the cup to his lips again. "Did my illness turn you against me?"

She was stunned by his query. "Of course not," she said firmly. "I don't know what would make you think that."

"Don't you?" He rested the cup on his lap and gave her his full attention. "I'm assuming that, in the course of events, you were given a bird's-eye view of my legs. Or what remains of them. Am I right?"

She cleared her throat. "Yes, of course I saw your legs. There was no help for it. I helped the doctor care for you, and then I spent the night in this room."

"I remember parts of it," he said. "I knew who you were when I awoke and found you with me. Quite often, I'm lost in dreams or memories that sweep through me like the ocean tide."

"You had a few of those, too," she said, remembering the cry of anguish he'd released. *Don't let them do it.*

His mouth curved. "Did I? I hesitate to ask about them." He rested his head against the headboard. "I'm not as strong as I'd thought. Perhaps I should wait and drink the rest of the tea later. Would you mind taking it away?"

She bent and removed it from his hand, noting the trembling of his fingers. He was shaky, unwilling to admit just how weak he still was, but she was smart enough to recognize that he had not fully recovered his strength.

"I'll let you rest now," she told him. "Perhaps I can make some soup for you. I'll have it ready for you later today, after you sleep for a bit."

"You're determined to make an invalid out of me, aren't you?" he asked dryly. Scooting down amid the quilts, he found a comfortable spot and drew the sheet up to cover his chest. She'd never seen such an expanse of bare male skin before in her life, and from the look in his eyes, he was mightily enjoying her discomfort.

"You're my wife, Alicia," he said softly, as if he would remind her that their situation was not in any way against the rules of good taste. "You're allowed to see my chest, you know."

"I saw more than that," she said sharply. "Looking at a man's nakedness is not my usual behavior."

"Well, since you've never been married before, I suppose I understand that." He smiled, his grin triumphant, and then closed his eyes. "Let me know when the soup is done," he said, turning his head aside and dismissing her abruptly.

She left him, turning on her heel and leaving the room with a swish of her skirts that spoke a language he would have no doubt recognized had he been watching. The man was crude, she decided. Either that, or he was protecting himself against the thought of her eyes beholding his body; if that were so, she could understand.

The soup was vegetable, begun with a pint of the beef Rachel had cooked up for Jake's use last year. Alicia added vegetables from the garden; peas and carrots, a handful of green beans and a large onion. A cabbage was ready to cut from its roots, and she sliced thin pieces from it and placed them atop the simmering mixture. By the time it was ready to eat,

Jake had been asleep for three hours, and she was aware that he needed nourishment more than he needed rest right now.

She placed a bowl of steaming broth on a tray she'd found in the pantry, then carried it in to him. He roused when she walked across the room and blinked at her, as if he were confused about her presence there.

"Are you hungry?" she asked, and his eyes focused on her.

"Yes, as a matter of fact," he answered. "I'm feeling much better. I think I'm well on the road to recovery."

She sat beside him, uncomfortable with his nearness, yet aware that the hot soup could prove to be dangerous should he slip and spill it on his lap. He allowed her to help, watching as she held the bowl in front of him, then handed him the spoon. He savored one sip, then he sighed. "I've married a woman of many talents, Alicia. You not only know how to tend a sick man, but you are capable of feeding him food fit for a king."

"It's only soup," she said. "Not the nectar of the gods."

His brow tilted a bit. "Don't argue with me. I'm the one who's sick."

He was teasing her again and she felt suddenly more at ease. The soup was finished readily, and he looked at her pleadingly. "Do you suppose I could have some more?"

"Later on," she said, bargaining with him. "If this

doesn't upset your stomach, I'll fix another bowl in an hour or so."

"You strike a mean bargain, Mrs. McPherson." His eyes made a slow survey of her and she felt the heat of his appraisal. "You look nice in that dress," he said. "I haven't seen it before."

She'd pulled it from the wardrobe, a brightly flowered gown that had struck her fancy in the store one day, and then had hung, unworn, for the past year. Too bright for the schoolroom, and definitely not subdued enough for Sunday church services; she'd rued the day she spent good money for such a frivolous garment.

Now, as he looked at her with admiring eyes, she found herself flustered by his words.

"Thank you. The colors are brighter than I usually wear."

"It brings out the pink in your cheeks," he told her. "Makes your eyes look blue."

"My eyes *are* blue," she said, wondering where this conversation was heading.

"Bluer, then," he told her.

She picked up the tray and rose and he leaned back, never moving his gaze from hers. "Thank you for looking after me," he said, teasing aside now.

"You'd do the same for me." And then she paused. "Wouldn't you?"

"Would I strip you naked and sponge you off?" He

paused as if considering the question, then grinned. "Why, of course!"

"That's not what I meant," she retorted, not knowing where to look as she cringed from the picture his words brought to mind.

"I'm teasing you, Alicia," he said quietly. "Come back in later, will you? I want to talk to you."

She escaped to the kitchen, and then stood thoughtfully in the middle of the room for a calming minute. Things were out of hand. The relationship they'd managed to keep on an even keel was rocking like a small ship on a large ocean. She felt the waves lapping at her feet and knew a moment of panic.

What if…. The thought of him actually doing such a thing, of his hands removing her clothing, was too frightening to contemplate.

She dished up a bowl of soup for herself and took it out onto the back stoop, sitting there in the late afternoon sunshine, wondering what he wanted to talk about. Maybe Jason would be home tonight. Certainly Cord or Rachel would be bringing him back. And yet, Rachel had said a day or two.

If Jason was having a good time with his cousins, and if Rachel's brothers, the two Sinclair boys, who lived and worked on the McPherson ranch, were about, Jason would be more than happy to extend his visit.

He'd sung their praises several times during the summer, speaking of Henry and Jay in the language of hero worship.

Back in the kitchen, she worked to clean up the stove, storing the remaining soup in another, smaller pan, and then decided to see if Jake had a taste for more of it now.

"Are you still hungry?" she asked, poking her head around the doorjamb of his room. He nodded and she backed away, pleased to be busy after lollygagging around for most of the day.

When she returned he took the bowl from her and ate in silence for a few minutes, as if his appetite had returned full force. "Do you know how to play checkers?" he asked, pausing in the midst of lifting the spoon to his mouth.

She only looked at him disbelievingly. "Everyone knows how to play checkers," she said. "I can play checkers, jacks, mumblety-peg and poker. I know how to jump rope, and I've played a mean game of hide-and-seek in my day." She reconsidered the last statement. "That is, before my mother and father decided there were more important things to do than run and play."

"Were they very strict with you?" he asked.

She nodded. "I wasn't unhappy, mind you. Just restricted from the common, ordinary games that most children play. I was trained from an early age to be a schoolteacher, given the best education they could afford, and then turned loose in a classroom when I was nineteen years old."

"Eleven years? You've taught for eleven years?" Jake asked, amazed. "That's almost half your lifetime."

"Sometimes it seems longer than that," she admitted. Then she shook herself mentally, as if to set aside the sadness she'd felt for a moment. "To get back to your question, Jake. Yes, I can play checkers. Are you asking me to give you a game?"

"It would make the evening pass quickly, wouldn't it?" he asked. "Then maybe you could read to me, pretend I'm an invalid in need of care."

"Poetry?" she asked, thinking of the ladies in the general store who'd thought a book of poetry might be a welcome gift for him.

He looked up at her, his eyes narrowing. "Now that you mention it, I like some of the poets. Although fiction is more to my liking. I have some books on the shelves here."

She rose and walked to browse among them, selecting two from the shelf and opening them at random. "I enjoy reading aloud," she told him, and placed both books on the table beside the bed. "I'll find a lamp to bring in here and use it to read by later."

HE DECIDED THAT LAMPLIGHT was kind to Alicia. It magnified the hollows in her cheeks, made her eyes appear larger and once more changed her hair to a hue not unlike the mahogany banister's richly polished surface. She read well, but then he'd known she would. The woman did everything she tackled as if it were of utmost importance in the general scheme of things. Whether it was a simple task such as sewing on a button or putting together a meal fit for a king, she was adept in each part of her life.

Now she read, and he found that he was not following the storyline, but instead relishing the pleasant sound of her voice and the animation of her face. He was simply enjoying her company, he decided, never mind the fact that she was devoting her evening to his entertainment.

They'd played four games of checkers, and she'd beaten him soundly three times before he called it quits. The final game had ended when he lifted his knee and scattered the checkers over his lap, and then frowned as if he were truly repentant. "I was no doubt going to win that game, too," he'd said regretfully, and been pleased at her hoot of laughter.

Now he lay back against the pillows and concentrated on the sound of her voice, its resonance lending depth to the words she read, even as he listened with half an ear to the tree frogs outside that filled the night with their music. He could have written a symphony, he decided, using the simple chirp they produced, varying it and elaborating on its melody.

No, he couldn't. The thought of what composing would entail—the long hours at the piano, the sheets of paper he would fill with notes, and the very act of fingering the keys—was enough to make him retreat into brooding silence.

"Jake? Are you all right?" Alicia's voice called him back, and he blinked as he focused on her expression and the concerned look that darkened her eyes.

She was attuned to him, he'd found. When his mood changed, as it so often did, she became aware of it, casting him long looks and biting her lip as if she would inquire as to his thoughts, but felt constrained by his belligerent silence. Now he forced himself to look beyond the perplexed expression she wore, knew a moment of guilt as she closed the book and placed it in her lap.

"I'm fine," he said. "Put the book back on the shelf, Alicia. I told you earlier we needed to talk. I think this is a good time for it." He watched her as she rose, her hips swaying as she replaced the book where it belonged, and then she turned and gave him her full attention.

"Come here," he said, patting the bed beside himself. She was hesitant and he smiled. "I won't bite you," he murmured, quirking an eyebrow.

"Don't be foolish," she muttered, stepping closer. "I hadn't even thought of that."

You should have. The thought sprang full-blown to his mind as she walked closer, and he reached to grasp her hand, held those long, slender fingers in his palm and drew her to sit on the edge of the mattress.

"What do you want to talk about?" she asked him. "Jason?"

He shook his head. "No, not Jason."

She seemed perplexed, shaking her head a bit, and then as his thumb moved slowly, carefully across her palm, she stilled, as if threatened by some unknown force. He rested her hand, fingers entwined with his, on his lap and decided quickly that it had been a mistake. She was too near that part of him that responded so readily to her proximity of late.

"Jake? What are you doing?" she asked, a look of panic shining in his direction.

"Just holding your hand. You're my wife, Alicia. Don't I have that right?"

She touched her upper lip with the tip of her tongue. "I suppose so." And then she shifted uncomfortably.

He raised her hand and brought it to his mouth, his lips forming a kiss against her knuckles. All the while, he watched her, feeling like a lion who has come to the water hole to drink, only to find a gazelle there, unaware of the danger. As was Alicia.

"Do you remember," he began, "that evening in the parlor, when you asked me to kiss you?"

She tugged, trying to loosen his grip on her hand, but to no avail. "Don't embarrass me, Jake. Of course I remember. It was foolishness on my part and I fear I put you in a spot."

He smiled. "I enjoyed it," he admitted. "I hadn't kissed a woman for a long time. And I'd never kissed a woman like you before."

"Like me?" she asked, her voice climbing. "What is *that* supposed to mean?"

"A woman so innocent, so naive, that she did not know what her kiss could do to a man."

"Do?" she asked, catching her breath as his tongue touched the tips of her knuckles and dampened its way across the small mountains they formed on the back of her hand.

"Shall I show you?" he asked, and then awaited her reply, knowing that if she withdrew from him, he would be obliged to let her go. He would not force her in this.

She was silent, looking confused and bewildered. And then she whispered the single syllable he waited to hear. "Yes."

He drew her closer, catching her across the shoulders with his free arm and pressing her against himself. Her head tilted, pillowed against his shoulder, and she turned her face up to his, then relaxed a bit, adjusting her position and leaning more fully against him.

He kissed her then, carefully, with a restraint he clung to with ferocious strength. It would not do to frighten her away when he was only just beginning to make a bit of progress with her. His mouth took hers, relishing the firmness of her lips, the soft pressure she offered in return and the scent of her that invaded him with the essence of woman.

She smelled of soap and starch, of fresh bread and cinnamon. The sweet aroma of a wife, he thought, and wondered how he'd become so fanciful. Her eyes closed, long lashes lying against her cheek, and he wished for another glimpse into their blue depths. He would settle for this, he decided, bending to her again and testing the line between her lips, his tongue pressing for admittance, even as he dared move his hand to touch the front of her bodice.

The first button came undone with ease, and then she stiffened in his arms. "Jake?" Panic underlined the single word she spoke, and he shushed her quickly, his mouth against hers, his lips whispering words of comfort.

"I won't hurt you, Alicia. I only want to touch you."

"Touch me?" She covered his hand with her own and his fingers moved beneath its fragile weight, undoing the next button, then the third. She did not call a halt to his shenanigans, only inhaled sharply as his index finger touched her skin.

"Touch you," he repeated quietly. "I've looked at you often, you know, wondering how you would feel in my hands."

"You have?" She sounded honestly surprised, he thought, and blessed the innocence of the woman he held. No other man had held her thusly, no other hand had invaded the valley between her soft, abundant breasts. He felt exultation sweep through him. Then he pushed aside the halves of her bodice, making room for his hand to enter beneath the fabric.

Her vest was fitted with tiny buttons and he found that his fingers worked well on the fragile fastenings. Alicia watched him, her eyes on his face, color rushing to her cheeks, and a sheen of some new emotion shading her eyes. He opened the vest wide, revealing twin mounds of soft flesh.

"I'm too big," she whispered. "My mother said so."

"Your mother didn't know what she was talking about," he murmured, wondering what fool of a woman would so mark her daughter with words of scorn. "You're exactly the right size." He covered one breast with his palm, its fullness plump and firm under his outspread fingers.

He bent closer and his lips touched her skin where the pink crest puckered as he breathed against it. His mouth opened and his tongue tasted her; he wondered at the shiver that spun through her body like heat lightning.

"Do I frighten you?" he asked softly. "I don't mean to."

"Nooo…" The single word was three syllables long as she drew it out.

He squeezed gently, admiring the pretty curves he'd uncovered, allowing her to become accustomed to his hand against her bare flesh. He released her then and drew back the vest more fully, exposing the second breast to his sight. The nipple puckered as he watched and he could not resist, lowering his head to take it between his lips, aware of her soft cry of surprise as he tasted of her.

"I didn't know…" Her words trailed off as if she could not speak her thoughts.

He looked up at her and smiled, loving the confusion she wore like a second skin, aware that the treasure he held was magnificent and worthy of his most careful attention. "You didn't know that your breasts could enjoy this? That this part of you was made for loving?"

"Loving? Is that what this is?"

He nodded. "What goes on between a man and his wife is loving of the very best kind, Alicia. Whether they consummate their relationship by physically joining their bodies or simply give each other pleasure in any way that pleases them, it's loving, and always right and proper."

"Are you sure this is a wise thing to do, Jake?" she asked, her voice trembling.

"Oh, yes," he said. "Unless you aren't enjoying it. Or unless I'm hurting you."

"No, of course you're not hurting me," she protested. "I doubt you'd ever do that."

"Then you aren't enjoying it?" he asked, bending his head to her again, aware that her tension was mounting with each touch of his fingers, each movement of his mouth against her skin.

"I am," she whispered.

"Am what?" he asked, forcing himself not to show his amusement in any tangible way, lest he hurt her feelings.

"You're teasing me," she said, wiggling against his lap as he took more of her breast into his mouth and suckled. The sound that passed her lips was a whimper of pleasure, a sound of yearning he could barely resist.

So intent was she on the attention he lavished on her breasts, she seemed barely to notice when he undid the remainder of her buttons and allowed her dress to fall from her shoulders and settle around her waist. His arms enclosed her as he felt the warmth of her lush form, and he knew a moment of aching need he'd thought would never be his again.

"Let me take off your clothes," he whispered, and knew the moment his words registered with her.

She stiffened against him and shook her head. "I can't," she said. "I just can't, Jake. I can't let you see me without anything on."

"You saw my legs, Alicia. Didn't you?"

"I tried not to look," she told him, and he smiled, his head bent as he heard the unspoken confession of her lapse. "I couldn't help it," she said. "I was helping the doctor take care of you."

"I want to take care of you now," he told her. "But I can't do it with all these layers between us."

She thought for a moment and then lifted her head to look at him. "Will you let me blow out the lamp?"

"If you need to." He wanted to see her in the light, but right now, he'd take her any way he could get her.

She leaned toward the lamp to blow out the flame, and then settled back in his arms. The darkness was absolute at first, and then the light from the window began to allow him small glimpses of her. "I can't get undressed this way," she complained. "I need to stand up first."

"By all means," he said judiciously, willing to allow her to stand before him and strip from the layers of clothing that hid her from his view.

She was pale in the faint glow from the windows, her arms pulling the vest from her body, then pushing her dress to the floor. She undid the ties of her petticoat and it followed the dress, leaving her in a pair of drawers that covered her thoroughly. He reached for her then, loosening them and pushing them from her hips. They fell at her feet and he murmured words that vibrated in his throat.

"Step out of them," he said hoarsely. "And take off your stockings."

She did as he asked, holding his shoulder for balance as she rolled the stockings to her ankles and then pulled them off. Standing before him, she was a woman blessed with a bountiful form, a woman who would have been beloved by the painters of the past, he thought, when such full-figured females were the most honored and respected of all women.

And she was his…every round, warm part of her was his to hold in his arms. In that moment he knew that he was blessed indeed to have the ripe perfection of Alicia McPherson before him.

His hands caressed her hips, cupped her bottom, and he felt her squirm against his palms. He was on the edge of the bed now, and he drew her to stand before him, then leaned forward to press his mouth against the curve of her belly, inhaling the sweet scent of her.

"I don't think you should—"

"Don't think at all," he said, silencing her protest. "Just know that I'm loving you, Alicia, that you are my wife and every part of you is precious to me." He looked up to where her face was a pale oval, her features not discernible. But he knew what she looked like, for he'd examined her from every angle over the past months, had made it his business to learn the lines of her form, the gentle sweep of her brow and the bow of her mouth.

"Will you lie down with me?" he asked gently. "I'm not as other men, Alicia. You know that, and what we do together will not be as it might have occurred if you'd wed another man. But I know we can find pleasure together if you'll give me a chance to make it happen."

She bowed her head, her lips pressing against his brow, and nodded, as if the words were hard to come by. And then he moved back, making room for her beside him.

CHAPTER THIRTEEN

HER HEAD FOUND a comfortable place on his shoulder and she snuggled close to him, her innocence leaving her unaware of the potent arousal that was making itself known beneath the sheet. He was warm, his body radiating heat—not with the fever that had possessed him last night—but with the healthy glow of a man whose body is preparing to take possession of his woman. He yearned for the patience to please her, to bring her a knowledge of pleasure.

"Jake?" She sounded curious and he turned a bit to face her, knowing that his manhood was surely becoming obvious to her now. She raised her hands to his chest and her fingertips pressed against the dark hair that centered his body, that ran in an arrow downward to where he felt an urgency he wasn't certain he could contain.

"I don't know what to do," she whispered.

The sound he made was almost a growl, a groan uttered deep within his throat, and he recognized the primitive part of himself that responded to her words. "Don't worry, sweetheart," he said, his voice husky with desire. "I know enough for both of us. All you have to do is let me love you, and try to be patient with me. I haven't done this for a long time, and I'm not sure my body will do as I want it to."

"I'll do anything you say," she told him, brave soul that she was, totally unaware of the effect her words had on him. She was giving him permission to lay claim to her, to possess her body without delay; but not for the world would he bring her undue pain.

"Then let me do this," he said to her, rolling her onto her back and leaning over her. He touched her breasts again, then lowered his head to suckle there, burying his face in her softness. She was so sweet, and he thought for a moment that he would lose control, that it would be over before it was barely begun.

His lips opened against her skin, and he kissed her shoulder, the line of her collarbone, the hollow of her throat, noting the quick intake of breath as she shivered beneath his touch. He ran his hand lightly over her form, admiring the smooth skin, the rounding of her hips, the width of that place where she might one day carry his child. His fingers moved between her legs, caressing her womanhood, and she raised herself slightly to meet his touch.

"Jake?" Her voice was high, breathless, and her

face turned against his shoulder, muffling the response she could not contain.

"Do you like that?" he asked, exploring farther, seeking the proof of her arousal.

She nodded against him and he nudged her legs apart, smiling when she obeyed his unspoken command. A moan of pleasure reached his ear and he bent to her breast again, seeking the puckered tip and tugging it inside his mouth, while his fingers found the sleek entry he sought.

"Let me, Alicia," he whispered. "Please don't turn me away."

She relaxed, allowing the intrusion, and he found the soft tissues that were ready for his entry. There would be pain for her, for she was untried and tense. Not for anything would he deliberately hurt her, or make her feel trapped beneath him.

Holding himself above her would be difficult, though he knew from past experience with Rena that he was capable. But for Alicia, for this first time, he wanted her to have the freedom to move as she would. He rolled with her until they faced each other, then spoke carefully, moving her aside as he straightened in the bed and sat leaning against the headboard.

"Come and sit on my lap," he said, taking her hand and drawing her to sit astride him. She was compliant, eager to please, and she lowered herself against the length of his manhood.

"Do you think it will fit there?" she asked, looking down as if she might see the matching of two parts. And well she might be dubious, he thought. His fingers had invaded the narrow passage, but this was another thing altogether.

"We'll work it out," he promised, and coaxed her to rise a bit, positioning himself beneath her. "Will you do this for me?" he asked. "Will you bring us together, sweetheart?"

"I don't know if I can." Her breathing was rapid and she trembled in his embrace, but he was careful, his hand between them, his fingers caressing her with deliberate movements that brought her to the very brink of pleasure.

"Jake?" Her whisper was one of surprise, as though some wondrous event was hovering just over the horizon, and if she were to reach out she might possess it for her own.

He lifted her gently, then eased her downward to take the full length of his manhood within her body. She tilted her head back and clenched tight muscles around him, milking him with an unconscious urgency. A sharp cry split the air as he pushed his way through her maidenhead, and then he was fully seated and she leaned forward to rest her head against his.

"Lift a bit, then come back down on me," he whispered, helping her to establish the rhythm that would bring her to release. His fingers touched her again and she wiggled against him, unable to hold the pace he had set.

She clenched him tightly, then moved more rapidly, crying out, speaking his name as she rose and fell against him. He joined her then, his body barely able to restrain the thrusting he feared would cause her distress. But she was beyond pain, her cries making him aware that he had brought her pleasure, a joy that far outweighed the brief hurt when he'd pierced her innocence and truly made her his wife.

She slumped against him and he turned with her, rolling her to her side before he slid down to take her in his embrace. She curled against him, her face damp with tears, and he felt a moment of guilt that he'd given her pain, yet his heart rejoiced that she had known her first loving at his hands.

"Don't cry, Alicia. It will be better next time. I'll never hurt you again. Only this once."

"It couldn't be any better," she whispered. "It hurt, but not more than I'd expected it would. And you made me fly, Jake. I thought I'd taken wing like the birds who soar through the heavens…" She ducked her face against his chest.

"You'll think I'm silly."

"No." He shook his head and held her close. "Never, sweetheart. If I brought you a measure of enjoyment,

I'm happy." He tilted her face up to his. "You've given me more than you know, Alicia. You've given me a new lease on life."

JASON CAME HOME THE NEXT afternoon, making a beeline for his father's room as soon as he burst in through the back door. His sack of belongings landed on the kitchen floor and Alicia picked it up, smiling as she watched him hustle past her. He called to Jake, his voice high, excited and filled with anticipation.

"Pa? Are you better, Pa?"

She heard the low rumble of Jake's reply, followed by the familiar laughter of a nine-year-old boy.

Holding the sack at arm's length, Alicia opened Jason's bag and emptied out the contents. It was about as she'd figured. Clothing soiled with grass stains, mud and more than a touch of food spills met her eye. She dumped the lot in the laundry basket that was kept in the back room, just off the porch. The wash lady earned her money, and more, she decided, shaking her head.

"Alicia?" Jake called her, his usual demanding tone apparent today. If she'd expected a miraculous turnaround in his behavior, she'd have been disillusioned. Jake was Jake, and would always be the same temperamental, obstinate creature she'd met last spring. That he had softened in the important things was all she expected of him. His eyes had touched her with warmth this morning, his hands had learned her body with patient loving care during the long hours of the night, and his lips had blessed her with an abundance of kisses several times today already.

She crossed the kitchen and went to his room, standing in the doorway, smiling as he beckoned her toward the bed. "Come on over here," he said. "Tell my son that I'm fully recovered from my bout. He won't believe me."

"He's still in bed, Miss Alicia," Jason said, his expression begging for reassurance. "If he was feeling all right, he'd be up in his chair. Wouldn't he?"

"I made him stay in bed a little longer, Jason," she told the boy. "He would have gotten up and dressed this morning, but I knew he needed another day to recuperate."

"Recuperate?" Jason asked. "Is that a new word like *exemplary* was?"

"It means to get better, to become the same as he was before," she told him.

Jason tilted his head and looked searchingly at his father. "I don't know, ma'am. He looks pretty good to me already. Maybe even better than before he got sick. I'd say he's all recuperated already."

"I'm feeling mighty fine," Jake said, emphasizing the words as he looked up at Alicia. His smile seemed carefree, she thought, his hair tousled, and his eyes sparkled with laughter. The unspoken message being sent in her direction was giving her the credit for his recovery, and she felt her lips curve in a bashful smile as she responded to his foolishness.

"I want you to do something for me, son," Jake told the boy.

"Sure, Pa. Do you need a drink of water? Or one of your books from the shelf?" Jason was poised for action, Alicia thought, willing to fetch and carry for his beloved father at the drop of a hat. And then Jake made a request that stunned Alicia and brought a soft exclamation from Jason's lips.

"I'd like you to go upstairs with Alicia and help her move her things down here to my room," he said. "I don't want her carrying the heavy things by herself. You'll have to lift one end of her trunk for her."

"What for, Pa?" the boy asked, truly perplexed by the request. "If you're not sick anymore, why does she need to bring her stuff to your room?"

Jake looked at Alicia, his expression guarded, and his reply said it all, she decided. "Alicia is my wife, Jason. She should have been in my room from the beginning. We're going to set that to rights today. She belongs here with me."

"But this was yours and Mama's room," Jason said, his eyes wide, his voice quavering.

"Your mama is no longer with us, son," Jake told him quietly. "And she would want Alicia to use this room. Wives and husbands share a bedroom."

"But…" The boy looked at Alicia and she was stunned by the resentment she saw in his face. "I don't want her in my mama's room," Jason said with stubborn determination. "I'm not gonna help her bring all her stuff down here."

"It's all right," Alicia said quickly. "I'll take care of it, Jake. We can talk about it later on." And she'd make certain Jake knew that his decision should have been discussed with her first, before springing it on the boy.

"Jason will help you," Jake said forcefully. "We've talked about this before. He needs to obey, Alicia, whether or not he chooses to agree with the order. If either of us asks him to do something, he'll do it. Or I'll know the reason why."

She shook her head in silent reproof, aware that Jason could not see her, his attention focused on his father.

"*Now,* Alicia." Jake would not back off from this thing, and she refused to argue with him in front of his son.

With a shrug, she turned aside and left the room, hearing Jake speak in a firm tone. She'd begun cooking supper and so she returned to the kitchen, where she was stunned to find Rachel at the big round table.

"What's going on?" Rachel asked. "Jake sounds like he's on the warpath. I assume he's better." Her smile was rich with understanding, and Alicia felt the sudden urge to cry.

She settled across the table from her sister-in-law and folded her hands before her. "I don't know what to do, Rachel. Jake told Jason he has to help me move my things downstairs, into his room. And the boy put up a fuss."

"You're moving into Jake's room?" Rachel asked, filled with surprise. "What on earth happened over the past day or two?" Then she coughed as though she'd choked on something too big to swallow and began to laugh. "Never mind, it's none of my business," she said. "But I'll tell you this. It's what I've been hoping for all summer long, Alicia. I told you not long ago that—"

She came to a sudden halt as Jason burst through the kitchen door and stomped his way past the table. Alicia reached out to grasp his arm. "Whoa there, young man!" she said firmly. "What do you think you're doing? That sort of rude behavior is not allowed and you know it."

"You aren't my mother," he said, his face twisted in a scowl.

"I never said I was," Alicia told him, feeling her heart pound.

"Well, my mama used to sleep in that bedroom with my pa, and she wouldn't like it if you was to move in there instead of her."

"Your mama is dead," Rachel said quietly. "And I beg to differ with you, Jason. She would approve wholeheartedly if she knew what your father has proposed."

"Well, I'm not gonna do it." The boy planted himself before them and his bottom lip formed a stubborn line. "Miss Alicia moved in to look after me and to cook and stuff like that. I heard my pa talkin' to her a long time ago about what she was gonna hafta do after they got married."

He shot an angry look at Alicia. "Now you think you're gonna be my mother, but you're not. You're just a teacher, and you're lucky we let you live with us."

Alicia was stunned, her hand falling from Jason's arm as she attempted to digest the words he'd spoken to her. Across the table, Rachel rose hurriedly and followed Jason as he tromped his way to the back screened door and allowed it to slam behind him. Alicia heard her call the boy's name, and then Cord's strong tones joined in.

She hadn't known Cord was out there, had assumed that Rachel's arrival had been a quick trip to town for the purpose of returning Jason home. Now she stepped to the door and looked out into the yard. Rachel was clinging to Cord's arm, looking up at him and telling him something. She glanced back at the house and caught Alicia's eye.

"I think he went into town," she said, releasing Cord and hurrying back to where Alicia stood, just inside the kitchen. "Cord will go after him."

"He won't want to come home," Alicia said dully.

"And I don't know what to do about it." From behind her, the sound of Jake's chair rolling across the floor caught her ear and she turned to face him as he crossed the kitchen. His trousers were only halfway buttoned, the pant legs lying unpinned, and he was bare-chested.

"Where'd he go?" he roared, pushing his way to look out the door.

Cord looked back from the edge of the yard and waved at his brother. "I'll find him," he called. "Rachel, stay with Alicia and Jake. This shouldn't take long."

"What did he say to you?" Jake asked, his dark eyes piercing, his tone harsh. "Damn it, Alicia, answer me. I want to know what he said to you. You look like a ghost—like someone just walked across your grave."

"Well, thank you, sir," she said. "I know I'm not the prettiest girl in town, but that description beats all, if you ask me." She turned away from him, unable to repeat the words Jason had uttered, unwilling to tell Jake how cruel the boy had been.

"I'll tell you," Rachel said. "Alicia doesn't want to get Jason in any more trouble than he's already in, but I have no such qualms, brother dear."

Jake leaned forward in his chair and his jaw jutted stubbornly. "Let's have it."

Rachel reached for a chair and nodded at Alicia. "Why don't you sit down?" she suggested. "Jake's right. You look terrible."

Alicia pulled a chair from the table and sat on the edge of the seat. With swift movements, Jake was beside her, his hand touching hers, clasping it in his palm. "All right, Rachel," he said. "Tell me."

Rachel repeated what the boy had said. In her calm voice the words didn't seem nearly as harsh and cruel, until she told Jake how Jason had designated Alicia's place in the home. "He said Alicia was lucky that the two of you let her live with you."

"I didn't think he'd feel that way about Alicia taking her rightful place in my life."

"Moving into your life doesn't seem to be the problem," Alicia said quietly. "What he objected to is my moving into his mother's bedroom."

Jake's expression turned stormy with anger. "Well, he'll just have to get over it, Alicia. He isn't going to tell me, or you either, what we should do with our lives. This is an adult decision, and not up for discussion. A nine-year-old boy is not going to run my household, no matter if he is my son."

"Maybe we should put off my making such a move for a while, Jake," she said, her voice trembling. "We could give him time to get used to it."

"That isn't going to work, either," Rachel said quickly. "He needs to know that his word is not law, that he doesn't make the rules. He's not allowed to speak to you the way he did." She bit at her lip. "I'm sorry. It's not my place to make a statement like that. It's not my business, actually."

"Yes, it is," Jake told her. "We're a family, Rachel. You've been involved in my life for a lot of years, most of them good years. And throughout the bad times you didn't give up on me, did you?"

"Never," she said vehemently.

"Well, I value your opinion, sister of mine, and I totally agree with what you said. The boy owes Alicia an apology, and I owe him a good trouncing."

"Cord may have already done that by the time he hauls him back here. He was furious when I told him what Jason said to Alicia."

"He'll have my blessings, then." Jake patted the back of Alicia's hand and rolled his chair to the back door, looking out through the screen. "Which way did he head?"

"Toward town," Rachel said. "He could be anywhere by now." Then at Alicia's soft sob, she backtracked a bit. "Of course, Cord may already be on his way back with him. I doubt Jason will go far."

"Should I find the sheriff and let him know that Jason is missing?" Alicia asked, feeling a degree of helplessness she'd never before known. "I feel like I should be doing something, not just sitting here."

"Let's give Cord a half hour or so and see what he comes up with," Jake said, turning his chair and moving to face her. He bent forward and cupped her cheeks with his hands, brushing at the tears she could not control. "This isn't your fault," he said forcefully. "It's mine, in that I didn't talk to the boy after we got married and prepare him for the eventuality of this happening."

"My moving into your room?" Alicia asked in a whisper, her eyes wide with surprise at Jake's words.

He looked at her with a softening in his gaze that touched her heart. "I knew for the past couple of months that this would come about, Alicia. I just didn't know when, and I didn't have any idea how it would happen."

"You knew?" She felt stunned by his disclosure. "I didn't know," she said. "It didn't even enter my mind." Then she blushed. "Well, that's not entirely true. I wondered what it would be like to…" She whispered the final few words and then decided she'd said enough. This might be confession time for her and for Jake, but getting Rachel involved in their conversation was probably not a good idea.

Rachel seemed to share her thoughts, for she rose and walked to the back door. "Don't pay me any mind," she said with a chuckle. "I'm going out in the yard."

Jake moved his chair, rolling it to sit beside Alicia. His arm circled her shoulders and he tugged her against him. "Kiss me, sweetheart," he said, and she turned her tear-stained face toward him. "I need to know you care about me." His words were husky, as if they were hard to come by, and she recognized the amount of pride he'd shed in order to admit his need.

She reached up to touch his face, then her lips met his, and she put her heart and soul into the kiss. His big hand cupped the back of her head and he held her in place for a gentle assault. She may have begun the kiss, but Jake was taking control, and doing it well, she decided. Her mouth was invaded by his tongue and she opened to him gladly, having learned well the intimate play he instigated.

Then he leaned back a bit. "Does that tell you anything?" he asked. "Do you believe what I'm telling you, Alicia? I need you in my life, I want you in my bed, and my son is not going to lead me around by the nose."

She was breathless, her mouth feeling swollen by the thoroughness of his kiss. "Yes," she murmured. "I believe you, Jake. I also believe that Jason is terribly hurt right now and we need to try to understand his side of this."

"I married you so that he would have a stable home life," Jake told her. "But everything changed over the summer, and our own wants and needs became just as important. Jason has not suffered by our marriage."

"He misses his mother." Alicia spoke the simple words, remembering Jason's contempt as he spoke his mind. "You're not my mother." He'd been so vehement in his statement, effectively putting her in her place. "I can't take Rena's place with him."

"Nor with me," Jake said quietly. "But you've made a place of your own. I'll always have a spot in my heart for Rena. But life goes on—and if that sounds trite, I can't help it. It's the truth. I mourned for more than two years and what did it get me? A lousy reputation in town and a dirty house. A boy who was the town terror and a whole string of housekeepers and cooks who were half afraid of me and refused to work here."

"And how has Jason coped with the loss of his mother?" she asked. "He was crying out for his father's attention, doing everything he could to make you sit up and take notice, Jake. He was destructive and mischievous. He was mean to the little girls and fought with the boys. Then what did we do? We gave him someone to take care of him and see to it that he had a stable home life. Now we've asked him to set aside the memory of his mother and watch me take her place."

"That's not true," Jake said. "I don't want him to forget Rena."

"Nor do I," she told him, "but he thinks we do. So long as I was upstairs, I was the cook and the housekeeper. Once you decided I should sleep in your room, I became a threat to him."

"You're making too big an issue of it," Jake told her. "It's much simpler than that."

She rose and walked to the kitchen window, looking out into the yard. Rachel stood by the back fence, looking down as if she were deep in thought…or perhaps praying, Alicia thought. The sun was sinking below the horizon and the moon was a faint glow in the sky.

And Jason was not yet home.

CHAPTER FOURTEEN

"HE'S IN JAIL." CORD stood in the kitchen, tired and irritated after the day's events. "I can't believe what the boy did. Went up to the sheriff's office and banged on the door. Somebody told him the sheriff was gone home for supper, so Jason just broke in the door, anyway, and got inside."

"How'd he do that?" Jake asked. "Why would he do such a stupid thing, anyway?"

Cord shrugged. "Who knows why kids do the things they do sometimes? As to how, he picked up a rock and smashed the lock. I shudder to think that our jail was secured by a lock that a nine-year-old managed to break so easily."

"Were there prisoners in the cells?" Alicia asked, already dreading the reply.

"Oh, yeah," Cord said. "There sure were. Three of 'em. And they're all on the loose right now. Jason took the keys from the sheriff's desk drawer and unlocked the cells. They all skedaddled like white lightning."

"Have you seen him?" Jake asked, his face pale and drawn as if he could not bear the message Cord had brought him. "Is he all right?"

"Cocky as hell," Cord said. "When the sheriff came running back after somebody went and dragged him away from his supper table, he found Jason perched on his desk. Apparently he admitted right off what he'd done, and asked the sheriff what he was gonna do about it."

"He put him in jail." Alicia said the words before Cord could repeat them to Jake. "Now what do we do?"

"He's only nine years old," Rachel said quietly. "Can they do this to him?"

"He broke the law," Jake said. "This isn't just mischief any longer, Rachel. He's in real trouble, I'm afraid."

"I'd say so," Cord agreed. "I talked to the sheriff and he's got six men out right now trying to follow the tracks of the men who walked out of the jail."

"Why were they there to begin with? Are they really bad men?" Alicia asked, hoping against hope that charges levied against the prisoners were along the lines of drunk and disorderly, rather than cattle-rustling or murder.

"Well, Tom Erickson struck his wife once too often and she filed charges. Another is one of the rustlers who stole horses from Simon's place. He was still waiting for the judge to show up and sentence him. The third fella was arrested for a shooting at the saloon the other night. They don't know if the man he shot is gonna live or not."

"They're all long gone, I'll warrant," Jake said. He looked up at Alicia and his eyes were dark with pain. "What will happen to him, do you suppose?"

"I'll go see the sheriff and find out if he'll let us bring him home if we'll guarantee his appearance in court when the judge gets here." It seemed like the logical thing to do, she thought, but Cord disagreed, shaking his head.

"Doubt if he'll hear of it, Alicia. This is serious stuff. The boy has really done it this time."

"Have you seen him?" Jake asked.

Cord nodded. "I went in the jail and back to the cell where he's cooped up and he wouldn't even look at me. Just lay down on the bunk and faced the wall."

"He's safe enough there, isn't he, Cord?" Rachel asked. "No one can get to him, can they?"

"I doubt it, honey," he said. "There's gonna be some folks awfully mad at him, but they aren't going to face down the sheriff to do Jason any harm."

"I think he needs to be given a good dose of being left alone to take his medicine," Jake said quietly. "He thinks someone will come to his rescue, and we're not going to do it, Cord. He'll just have to stew over this, all on his own."

"Oh, Jake," Alicia said, her heart aching for the boy who had been so hurt. "He's only angry because he thinks you've turned against him. Telling him…" She hesitated and then plowed on. "When you told him I was moving into your room, he took it to be a rejection of his mother, and he couldn't handle it. He thinks you've forgotten Rena."

"I told him differently," Jake said firmly. "It was his choice not to believe me."

"He's only nine years old," Alicia said. "A child who's still missing his mother, and terrified that he's the only one who cares that she's gone."

"He knows better than that," Cord said. "You'd think he'd be tickled to death that things are getting more cheerful around here."

"But he doesn't *care* about that," Alicia said, determined that she was right in this. "All he cares is that I came in and tried to take the place of his mother. As long as I stayed upstairs, he could tell himself that I was the cook and his father had married me to look after the two of them." She looked at Rachel appealingly. "You heard what he said, Rachel."

"I think Jake's right, though," Rachel told her. "You can't let Jason run this household. He's only a child and he needs to learn who's in charge."

"Well, right now, that's neither here nor there. Jason is stuck in a jail cell until the judge comes to town or the sheriff decides to let him come home on parole," Cord said.

"Do you think he will?" Alicia asked hopefully.

"I wouldn't hold my breath." Cord looked grim as he rose and walked to the back door. It was fully dark outside, the stars out in profusion and the moon shining in a cloudless sky. "We need to head for home, Rachel," he said. "We can't do anything more here. Jason is stuck right where he is for tonight."

"I hate to leave," Rachel said slowly, touching Alicia's hand in a comforting gesture. "Do you need me to stay?" she asked.

Alicia shook her head. "No, we'll be fine." Then she looked at Jake and wondered at the truth of those words. Jake looked anything but fine. His face was drawn and his jaw was firmly set.

"Go on," Jake said, with more than a trace of his old harshness. He waved dismissively at his brother. "You can't accomplish anything here, Cord. You've found the boy, that was the most important thing. He's got himself in a mess, but there isn't a damn thing any of us can do to change things for tonight."

"You're probably right," Cord agreed. He took Rachel's arm. "Come on, honey."

"My brother Jay is at home," she said. "He'll be looking after Matthew and Melody." She allowed Cord to hustle her to the door and then looked over her shoulder at Alicia. "Will you send someone out to get us if anything happens?" she asked.

Alicia nodded, hoping against hope that no such event would occur.

She closed up the house as soon as Cord's surrey rolled down the street, checking to be sure the parlor windows were shut, although the sky looked clear enough. It probably wouldn't rain, but the nights were cooling off rapidly. Jake didn't need to take a chill. He was barely over the attack that had precipitated this whole mess, and she couldn't take the chance of him having a relapse.

"Leave one of my windows open," he said, rolling into his bedroom and then turning to face her. "Go get your nightgown, Alicia. You're sleeping here with me tonight."

She opened her mouth to protest, aware that this was the very thing that had brought about Jason's run-in with the law, but the look on Jake's face silenced her. He wasn't in the mood to argue, she decided. His eyes were piercing, his jaw set aggressively and his knuckles were white as he gripped the arms of his chair.

No power on earth could make her defy him tonight, she decided. It was too important for Jake to feel in control right now. He'd lost his authority over Jason, and that was something he was trying to deal with, a burden he was barely equipped to bear. All that was left to him was the wife he'd chosen to protect and establish in her proper place, over the protests of his son. She had no intention of hurting him further.

"I'll be there in a minute, Jake." After lighting a candle to light her way, she climbed the stairs and paused in the doorway of Jason's room. He'd thrown the quilt over his bed in a haphazard manner, but most of his things were in fairly tidy condition. The boy was trying, she decided. Her own room was spick-and-span, the bed neatly made, her clothing in good order, her nightgown tucked beneath her pillow.

She snatched it up, gathered her brush and clean undergarments for tomorrow and, picking up her candle, left the room. Jake had lit a lamp beside the bed and pulled back the sheet and quilt, preparatory to undressing. He looked up at her and hesitated.

"Would you rather I get undressed in the dark?" he asked.

She shook her head. "No, of course not." Her smile was quick. "However, if you'd rather not be exposed to *my* particular set of imperfections, I'll be happy to blow out the lamp for you."

"You know better," he said gruffly, pulling his shirt off and tossing it toward the laundry basket she kept in his room.

She felt constricted by his attention, wished he

would turn his gaze elsewhere as she undid her buttons and slid the dress from her shoulders to drape at her waist. Her vest was quickly removed and for a few unguarded moments her upper body was bare of covering before him. Then the nightgown was pulled over her head and she undid the rest of her clothing beneath its sheltering folds.

"That's unfair," Jake told her, undoing his trousers.

She buttoned the gown and stepped out of the circle of clothing she'd shed. "It's the way I get undressed every night."

"I can see we'll have to make some changes in your routine," he told her. And then his expression softened, as if he were setting aside for a moment his anger at Jason. "I know you think I'm harsh and unfeeling about my son, Alicia. I haven't forgotten about Jason and where he's spending the night. But right now, I need you with me. I need you in my bed."

"If having me with you is any comfort, then I'm here, Jake." She meant the words from the bottom of her heart. Her throat tightened with emotion as she offered herself as consolation to the man who bore wounds of the spirit as well as the body, whose aching heart might be eased by her presence.

He reached out his hand to her and she walked toward him, accepting the touch of his fingers, leaning over him to press her lips against his forehead, then his jaw, where whiskers had formed during his illness, making him seem dangerous and disreputable. Jake was a good-looking man—clean shaven, he had proud and noble features.

Now, with the shadow of a beard present, his face took on a darker image as though the stronger facets of his personality were given leave to emerge. A twinge of apprehension gripped her, even as a thrill she could not describe sent a shiver down her spine.

She noted the difference with senses more acute than ever in her life. It seemed he lacked the delicacy of the night before, for he looked at her with eyes that glittered, touched her with hands that demanded rather than coaxed her submission.

"Come to bed," he said, his tone urgent, his fingers firm around her wrist as he guided her toward the turned-down sheet. She obeyed, sliding to the opposite side of the bed and pulling the sheet up to her breasts.

He stripped from his trousers and reached for the trapeze that hung over his bed. With practiced movements, he lifted himself from the chair, balancing himself with the remnants of his legs and sank into the mattress beside her. His chest was bare of covering, but his drawers hid the lower part of his body.

Alicia lay quietly beside him, unable to decipher his thoughts. If he needed the possession of her body to give him some sort of comfort tonight, she was willing to oblige. If he only needed her presence beside him, she would be pleased to do as he asked. Then he turned to her swiftly, raising himself on one elbow to loom over her, and her breath caught in a gasp of surprise at his sudden movement.

His hair was ruffled, his face shadowed and his voice when he spoke was ragged. She felt his pain as he spoke, fearful that his son's betrayal had hurt him deeply. "I won't blow out the lamp, Alicia," he said gruffly. "You can't hide beneath that gown tonight. I won't let you. Any more than I'm planning to wear these damn drawers for any longer than it'll take me to get them off."

"All right," she said, reluctant to shed the gown but unwilling to put up a fuss when Jake was so obviously agitated. She sat up and unbuttoned her bodice, then pushed it from her arms and to her waist. Wiggling beneath the sheet, she pushed it to the foot of the bed, then kicked it from beneath the covers.

She'd never felt so naked in her life. Last night shedding her clothing had made her self-conscious, but at least the room had been dark. Tonight was altogether different. And Jake was making no effort to put her at ease; his gaze was all-encompassing as his hand pulled back the sheet from her breasts. Then he made a demand she could barely countenance.

"Take off my drawers, Alicia. Unbutton them and push them off."

"What if someone comes, Jake? We'll both be..." She could not bring herself to speak the word. But apparently the situation would not be a problem, should it occur, so far as he was concerned.

"No one will be knocking at the door tonight," he said. "We know where Jason is, and the sheriff is aware of it. Nothing is going to change before morning." He lay back on the mattress and waited.

Alicia felt for the buttons that held his drawers in place and her fingers trembled as she undid the fastenings. He raised his hips, allowing her to push the soft knit fabric from him. She touched his upper leg, then moved downward till she came to the abrupt end of his thigh. Alicia looked up at him inquiringly, but his dark gaze was inscrutable. She was on her own.

She ran her fingertips lightly over the scarred flesh, her palm covering the area where once skin and bone had formed a knee. Their eyes met and held, seeming to form a bridge across which flowed her aching need to reassure him. He flinched once as her fingers explored the rough ridges of flesh where once a cruel saw had deprived him of the power to stand and walk as a man.

"Do I repel you?" he asked, his words harsh and biting. She felt him withdraw from her, and then he reached to push her hand from his leg.

She would not have it, would not allow him to force her from the path she had chosen. "No, you don't repel me," she said smartly. "Quite the opposite, in fact. You have my admiration, Jake. With all of your pain and the sorrow you've lived with the past years, you're still more a man than any other I've ever known."

When she would have resumed her caress, his grip tightened on her wrist. "You're hurting me," she said quietly. "I'll wear bruises tomorrow." But she refused to give way, would not allow him to force her retreat. Rising to her knees, she shed the covering that hid her from him, the sheet falling aside. She bent low, her breasts brushing his belly and the place where his manhood was not yet fully aroused.

Her mouth was open against him, pressing kisses against his leg, her tongue touching the scars, her lips leaving behind the caress of a willing woman, a wife who knew her husband's flaws and was willing to accept them as a part of the man he had become. Jake released her wrist, and with a groan that seemed wrenched from deep within him, his fingers moved to touch her hair, weaving into the coronet of braids she wore, pressing her closer to her goal.

She held his scarred thigh between her hands, caressed it gently, and blessed it with a multitude of

kisses, then lifted his other knee and sought the short
length of leg it possessed.

"Alicia." His voice was raw with pain, with a sorrow she could only imagine, for nothing in her life had
prepared her for the reality of Jake's wounding. "You
don't have to do this."

She looked up at him. "Ah, but I do," she whispered.
"I have to make you understand that it isn't the absence
or presence of your lower limbs that makes you the
man I love. This is but a part of you, an essential part,
but not the most important part." Beneath her breast,
his manhood was coming to life, nudging her skin,
making itself known to her. She smiled, shooting him
a warm, inviting glance.

Suddenly he reached for her, grasping her shoulders
and drawing her upward.

She shook her head. "Wait, Jake. I need to tell you
why I love you."

"You love me?" He looked disbelievingly at her.
"I've given you little enough reason to even *like* me."

"Well, it's true," she said firmly. "I knew months
ago that I was in love with you. Although how I knew
is beyond me. I've never felt this way about a man before and, as you pointed out, you haven't given me
much reason to feel like this. But at this point, I suspect it isn't something I can control."

"I'm mean and harsh and arrogant, Alicia," he said

crossly. "You told me that yourself. Surely if you were going to fall in love, it wouldn't be with a man with no redeeming qualities."

"Oh, you have a few." She faced him then, lying halfway across his body. "You're smart and quick-witted. I like your humor, and the way you respond to me. You don't get angry…well, not very, anyway, when I speak up to you. And for the most part you've been fair with me."

She reached out and traced his jawline with her index finger. "Even with these whiskers, you're a hand-some man, Jake McPherson. I don't know why you ever decided I was a good candidate for marriage, but I'm happy that you made that move in my direction."

"You're a good wife, Alicia," he told her. "Even if you'd never allowed me to coax you to my bed, you'd still be a wife to me. You've taken care of me and put up with my moods and been good to my son. This—" he touched her hip, his hand widespread against the firm flesh "—this is just a gift." His other hand cupped one breast, the abundant roundness fill-ing his palm.

"I feel so lucky to have you. To know that you aren't—" As though he searched for a word, he paused, then pulled her closer. "Kiss me, Alicia. Please give me your warmth tonight. I need you badly."

She met his lips with hers, still tentative, even after

the long hours spent in his arms. "I'm not very good at this," she murmured, raising her head to look down at him.

"If you were any better at it, I'd be in deep trouble," he whispered. "As it is, I'm not sure how long I can hold out, sweetheart." He touched her temple, ran his index finger through a lock of her hair that had come free of the braid she wore. "Will you take down your hair for me?" he asked. "I wanted to see it last night, but we got too involved too quickly, and besides it was dark. I'd like to watch it ripple around your shoulders."

"It's a mess when it's undone," she warned him. "I've thought of cutting it off. It takes forever to dry when I wash it, and keeping the snarls brushed out is a daily task."

"No, I don't want you to cut it," he told her fiercely. "It's lovely. Leave it long." Then he sought the pins that held it in a coronet. One at a time, he removed them, holding them in one palm as the fingers of his other hand tugged them from place, until the long braid swung free against his chest.

She felt ill at ease, for her mother had often said that a woman's hair must be kept tidy at all times. That it was vanity that made women allow it to lie loose against their shoulders, that men did not admire a woman who was slatternly in appearance. But Jake had bid her loosen the braid, allowing the crinkled mass to flow freely.

She did as he asked, undoing and running her fingers through the free strands of hair, watching as he reached to grasp a handful and clutch it between his fingers and palm. It was indeed long, hanging well beyond her waist, and before she was finished he had pulled it to either side, displaying it like a living shawl over her shoulders and breasts.

"It's beautiful," he whispered. "It looks just as I thought it would."

"When did you ever think about my hair?" she asked, a dubious frown appearing.

"Frequently." Absorbed in his task, he placed the long locks where he would and then smiled, as though pleased with his work. "I'll brush it for you in the morning," he offered.

"I may just take you up on that," she said. "By the time I sleep on it, it'll be a mess."

"Come here to me," he told her. "Lie beside me, Alicia. I need to love you tonight."

"Beside you?" she asked, frowning. How this thing could be accomplished in such a way was more than her mind could fathom, but it seemed Jake had no such problem, for he took but moments to adjust their bodies, lifting her leg across his hip, so that he could reach her with ease, his hands once more making magic against her flesh.

"See?" He breathed the single word and she could

only nod in response, unable to voice her delight at the sensations he elicited from the places he chose to visit. He bent to her breasts and suckled there, holding her against himself with hands capturing her legs and the width of her hips.

She obeyed his every command, gave him that which he asked from her, and rose with him to the heights as he bid her follow his lead. He moved within her, filling her with the very essence of his manhood. The thrill of his possession brought tears to her eyes and joy to her heart, and she gladly gave in return the love she had stored within her heart for just such a moment.

He was not gentle, but she had not expected his taking of her to be as it had been the night before, when she was totally untried. Tonight, he demanded more of her, fitting her to himself and turning loose his passion on her willing flesh. Again, she knew long moments of fulfillment, once more realized the joy of accepting his seed into her body, and clasped him in spasms of pleasure beyond any she had imagined.

"Alicia." He spoke her name in a voice that murmured of passion spent, of desire satisfied by the woman of his choice. "Alicia." He repeated the syllables slowly, enunciating them as if tasting each one, whispering her name in a rhythm that spoke of delight and brought her joy.

He might not love her, for he'd not said those words

aloud. But he needed her, he wanted her beside him and he had been pleased with her. For tonight that would be enough.

CHAPTER FIFTEEN

"THE BOY MAY ONLY BE nine years old, but he committed a crime." The sheriff was adamant, and Alicia found it difficult to disagree with him. Jason had gone far beyond a simple prank this time.

Wrecking a flower bed was one thing. Releasing three prisoners quite another.

Visiting Jason in jail was an experience she'd just as soon not repeat, she decided. Since Jake could not make the trip, it was left to her to speak with the sheriff and see Jason in his cell. After being patently ignored by the boy and noting his blatant stubbornness, she found herself agreeing with the lawman.

"Is it legal to keep him here?" she asked. "His father is talking about having him at home and keeping track of his whereabouts until the judge decides what should be done."

"I reckon I can do pretty much whatever needs to be done with the boy," the sheriff said firmly. "He needs to learn a lesson, and turning him loose ain't gonna do the trick. He's safe and sound where he is, Mrs. McPherson. Nobody's gonna hurt him, and there ain't even any other prisoners back there to have a bad influence on him—thanks to his turning them loose."

It seemed her trip to the jailhouse had been for naught, Alicia thought glumly. Going home and facing Jake with her failure was not palatable, but she'd done all she could to solve the problem, with no success.

"I brought Jason some clean clothes," she said, offering the bundle of personal items into the lawman's hands. "Is he able to bathe in his cell? And Jake wondered what he's eating."

"All taken care of, ma'am. My wife does the cooking for the prisoners, and she's a good cook. Makes plain, everyday meals. Nothin' fancy, you understand, but I manage to get along on it. I reckon Jason will, too." He grinned then, as if a thought had amused him.

"Far as keeping clean is concerned, I can only provide soap and water and a bucket. It's up to him what he does with it. If I remember right, my own boys weren't any too fond of washin' up at that age. No guarantees there, ma'am."

Alicia's heart ached for the boy, and yet no one could solve his problems for him. Somehow he had to come to grips with the changes in his life, and how that would come to pass was a mystery to her. Jake had been abrupt with him. She had probably been too le-

nient at times. And Jason was a stubborn boy, not unlike his father. A boy who was still in mourning for the
mother who had left him…not willingly, but permanently, nevertheless.

She walked from the jailhouse. Rescuing Jason was
not going to be a simple matter. And she wasn't at all
certain that rescue was what he needed. Maybe this
was, indeed, a wake-up call, a rough spot in his life that
would eventually set him in the right direction.

The general store was almost empty, and for that
she was thankful. Facing a whole raft of women, all
of them set on quizzing her or commiserating with
her problem, was not appealing this morning. She
placed her order with Mr. Harris, then left him alone
to fill it for her while she wandered through the store.
Fresh eggs on the counter reminded her that her own
supply was low, and she turned back to add them to
her list.

Only to run almost headlong into Toby's mother.
The woman looked mighty uncomfortable, but spoke
nicely. "I'd like you to pass along a message to your
husband, Mrs. McPherson," she said timidly. "Toby is
like a different boy since he's been taking lessons from
Mr. McPherson. You know we don't have a piano of
our own, but the minister over at the church lets him
practice there pretty near every day."

She leaned closer, her voice dropping in volume as

if she feared being overheard. "The church pianist, Mrs. Howard, doesn't approve of the music Toby is learning, but she hasn't been able to discourage him from it, and the minister is agreeable to the boy playing whatever your husband gives him to work on."

She fussed with her reticule and then met Alicia's gaze with eyes that filled with tears. "I'm so sorry about Mr. McPherson's boy, getting in trouble and all. He's had a bad time of it, losing his mother and his pa being a recluse and all. It's a wonder to me that the boy hasn't been in more trouble than—well, anyway, I just want you to know I'm sorry."

Alicia was moved by the offer of sympathy. She reached to touch the woman's arm and smiled, hoping she could convey her appreciation without going into a great deal of explanation. "Jason is in trouble, all right. But his father and I are hoping he'll learn from this experience."

"Well, I just know that I'm thankful for what Mr. McPherson has done for my Toby," the other woman repeated. "He can hardly wait every week for the day of his lesson." She leaned closer. "I sometimes wonder how I managed to birth such a child."

"I'm sure you're a very good mother," Alicia told her. "There are miracles every day of our lives, you know. Perhaps having Toby sent into your home was one of them."

Mr. Harris raised his hand, signifying that her order was ready, and Alicia took her leave of the woman, pleased that she would have one bit of cheer to offer Jake when she arrived home. Although the notion that he could reach another child, yet not have the impact needed on his own son, might not be the best news she could carry to him.

"Thank you, Mr. Harris," she said, checking the contents of her basket quickly; reassured that her list was well represented, she was ready to leave. "Please put this on our bill," she said, to which the gentleman smiled and nodded.

The basket Alicia carried was heavy and she lifted it with an effort. From behind her a familiar voice spoke her name, and she turned with a smile to greet Cord.

"Good morning," she said, and then lowered her voice. "Have you stopped by the jail?" she asked. "Did you talk to the sheriff?"

"Yes, on both counts," he answered, shaking his head. "Jason is pulling his stubborn act, refused to talk to me, in fact."

"I couldn't get him to look away from the wall, either," she admitted. "I don't know what I'll tell Jake. He's going to want to know every detail of this jaunt to see the sheriff."

"I'm going by your place right now," Cord told her. "Come on. I'll give you a lift." Without asking, he took the basket from her and she followed him to the door, then on out to where his farm wagon was tied to a hitching rail at the end of a long line of shops. He gave her a hand and she climbed to the seat, where she settled herself, thankful that he'd come along to tend her heavy basket.

If the buggy Jake had given her were to be kept at the house, she might have used it this morning. As it was, the shed-building kept getting postponed for one reason or other.

Cord passed along word from Rachel, mentioning the last of the garden that was keeping her busy in the kitchen. Melody was learning the fine art of putting a meal on the table these days, what with Rachel involved in canning the produce. Cord mentioned the fact in passing and then sighed. "She's not yet the cook her mother is, but Rachel says I have to be properly appreciative of her efforts."

In no time, they arrived at the house. Jake was in the kitchen when Cord carried in the basket. Alicia busied herself putting away the assortment of canned fruit and the staples she'd needed, listening with one ear to the two men as they spoke of Jason.

"It's got me hangin'," Cord said with a dour expression on his face. "I felt like snatching him up from that bunk and shaking the stuffing out of him." Then he relented, smiling a bit. "Well, maybe not quite, but doggone it, Jake, he doesn't seem to be showing any re-morse at all for what he did."

"I need to see him," Jake said. He looked down to where his trousers hung, empty. His face tightened. "Damn." It was a curse that Alicia could not have denied him, conveying his feelings of helplessness at this moment. His son was in jail, less than a half mile away, but it might as well be ten miles, for all the chance Jake had of dealing with the boy.

"Maybe we can figure something out," Cord said. "I'll bet between Alicia and me, we could get you out the back door. There's only two steps there, Jake, and I could pull the wagon around from the front of the house. There's room for it at the end of the picket fence. I'd figure out how we could hoist you up to the wagonbed, and maybe the sheriff would let Jason come out and see you."

"And maybe pigs will fly," Jake said bitterly. "I'm not going to be carted around town like a freak at a sideshow, Cord. You know better."

"You used to go to your office when you worked for the opera company," Cord reminded him quietly. "We had a ramp for you and—"

Jake's raised hand effectively cut off his brother's reminder of better days. "And I had the damn ramp torn down the day after Rena's funeral, if you remember. We're not going that route again. Those days are over, and you might as well get used to it."

Alicia closed her eyes, standing in the pantry, listening to the brothers, and feeling Jake's pain as he spoke the brutal truth as he saw it. She might never make things any better in this house than they were at this moment, she thought, bowing her head, taking note of the hot tears that fell against her hands. Jake had been so badly hurt by Rena's death he might never fully recover.

Her own helplessness tore at her heart. She could only do so much, and she'd been fooling herself when she'd dreamed of Jake going to church with her and even socializing on occasion.

Even the Fourth of July picnic had come and gone without a mention, except for Jason running off early in the morning and not returning until after dark. "You know where he is," she'd told Jake midway through the day. "I can't blame him for wanting to attend, and if you'd be honest with yourself, you can't, either."

"He didn't even ask permission," Jake had said harshly. "Just ran off."

"Every other boy in town went to the picnic," Alicia reminded him. "He's been looking forward to seeing the fireworks and playing in the games. The only thing that would have pleased him more would be to have you along."

Morosely, Jake had retreated for the day, and Alicia had not attempted to coax him into a better mood.

Now she wiped her eyes and made ready to leave the pantry. Jake was in the midst of telling Cord why it was impossible for him to leave the house, and Cord was arguing the point with flashing eyes and a grim frown creasing his forehead.

"Never mind, Cord," she said quietly. "He won't go, and you'll just get upset for nothing."

"Stay out of this," Jake said sharply. "I can speak for myself, Alicia."

She shrugged and turned to leave the kitchen. "I'm well aware of that." As a final remark, it left a lot to be desired, but right now it was the best she could do without displaying her discouragement by shedding tears in front of the two men…and *that* she refused to do.

"Alicia!" Jake called her name, but she kept walking, past his bedroom and to the staircase. She heard the wheels of his chair on the floor as she climbed the stairs, refused to look back at him, and closed the door of her old room with barely a sound. She ached to slam it, but was determined he would not have the satisfaction of knowing he'd frustrated her to that point. Her bed was made and she broke her own long-standing rule to lie down atop the quilt.

She'd been taught as a child that a lady must not succumb to laziness, and naps were for children. Today she didn't give a hang what her mother might think of her actions, and hugged her pillow to herself as she curled up in the middle of the big bed.

THE SHERIFF ARRIVED JUST after suppertime and, seemingly oblivious to the tension in the air, walked through the hallway to the kitchen, where Jake was still sitting at the table. Jake watched Alicia cleaning up the dishes, and thought of what he might say to break the silence. She didn't seem angry, so much as discouraged. She'd retreated from him today, and it wasn't like Alicia to do so. She barely had a smile for the sheriff, in fact.

Having the lawman come to call was the icing on the cake, he decided, and he turned his chair to face the intruder. The fact that the man was well within his rights in keeping Jason in custody was immaterial, so far as Jake was concerned. The boy belonged at home, with his family. Jake was ready to handle the whole mess, and had spent the better part of the day forming a plan.

"Come on in to the parlor," he told his visitor, then looked long and hard at Alicia. "Will you bring us some coffee?" he asked.

She only nodded, and he watched as the sheriff raised an eyebrow and grinned. He followed Jake down the hallway and murmured his opinion aloud. "Looks like your wife is pretty upset with you."

Jake turned in the middle of the parlor to face the sheriff. "Hell, I was pretty ornery to her."

"She's a good woman," the sheriff said bluntly. "I'd say you're a lucky fella to have her."

"I'd say you're absolutely right," Jake admitted readily.

He heard Alicia's footsteps outside the parlor door and watched as she carried a small tray with two cups of coffee on it. "Here you go, Sheriff," she said nicely, handing him a cup. "I hope you like it black. If you need sugar or cream I'll fetch some."

"No, I decided a long time ago not to ruin perfectly good coffee by addin' stuff to it," he told her.

Jake watched in silence as Alicia brought him his cup. He reached for it and murmured thanks, hoping she wouldn't dump it in his lap. She took a seat on the couch. "May I join in this discussion?" she asked. "Or would you rather I not be included, Jake?" She looked at him with a glint in her eyes that dared him to relegate her to the kitchen, and he was quick to shake his head.

"No, you have a perfect right to be here," he told her.

The sheriff leaned forward, speaking directly to Jake. "I'll tell you right off, McPherson. I won't let your boy loose till I'm satisfied that he's paid for what he did. I haven't figured out yet just what we'll do to set him straight, but he's the one who involved the law in this."

"I understand," Jake said. "But the bottom line is that Jason is only nine, and he's sitting in a jailhouse built to house criminals. I fear he'll only be more resentful than ever by the time he's turned free."

"Well," the sheriff began, "I fear that he won't appreciate the problems he caused by turnin' loose those fellas, unless he's punished for it."

Alicia spoke up. "I tend to agree with you, sir," she said, and then looked at Jake. "And I understand your concern with Jason's well-being. There must be a middle ground here. How long will it be until the judge shows up?"

"Middle of next week," the lawman replied. He looked down at his coffee cup. "I was thinking about putting Jason to work around the jailhouse in the meantime."

"Doing what?" Jake asked darkly. "I don't want everyone in town looking at him and pointing their fingers."

The sheriff lifted his head and gave Jake a long, steady look. "He should have thought of the town's disapproval when he pulled this stunt, McPherson. He's gonna learn a lesson if I have anything to say about it. I don't want to be hauling him into custody a few years down the road, just because he thinks he can get away with breaking the law now."

"What sort of work do you have in mind?" Alicia asked, as if she would try to smooth ruffled feathers.

"Sweeping the floors and the sidewalk every morning," the sheriff said. "And washing the windows a couple of times a week. My wife will appreciate that, seeing as how it's been her job up till now. He's gonna miss school as it is, so I thought you could give him some schoolwork to get him ready for going back to classes."

"That wouldn't hurt, I suppose," Alicia said slowly. "And the rest of it might be good for him." She cleared her throat, and Jake aimed a questioning look at her. She was about to speak her mind if he was any judge of it.

"I wonder if he might not be sent home for a certain number of hours each day, perhaps do some chores here to keep him busy, and at the same time give his father time to spend with him. I think Jason needs to know that we love him and we're concerned about him, Sheriff."

The lawman leaned back in his chair, settling his coffee cup on the end table. "Now, I don't know about that Mrs. McPherson. It might jeopardize keeping him in custody."

"If it were a simpler crime, would it be feasible?" she asked.

"Sure," he said agreeably, "but it's not. And I don't know how the judge will feel if he comes to town and finds the prisoner off doing chores at home."

Alicia leaned forward in her chair. "The whole thing is, Jason is a boy, and he needs the influence of his father. As I said, he needs to understand that his father loves him and cares about him. That's the whole crux of this matter, Sheriff. I fear the boy was trying to get our attention in a big way, so we seem to bear part of the blame for what he did."

The man eyed Alicia with respect. "You might be right, ma'am. I'll think about it and see if Jason is willing to listen to me. Maybe we can work something out here." He rose and took his leave, shaking Jake's hand and following Alicia to the front door.

Jake waited impatiently for her return, but in vain. She walked past the parlor door and back to the kitchen. "Damn," he muttered under his breath, and rolled his chair in her wake. "Fool woman is bound and determined to fuss with me."

She was in the pantry and looked up as Jake wheeled his chair to block the doorway. "We're gonna talk," he said bluntly. He looked down to where his hands lay, seemingly helpless, in his lap.

He'd give much to be able to touch her right now. But she was aloof, and unless he missed his guess, Alicia was not fond of him right now. He'd come to the awareness that he was becoming more than fond of her, which presented a real problem.

"I don't know any other way to say I was wrong," he continued. "You've been good to me, and Jason, too, for that matter. You have as much right as I to put in your two cents' worth with the sheriff or with my brother. And I can see how frustrated you are with me and my refusal to leave this house."

He risked looking up at her, noting the sadness that drew her mouth into a soft line and gave her blue eyes a sheen of sorrow. He'd hurt her, and words were not adequate to convey his deep regret. "I seem to be doing this on a regular basis, Alicia, this apologizing to you and trying to make amends for my behavior. I fear you'll reach the point of saturation with my bullheaded performances, and I don't want to see the back of you again, as I did earlier today."

"You do this so well," she announced, biting her lip, as if to hold back a smile. Then the smile was there, a bit weak, but present, nonetheless. "You make me feel as if I'm beating my head against a stone wall sometimes. I'd hoped to remain untouched by your shenanigans, but it hasn't worked out that way."

His brow tilted in surprise and she heard amusement color his words. "Shenanigans? I've been up to shenanigans?" And then he reached for her, bending forward to touch her hand. It lay within his palm, limp and unresponsive, and he looked down at it in surprise. Alicia was many things…sharp of tongue, amused at times, and always astute and observant. Never had he seen her as an unresponsive woman.

"Your hand is cold," he said quietly, and tugged her

forward a bit to lift her fingers to his mouth. His lips caressed the cool flesh and he bowed his head over it, his eyes closing as he murmured words he'd never spoken aloud to another woman.

"I need you, Alicia. More than I've ever needed another human being in my life. I know I've told you this before and, understand, it's not easy for me to admit my dependence on you, but there it is."

He looked up at her. "You've become the center about which this house revolves. Both Jason and I owe you a great debt. The only problem is that he's too young to understand just what you've done for him. I appreciated your suggestions to the sheriff today. I hope he listened well. Maybe he'll consider doing as you asked."

She nodded at him, and he knew she suppressed tears, tears she was unwilling to shed in front of him. Alicia had her pride, too.

"Will you reach the saturation point with me one day?" he wondered aloud. "Will I chase you away, Alicia?"

"It would take more than you've thrown at me thus far," she said quietly. "I told you, I love you, Jake, and that leaves me open to hurt. But there's always the chance of pain where love exists, and I've found that out in a mighty way lately."

"I'd like you to stay with me tonight," he said softly,

and bent his head to kiss her fingers once more. Then he released her hand and rolled backward from the pantry door. She left the small enclosure and he waited silently for her answer, knowing she would not walk away without some sort of reply.

He was not disappointed.

"I'll stay with you, Jake. I think we need each other tonight. Comfort is a warm blanket to my mind. And that's what I need from you right now."

His heart sang, the melody one he'd thought he might never hear again. He rolled his chair out of the kitchen and he heard the lamp chimney being lifted as she blew out the flame, leaving the room in darkness. Ahead of him lay the dim hallway, night having fallen as they spoke, the moonlight spreading across the wide boards through the narrow panes that framed the front door.

"Can you see all right?" he asked, his voice soft as suited the quiet gloom of the house. "Do you need to go upstairs for anything?"

"Yes," she said, "I can see just fine. I have enough down here for tonight."

She followed him into his room and crossed to the window. "I'm going to close this. It's getting nippy out and I don't want you to take a chill." Framed against the window, she pulled the sash down and then turned to him. In profile she seemed to exemplify the very foundation of his life she'd become. Strong and sturdy, womanly and giving, Alicia was a wife to be cherished, he decided.

To that end, he spoke her name. "Alicia? Get undressed and pull back the sheets for me, would you? I don't think we need the lamp or a candle lit. I'm used to doing this in the dark."

He unbuttoned his shirt and tossed it on the chair, then worked at his trousers. Down to the drawers he wore, he rolled to the bed where she'd drawn the sheets aside. As he watched, she fluffed the pillows, bent over the bed, wearing her vest and petticoat. From beneath the pillow she'd slept on, she removed her nightgown and drew it over her head, offering him the same view of her nightly performance he'd seen before.

"One of these days you'll leave the gown off," he told her. "When you're comfortable enough with me to know how I feel about you, you'll let me watch you."

She laughed softly and tossed aside her underclothing. "That may never happen, Jake McPherson. I've been doing this ever since I can remember."

"I yearn for the day when you no longer object to my eyes on you," he told her. "Then I'll know that I've convinced you of my regard."

"Regard?" she said musingly. "What a strange word to use."

"What would you prefer?" he asked, already knowing her reply.

"Maybe affection," she whispered. "Perhaps devotion, or fondness or maybe even love, one day. Any of them would do, Jake. But not unless they're from the heart. And I'm not sure you have any of those thoughts about me."

She sat down on the edge of the bed and reached down to remove her stockings. "I know you need me, you've made that clear, but eventually I want more than that from you. I'm not sure I'll ever get it."

He moved himself into the bed with his usual efficiency. His drawers were cast to the floor and he settled against the sheet, pulling it up to cover himself. Alicia punched her pillow, then turned to lie beside him.

"I'll do my best to speak my thoughts, Alicia," he said quietly. "I'm not good at this. I doubt very many men are. To speak of our affection aloud is difficult." He reached for her hand and lifted it once more to his lips. "I'll try. I'll do my best. That's all I can promise."

"Then I'll have to be satisfied with that, won't I?" She turned her head and her face was but a dim, ivory oval in the gloom. "I've not asked much from you, Jake. Only that you treat me with respect, that you allow me to speak my mind. I'm not asking you for your love. I'm not certain you are capable of giving it to me, anyway. But I need to know that what I do for you and Jason is important."

"Important?" He laughed, a rusty sound that choked

in his throat. "Only about as important as every breath I take," he admitted. "You've brought us back to life, Alicia. You've given Jason the presence of a woman in his life, and for that Rena would be thankful, if she knew."

"I think she does know, Jake. And I think she's at peace now," Alicia said gently.

He closed his eyes, grateful for her words of comfort. "She'd love you, Alicia. If she'd known you, she'd have wanted you as her friend."

"I think I agree," Alicia told him.

"I don't believe in ghosts, Alicia. Rena lives inside a corner of my heart, and maybe it's from there that I've felt her presence and heard her voice." He felt an easing of the loss he'd suffered with Rena's death, and he reached for Alicia, his fingers touching her shoulder, drawing her down next to him.

"Lie with me," he said. "Sleep beside me. Tomorrow we'll face all our problems. For tonight, let's just be at peace."

CHAPTER SIXTEEN

"DO YOU THINK I could try to play the piano, Pa? Maybe I could take lessons from you, too."

It wasn't a question Jake had expected, and he found himself groping for an answer. "I didn't know you were interested," he said after a moment.

"I might'a thought about it before, but you've had it all covered up for a long time," Jason said diffidently, halting in his raking of the front yard to look up at his father. Supervising from the porch, Jake had been surprised by the question, one he thought seemed to have come from out of the blue.

"So it has," he said, nodding his agreement. "But it isn't anymore, Jason. And if you'd be interested in it, I'd be happy to teach you."

Jason ducked his head. "I just thought if Toby can do so good at it, maybe I can try." He laughed scoffingly then, and his eyes glittered as he spoke. "Heck, even old Catherine can play with both hands now, Pa. There's hope for me, don't you think?"

Jake felt his heart swell within his breast. "Of course there is, son," he managed to murmur. "You're a talented young man, Jason." He watched his son for a few moments, aware of the boy's dark hair that curled against his collar, of his tongue stuck between his teeth as he concentrated on raking the leaves with precision.

Then he spoke his thoughts, deciding it might be better if Jason were aware of his father's concern. "I hate to think that you're having to pay such a high price for your actions lately," he told him quietly. "All your energy and your considerable talent should be going toward your schoolwork and the abilities you possess."

"Abilities?" The word seemed foreign to the boy as he paused in his work and looked up to meet his father's eyes. "You think I've got abilities, Pa?" His tone was dubious.

"You're a smart boy, Jason. You've just been directing your intelligence in the wrong direction over the past weeks. You'll make Alicia and me both very proud of you one of these days, provided you straighten up and do as you should."

Jason bent his head to his task. "I'm tryin', Pa," he said. "I told the sheriff I'd do whatever he wanted me to. I hate that you and Miss Alicia are—" He hesitated, searching for a phrase that would better explain his thoughts. "You're both kinda embarrassed about me, aren't you?"

"No, not embarrassed, Jason. Just wondering what we could have done to make things better for you. I know it was a shock to you when Alicia moved into my bedroom. But it was the right thing to do. You have to understand that, first and foremost."

Jason dared a quick look at Jake. "I guess I do now. It just made me mad, that she left me all alone upstairs and that she likes you better than me."

He hadn't thought of that angle, Jake decided; it would be worth his consideration. "Well, she likes you an awful lot, son. You just don't realize it."

"Yeah, I do," he said, shamefaced. "She's been good to me, Pa, and I didn't treat her the way I should've, did I?"

Jake shook his head. "No, you didn't. It's about time for you to make amends, don't you think?"

THE WALK BACK TO the jailhouse was getting to be a regular part of her schedule, and Alicia set out with Jason in tow right after supper. The sheriff had allowed him to spend most of the day at home, for which she was thankful. The judge was to arrive in the morning, and she planned on appearing at the hearing, as did Cord.

"I need to say somethin'," Jason said abruptly as they neared the center of town.

She looked down at him and nodded. "All right.

Have at it," she told him, and then waited, acknowledging that his words might not be to her liking.

"I really like you, ma'am," he said softly, glancing up at her as if to gauge her reaction. "I know I haven't always been real nice, and I know I said some things that were pretty nasty to you the other day." He drew in a deep breath.

"I'm really sorry, Miss Alicia. I didn't mean the stuff I said. I was mad at Pa and I guess I was feeling sorry for myself, that you wanted to move downstairs. I kinda liked you being upstairs with me." He shot her another look, bordering on hopeful, she decided.

"I liked being upstairs with you," she told him. "But your father is right. I'm his wife, and I belong in his bedroom with him."

"I won't give you any more trouble about it," Jason said firmly. "I don't want you to get upset and think about leavin' us."

"I'll never leave you, Jason. I'm here for the duration." Pleased at the effort behind his words, she refrained from her first impulse to lean down and press her lips against his cheek. He'd be humiliated should anyone see such a gesture, so she settled for a pat on his shoulder.

"Thank you for saying all of that," she told him. "I think we understand each other a bit better, don't we?"

He nodded, his steps slowing as they saw the sheriff in the doorway of the jailhouse, awaiting his prisoner's return. "Will you be here in the morning, ma'am?" Jason asked her softly.

"Of course I will. And so will your uncle Cord," she told him firmly. She raised a hand in greeting to the sheriff and spoke politely. "I hope we didn't make you wait too long," she said. "I cleaned up the kitchen first."

"That's what I left my wife doing," he told her, then his attention shifted to the boy beside her. "You ready for bed, young'un?"

Alicia thought Jason's answering nod held a degree of sadness, his shoulders slouching as he crossed the threshold into the sheriff's office. The lawman turned to her and winked. "It's gonna be fine," he said in an undertone, lifting her spirits immensely.

IT *WAS* FINE. In fact, Alicia thought it was downright wonderful. The judge peered over his spectacles at the prisoner, reading aloud the list of community projects Jason had participated in over the past week, then the long line of work details he'd completed at his home and around the jailhouse. Most important, the escaped prisoners had been captured without incident.

"I'd say you've complied with everything the sheriff asked of you, young man," he said in a booming voice. "I hope you recognize that you've been given a very light sentence for the seriousness of your crime, Jason. I'll tell you one thing. If ever I see you standing before me again, I'll not be nearly so lenient. Is that understood?"

Jason nodded and voiced a wobbly, "Yes, sir." His words spoken in a shuddering breath. He repeated the reply, this time more strongly, and raised his chin, his shoulders becoming straighter, as if he recognized that his ordeal was almost at an end.

"Go home to your family," the judge said. "And keep your nose clean."

Jake was waiting on the front porch when Cord's surrey pulled up in front of the house. He bent forward in his chair, his hands holding the chair arms as if he yearned to stand erect and meet his son halfway.

Alicia thought Jake's eyes were a bit damp, but she ignored it, focusing instead on the meal she had cooking on the back burner of the cookstove. "Will you stay for dinner, Cord?" she asked.

"No, I'll be in the doghouse if I'm not home by the time Rachel has mine on the table," he answered. "She was making chicken soup and had bread in the oven when I left."

"Maybe I'll go with you," Alicia said with a laugh. "We're only having leftovers." Turning to Cord, she offered her hand and her sincere thanks, the words unspoken but acknowledged by Jake's brother as he leaned forward to press his kiss against her cheek.

She swept through the screened door and into the house, her own tears close to the surface. *If only Jake had been there to support Jason with his presence.* Cord was a wonderful substitute, but a substitute, nevertheless. The prospect of convincing Jake to rejoin society seemed an insurmountable task to her today.

There must be something she could do. Some way of giving Jake the impetus to go out in public once more, yet she felt unable to find a solution.

She began setting the table. From the front of the house, she heard Jason's high-pitched laughter and she halted where she stood, a smile touching her lips. Then Jake's low, deeper tones of good humor blended with those of his son, and Alicia knew a moment of contentment such as she'd yearned for over the past days.

ALICIA WAS KEPT BUSY in the evenings, making certain that Jason was caught up with his classmates. The boy was eager to make amends, it seemed, and though she'd recognized his potential before, Alicia found herself astounded at the intelligence he displayed.

"Miss Alicia, the other kids are gonna think it's not fair for me to be having you teach me at home. It's like I have my own special teacher. They all liked you a lot, and I don't think that new Mr. Smithers is near as nice as you were to everybody. Now I get to have you here all the time because you're my…"

"Stepmother?" she asked, providing the word he had difficulty speaking aloud.

"Yeah," he agreed, relief apparent in his voice. "Seeing's how you live with us and all, I get a lot more attention than the rest of the kids in school. Maybe it's not right for me to—" He halted again and eyed her with a measuring look. "I know you're tryin' to help me, ma'am, but I don't want to take up all your time."

"What my son is attempting to convey in his own sneaky way, is that he's feeling put upon, Alicia," Jake said dryly. "He thinks you expect him to spend more time on schoolwork than the others do."

"You're right. I do expect more of him with his studies. He's a bright boy and I have reason to know that he's more capable than many of the other children. I want him to do his best." She studied Jason for a moment, watching as his cheeks reddened at her words. "If you like, I'll back off. I only want you to be all you can be."

"Yes, ma'am," he said agreeably. "Now, can I go read my book?" Fleeing from arithmetic problems seemed to be his goal; Alicia granted his request, then watching as he picked up the adventure story he was deeply involved in, choosing a spot to sit where the lamplight fell directly on his book.

"He reads more than I did at his age," Jake said quietly. "I was glued to the piano, even then."

"He might be, too, if you choose to give him lessons as he asked," Alicia told him.

"He hasn't mentioned it again," Jake said. "But I've been thinking about that. Maybe after Toby's come and gone this week, I can spend some time with Jason."

He did as he'd proposed, and on Thursday Alicia listened from the hallway as Jake introduced his son to the piano. It was more than half an hour later when she heard the first sound of impatience in his voice as he explained some small thing for the third time to the boy, and she swept into the room as if on a mission.

"I think perhaps we've had enough music for now," she said, shooting a warning glance at Jake. "I'd like Jason to wash up and set the table for supper."

The boy slid from the piano bench with a nod and headed for the doorway, turning back as he left the room to grin widely at his father. "Thanks, Pa," he said. "I'll do better next time."

"He did fine," Jake told Alicia with a wry look of impatience. "I was the one who was having a hard time. It's more important when it's your own child, I think. I can be patient with Toby and Catherine, but with Jason, I seem to want to teach him everything I know in one sitting. All he's ready for right now is locating middle C and learning the scales."

"Have you played for him?" she asked, knowing as she spoke that he would frown at her and shake his head in a negative reply.

"You know I don't play anymore," Jake said shortly. "Don't push me, Alicia."

She turned away. "All right. Supper is almost ready." Hurt stiffened her backbone as she walked from the room, but she hid the pain his quick temper caused.

He rolled through the long hallway behind her. "Alicia." He called her name and she halted by the kitchen door, waiting for him to catch up with her.

"I doubt I'll ever touch those keys again," he said. "It's difficult to teach when I have to tell my students instead of showing them, but that's the way it is. Try to be content with what you've accomplished."

"I'm trying." Opening the kitchen door, she stood to one side, waiting for Jake to roll past her, and pinned a smile on her face for Jason's benefit. "Let me check the potatoes," she said, and then looked at the table. "You've done well, Jason. Don't forget the napkins."

THE WEATHER WAS GROWING chilly, the nights bringing frost to paint the trees with the colors of autumn. Alicia had settled in nicely, arranging her nest with the confidence of a woman who knows her worth. She rose early each morning to prepare breakfast for the three of them, confident that a good meal would hold Jason in good stead during the long day he spent in school.

The next Tuesday morning began as any other weekday, with Jason dragging his feet, Jake sitting at the table with his coffee before him, and Alicia trying her best to keep them both happy. It would behoove her to snatch a piece of toast, she thought. Her stomach was protesting its lack of food, and even as she considered that idea, a wave of nausea swept over her.

"What do you have planned for this morning?" Jake asked, watching as she put together a thick sandwich for Jason's lunch. An apple from the pantry was added to Jason's lunch bag, and she counted out four cookies and wrapped them in waxed paper. Preparing food was not sitting well, she decided, reaching for a piece of bread.

"I'm going to help at the church for a couple of hours," Alicia said. "They're getting ready for a quilting bee and I promised to lend a hand."

"Have you thought about what you'll fix for our lunch?" Jake's eyes followed her around the kitchen and she turned to face him head-on as he spoke.

"Mrs. Bates will be here today," she said. "I'm sure she'd be happy to fix you a fresh sandwich or get out some chicken left from last night's supper."

"It won't taste as good if you don't make it." She thought his mouth drew into the same sort of pout as

Jason's when he was in a bad mood, and she almost laughed aloud at the sight.

"Did you forget that Cord's coming today to fix a trapeze in the bathing room for you? That'll keep you busy, giving him orders." She whispered in his ear, bending over to kiss him. "I'd have thought you'd had enough of my company. You kept me awake half the night."

He shot her a quick glance and she noted the smile he could not contain curving his lips. "Are you complaining?" he asked dryly. Reaching for her hand, he drew her back toward him and tugged at her until she bent again to kiss his brow.

"Is that the best you can manage?" he asked.

"For now, yes." With a look toward Jason, she mouthed words for Jake's benefit only. *Later. Much later.* He grinned, his mood cheered considerably by her foolishness and she felt relieved.

Turning to go to the bedroom where she would change into a nicer dress for her jaunt to the church, she felt a moment's dizziness and reached to balance herself on the doorjamb. It passed quickly and she covered the momentary lapse with an excuse, spoken in an undertone.

"I'm getting clumsy in my old age," she murmured, then came to a halt in the hallway in front of the back bedroom door.

Again, nausea rolled from her stomach to her throat, and the taste of bile was sour in her mouth. She closed the door behind her and fled across the room to where the chamber pot sat beneath a wooden table. Thankful that she'd already washed it out for the day, she bent over it and lost what little coffee she'd drunk and the half slice of bread she'd eaten.

"Oh, my word," she whispered, sinking down on the chair, wiping her forehead with a damp cloth from the basin. "What on earth is wrong with me?" Her hands were trembling, and as the dizziness returned she searched her mind for possibilities. Only one made itself known, and the possibility of that was highly unlikely, she decided.

A woman of thirty who'd never been married, never conceived a child heretofore, would not be prone, she thought, to have fallen pregnant so easily. Then again, she'd been sleeping in Jake's bed long enough for such a thing to happen.

She blushed as the thoughts circled in her mind. It could not be, she decided firmly. And yet, the niggling thought of monthly times, and the lack thereof, would not be banished. She'd known that her time was late, but that happened sometimes, especially to a newly married woman, she'd heard.

Didn't it?

With determination, she decreed it time to talk to

someone who knew a whole lot more about this situation than she did. Perhaps Rachel would be the best choice. For although she had a fine education, there were areas in which she was sadly lacking—and this one headed the list.

She dressed quickly and hastened from the room, almost plowing into Jake's chair as she met him in the hallway.

"What's wrong, Alicia?" His voice was stern, as though he would not swallow any excuses, and she sought a plausible explanation for her haste.

"I'm going to be late," she said with a smile. "I fiddled around too long this morning and now I'm having to hurry to make up the time."

"That's not what I'm talking about," he told her. "You weren't clumsy in the kitchen, and you know it. You're about the most graceful woman I've ever known, and losing your balance that way wasn't because you tripped." He looked at her, his eyes narrowing, his gaze seeming to penetrate her very pores.

"Now, tell me what's wrong."

She shook her head, unwilling to speak aloud the fears she harbored. *Fear* was the wrong word to use. For if she was indeed carrying Jake's child, it would be the most wonderfully exciting thing ever to happen in her life. As to whether or not Jake would feel the same, she had no idea, and this morning wasn't a good time to find out.

She bent to him and kissed him quickly, her lips warm and soft against his, seeking to distract him. It didn't work. He reached for her and his fingers grasped her wrist. "Alicia." It was a warning, one she recognized. Jake would not be thwarted in this. He wanted an answer.

"Hey, Pa. I'm leavin' now," Jason said brightly, sailing through the kitchen door and pausing momentarily beside his father's chair. Then he looked up at Alicia. "Are you walkin' to the church, Miss Alicia?"

"Yes," she said. "It'll be a few minutes till I'm ready, so you go on ahead."

They watched as Jason went out the front door, his jacket undone, his books under his arm. Jake shot her a look that she recognized.

He would not be denied.

Kneeling abruptly beside his chair, she leaned on his leg, placing her forehead against the fabric of his trousers. "Alicia, what is it?" His voice deepened, and his hand touched the crown of her head, where her braids were coiled and pinned in place. "Tell me what's wrong," he said firmly. "I won't let you go until you do."

"I don't know for sure," she said, her voice muffled against his knee.

"You don't know for sure." He repeated her words slowly as his palm moved to her nape and cupped it, rubbing the tender skin there with easy movements. "What don't you know for sure, sweetheart?"

"I can't remember if I've had a monthly time lately," she told him.

His hand ceased its movement, and she thought he'd stopped breathing. "Are you sure?" And then he laughed aloud. "Of course you're sure!"

She lifted her head and peered up at him. "Do you think...?" She could not finish the sentence, could not speak aloud the thoughts that spun through her mind.

"Yeah, I think," he whispered, and his hand cupped her chin now, lifting her higher on her knees until he could reach her lips with his own. "I think you're going to have my child, Alicia."

"I'm such a dummy," she whispered. "I didn't even think it might be that."

"And you weren't going to tell me?" His face drew into stern lines and he shook his head. "I'm not sure you're well enough to be helping at the church today."

She looked down at her lapel watch and inhaled sharply. "I'm fine, Jake. I feel up to snuff now, and I've got to hurry. I promised to be there early to set up the quilting frames." She smiled, the pleasure of this revelation building within her.

"I'm so happy, Jake. I didn't know how badly I wanted to have a child."

"Thank you for that, for wanting to bear my child," he said quietly, and then helped her to her feet. "Go on, then," he said. "I'll let Mrs. Bates in when she comes and ask her to start supper for us. I fear you'll be tired when you come home."

She nodded her approval of his plan and crossed to the hall tree where her heavy coat hung on a peg. Sliding her arms into the sleeves, she turned back to him, catching him with a foolish grin on his lips. With six long strides, she was beside him once more and she bent again to kiss him.

He laughed again and playfully swatted her bottom. "Go on now, before you end up staying home altogether," he warned her.

The nausea was gone, the dizziness had passed, and she felt invigorated by the brisk air as she marched along the road toward the church. The ladies were waiting for instructions, and since Alicia had volunteered to be in charge of this project, they welcomed her with open arms. Within minutes she had begun to organize things and the clutch of women set to with a will, Alicia tending to each facet of the preparation.

Yet beneath her surface calm there beat a heart that overflowed with anticipation. She felt as though she walked on a cloud, that her sensibly shod feet barely touched the wide-planked floor. Just to think, she'd be cradling a baby boy or girl by the time the flowers were in full bloom next summer.

CORD HAD HUNG THE TRAPEZE from the center of the bathing room, directly over the claw-footed tub. It rose and fell with a pulley and the rope could be bound around a fixture on the wall to keep it out of the way when not in use. Jake's pleasure at the arrangement was obvious, his grin wide as he showed the apparatus to Alicia after supper.

"Did you try it out?" she asked, attempting to visualize how the contraption would work. At Jake's negative response, she made a suggestion she knew would please him. "Why don't I fill the tub after a while, when Jason's gone to bed, and we can figure out how to do this?"

His nod signified instant acceptance of her suggestion, and he waited with a decided lack of patience until it should be bedtime for his son. Alicia had already put the largest containers on the stove and filled them with water to heat. In no time at all, she had carried them into the bathing room and emptied them in the tub, adding enough cold water to make the temperature of his bath comfortable.

"I want it good and hot," Jake said, reaching from his chair to test the waters. "You have no idea how I've dreamed of this, sweetheart," he said in a low voice. "Washing in bits and pieces is frustrating. I never feel like I've got all the parts clean."

"You've always been clean, Jake," she told him. "This will just make it easier."

"Not for you," he said, waving a hand at the empty containers she'd lugged over the threshold during the past fifteen minutes.

"Oh, I don't know," she said, rolling up her sleeves. "I'm planning on enjoying this."

"Oh?" His brow lifted as he watched her actions. "How's that?"

"I'm going to wash your back and lots of other places, as well," she said smartly.

His grin was wide and she thought for a moment that she barely knew this man, hardly recognized him as the same individual she'd met months ago. He'd gone from being a cantankerous recluse to the man before her, emerging from his solitude and learning to smile, to enjoy life once more.

Within moments, he was stripped from his clothing and had placed his chair next to the tub. Alicia lowered the trapeze, then secured the rope. Jake reached for it, balanced himself on the chair with his strong arms and then swung into the hot water, lowering himself to the bottom of the tub with a gasp.

"Damn, it's hot."

"You're the one who set the temperature," she reminded him, reaching for a bucket of cold water. Before she could add it, he held up a hand.

"It's all right now. I like it this way, Alicia." He leaned forward, balancing himself and reaching for the washcloth she'd placed on the side of the tub. But she would not have it, and snatched it from his hand.

"I'm doing the honors this first time," she told him, kneeling beside the tub and sloshing the cloth in the water. A bar of soap was handy and she rubbed it against the cloth, forming a lather that promised to cover his whole back with a layer of suds.

She began there, and listened to his groan of pleasure as she scrubbed the muscular lines of his shoulders and then down past his waist. The cloth was rinsed and she splashed water on him, allowing it to sluice away the soap. In turn, it was time for his chest and neck, his arms and hands.

As if he were a babe, she washed him, and he allowed it. His hair received a long sudsing and she rinsed it with cool water, bringing low growls of protest from him as the water made him shiver. Then she handed him the cloth.

"You get to finish," she told him firmly, nodding as he bent to peer through the sudsy water to where his male parts were showing proof of her efficiency. His arousal was apparent, and she felt a twinge of embarrassment as she recognized her effect on him.

"Coward," he whispered.

"Am not," she retorted firmly.

"Are, too," he returned. Then watched her with glittering eyes as she considered his state of readiness.

With a toss of her head she knelt beside him once more, took the cloth in hand and rubbed the soap against the fabric. "You asked for it," she warned him.

"Yeah." His voice was husky, the single word a satisfied groan as she completed the task she'd begun.

CHAPTER SEVENTEEN

ALICIA WAS HALFWAY HOME from the general store, the mare high-stepping its way down the street. As if anxious for more exercise than she received with these short trips to town, the horse pranced within the traces. If only she could somehow get Jake into the buggy, especially now that the shed at the house had made outings so convenient. A ride in the country would be just the ticket, and the mare would enjoy the outing.

The building of the shed and corral had gone quickly once Cord arrived to handle the project. Recruiting three men from the lumberyard and hardware store had been a good move on his part, Alicia thought, remembering the speed at which the small building had been erected. A lean-to on one side provided a place for the buggy and future plans included fencing in an acre of land for a pasture. Small, but sufficient for one horse. Now her horse and buggy were handy, requiring only a trip to the back yard, where she could harness the pretty mare to the shiny new buggy, and do her errands in style.

Her mind was spinning, awhirl with plans for the coming week. Christmas had ever been the most important day in the year, so far as she was concerned. Although she hadn't had much opportunity to celebrate in previous years, except for the services at church and being included in preparations in whichever home she was living at the time, she'd still been attuned to the holiday spirit, enjoying the music and decorations that made it such a wonderful time of the year.

Living with Jake and Jason opened up a whole new world of celebration, one in which she could indulge her fantasies to the fullest extent. Oblivious to everything but her own thoughts, she was caught by surprise by Cord's appearance. His farm wagon moved beside her as she traveled, pacing her, and his laughter caught her attention.

"You're in another world, Alicia," he said with a wide smile. "Here I've brought you a gift, and you're too wrapped up to take notice."

"Me?" she asked in surprise. "A gift for me? Whatever are you talking about?"

"Follow me to the house and I'll unload your present, and put away the buggy for you."

She turned to peer into the back of the wagon and her mouth dropped open in amazement. The tallest pine tree she'd ever laid eyes on was in the wagon bed, green and bushy and very obviously intended to be used as a Christmas tree. She looked at Cord and was filled with mixed emotions.

"Jason told me that Jake won't have a tree in the house since Rena died," she said sadly. "They didn't even celebrate for the last three years."

"Don't I know it," Cord said fervently. "Rachel about had a fit when she found out that Jake had deprived the boy of all the holiday fun. We ended up coming into town and taking him home with us for a couple of days. That might have been a mistake, since it only served to put Jake in the doldrums even more."

He waved at the tree with one gloved hand. "This is my solution to the problem this year. I figure you're capable of decorating the thing with Jason's help, and you can certainly hold your own against Jake, no matter how ornery he gets."

"Well, thanks for the vote of confidence," she said dryly. "I hope there's room for me out at your place if you're wrong."

Cord pulled his team up short in front of the big white house and jumped to the ground. Alicia slid quickly from the buggy and opened the gate, allowing Cord to pass through before her. At the porch, she turned and shot him a long look.

"Don't be surprised if he shoots the both of us," she warned him. "If he didn't want a tree decorated last year, I doubt if he'll have changed his mind." She opened the big door and watched as Cord carried the tree into the parlor.

"What the hell is that for?"

Closing her eyes, she sent up a brief prayer for patience, then scurried in Cord's wake, recognizing the need to serve as buffer between the brothers. "Isn't this fine?" she asked heartily. "Cord brought us a tree, and I was thinking I'd have to go out and find one on my own."

"We're not having a tree," Jake said harshly. "Cord can just turn right around and drag it out of here."

Alicia strode to where Jake sat beside the fireplace and faced him, determined he should not win this battle. If for no other reason than for Jason's sake. "You needn't be involved in this, Jake. If you don't want to enjoy our Christmas tree, that's fine with me. Jason and I can decorate it by ourselves. I've done a lot of things to please you, but this isn't going to be one of them. This tree will be put in a stand and will be placed in front of the big windows."

"The hell it will."

She'd never heard his voice so firm, never known his stance to be quite so rigid. For a moment, she hovered between backing down and taking a stand of her own. Her hopes for a joyous Christmas hung in the balance, and she determined that Jake McPherson would not rob her of the beauty of this season.

"I say the tree stays," she told him. "You can park in your room for the next ten days if you like, but the tree will be here in the parlor."

"Who gave you control over my life?" he asked bluntly, ignoring Cord's uneasy presence.

Alicia turned to Cord, refusing to be baited by Jake's sullen query. "Shall I find some pieces of wood to make a stand?" she asked.

"I'll handle it," he told her, obviously thankful to take his leave with haste.

She turned back to Jake, only to watch as he left the parlor, his chair heading at a rapid speed into the hallway and toward the back of the house. The bedroom door closed with a bang, and she felt quick tears come to her eyes.

"Miss Alicia?" From the kitchen, Jason called her as he stomped his way across the hallway, seeking her whereabouts. "What's goin' on?" he asked. "I saw Uncle Cord's wagon out in front." Then he caught sight of the pine tree, and his eyes opened wide. "Is that for us? Are we really gonna have a Christmas tree this year?"

It was enough to solidify her resolve. "We certainly are," she said firmly. "You'll need to show me where the decorations are, Jason. We'll do this together." She saw the boy's face light up and it was enough to make this whole fuss worthwhile, she decided. "Your father doesn't want it here, but it's staying, anyway."

"He's gonna be really mad at you," Jason murmured, looking over his shoulder as if seeking Jake's
presence.

"He already is," Alicia said agreeably. "He'll just
have to change his mind, won't he?"

CORD BUILT THE TREE STAND quickly, and Jason helped
him secure it in place before the windows, then called
Alicia in from the kitchen for her approval. She nodded, pacing from one side to the other, and then smiled.
"It's perfect," she announced.

"I took care of the buggy, put the mare in her stall
and hung up the harness," Cord said. "My good deed
for the day." He looked around with a frown. "Where's
Jake?"

"In his room. I suspect he'll be staying there for the
duration."

"Won't Pa come out to the kitchen to eat?" Jason
asked, his mouth turning down.

"We'll see," Alicia answered, not at all certain what
would be the outcome of this whole undertaking.

As it turned out, Jake chose to eat in his room, silent and morose, looking put-upon. As well he might
be, Alicia decided, trying her best to be fair with him.
This *was* his house and she probably didn't have the
right to override his objections. But the house was her
home, too, and she felt she was within her rights on

this issue. She'd thought he was beyond the foolishness of honoring Rena's death by denying the joy of
Christmas to his son.

Jason took her to the attic after supper and they
found dusty boxes of ornaments and candle holders,
plus a wooden, hand-carved set of angels and shep-
herds in a box. Beneath the miniature figures was a
manger, complete with a tiny child, and accompanied
by figures which could only have been meant to rep-
resent Mary and Joseph.

It brought tears to her eyes as Jason carefully explained that his mother had ordered the set made especially for the last Christmas they'd shared as a family.
Jason's fingers touched each individual piece as he spoke,
and Alicia was touched by the sadness in the boy's face.

"She'd be happy if she knew you were going to set
it up in the parlor this year," she told him.

"Do you think she knows?" Jason asked, his eyes
hopeful.

"I suspect she might," Alicia said carefully. "We
don't always know about things that are beyond our
understanding, Jason. So long as your mother is alive
in your heart, and you cherish her memory, she will
have an influence on you."

"She'd be mad if she knew I'd let those men out of
jail, wouldn't she?" he asked glumly. "She'd probably
have cried." He looked up at Alicia. "She cried one

time when I got in trouble with Pa, and she made him let me off easy."

"Your mother loved you, Jason. I'm sure she was sad when she realized she was leaving you."

"Miss Alicia," he began slowly. "Do you think my mama would be happy if she knew you were here with us now?"

Alicia's heart pumped more rapidly as she responded. "I'd like to think so. She loved you, and I'm sure she would've wanted you to have someone to look after you and make sure you were kept clean and well fed." She reached to him and ran her fingers through his hair. "Speaking of that, you need a haircut, young man."

He wrinkled his nose, a reaction she'd expected, and she laughed. "I love you, Jason." Before she thought, the words were spoken aloud, and the boy looked up at her with astonishment.

"You do?" he asked. "How come? I've been bad a lot, Miss Alicia."

"No," she said firmly. "You've done some things you shouldn't have. But you're not a bad boy, Jason. Don't ever think that of yourself."

She thought his eyes teared up, but it was difficult to tell, for he stepped closer to her and his arms circled her waist and his head pressed against her bosom. "If you say so, ma'am," he whispered. He looked up at her, and his smile was like sunshine on a dreary day.

"I love you, too, Miss Alicia. I really do. I'm glad you married my pa."

She sighed. "I'm not sure he's too happy about that right now," she murmured. "But I'm sure he'll come around."

It took two days. Two long, dreary days in which Alicia discovered the depths of Jake's stubborn streak. He stayed in his room, venturing forth finally on the third morning. "Why haven't you been sleeping with me?" he asked harshly, rolling his chair into the kitchen.

Alicia stood by the table, a knife in her hand, midway through slicing a loaf of bread.

"Are you gonna throw it at me?" he asked.

"The bread or the knife?" She continued her task as she spoke, averting her gaze from his.

"I'll take the bread gladly. I'm hungry," he told her.

"You know where the food is kept. You've no need to be hungry in this house," she said. She looked up at him. "Are you planning on eating breakfast at the table with me?"

"I suppose so," he answered, rolling closer to the spot where he normally sat for meals. "Am I welcome?"

"It's your house, Jake. As you so nicely reminded me the other day."

"So I did." He reached for a piece of the bread and she lifted the knife, pointing it in his direction.

"You can wait till I have the food on the table," she told him sharply.

"Yes, ma'am," he said humbly. But she thought she caught a glimpse of his rare good humor in the smile he had trouble suppressing. He folded his hands and watched as she finished with the meal preparations, his gaze fixed on the plate of eggs and sausage she placed before him. "I don't suppose you made pancakes, did you?" he asked hopefully. "I thought I heard them sizzling on the griddle when I opened the bedroom door earlier."

"I made pancakes," she said, turning to the warming oven to bring forth a platter rounded with the light, golden-brown circles.

"Oh, boy." Jason stood in the doorway, his eyes bright with anticipation as he surveyed the meal she'd prepared. "I'm sure glad it's Saturday, Pa. We got all day to do stuff for Christmas." Then his face sobered and he shot a brief glance toward Alicia.

"Can I help?" Jake asked quietly, and Alicia sent up a quick prayer of thanksgiving for the minor miracle wrought in this moment.

"We can use all the help we can get," she said. "I've cookies to bake, and Jason has something he needs help wrapping. The two of you can frost my cookies and cut up the fruit for my fruitcake."

"How come we hafta do all the hard work?" Jason

asked, his eyes twinkling as he shared the moment with his father.

"It's just the fate of the men in the family, I guess," Jake told him. "What would Alicia do without us?"

Jason sidled closer to his father and stood at his elbow. "Pa? Can I ask you something?"

"Of course," Jake assured him. "Is this a secret? Or can Alicia hear, too?"

"She doesn't know about it," Jason said quietly. "But I don't care if she hears, I guess. It's about her, anyway."

Alicia's hands stilled as she filled Jason's plate and delivered it to the table, and then turned back for her own. Her back was toward the two of them as Jason's words were spoken in a faint whisper. Words she'd thought never to hear.

"Pa, I think it would be good if I called Miss Alicia something else. What do you think?"

"You going to call her Mrs. McPherson?" Jake asked soberly, and Alicia caught the smile buried beneath the query.

Jason laughed aloud, and she turned as he shook his head and crinkled his nose. "Of course not. I thought I'd just call her my mama."

Alicia held her plate before her and placed it on the table, sliding into her chair when she found her legs felt weak. The boy wanted to name her as his mother.

She looked up at him and saw the hopeful look he could not conceal as he awaited his father's opinion.

"I'd be pleased if you'd do that, Jason," Alicia managed to say, then included Jake in her reply. "If your father thinks it's the right thing to do."

Jake nodded, and she suspected he was having a difficult time putting words together. His arm enclosed Jason in a firm grip. "Your mama would be pleased," he said. "I know it for certain, son."

IT WAS A MAGICAL TIME, Alicia decided. The baking, the decorating and the wrapping of gifts filled the house with a combination of scent and sound, of activity such as had not taken place within these walls in far too long. The candles were lit at dusk, and the parlor became a fairyland of lights and tinsel and the reflection of glowing, glittering lights in the big front windows.

Jake sat beside the couch, his hands at rest on his lap, his eyes fixed on Jason as the boy lay beneath the lowest branches of the tree and looked upward into the greenery. "I can see the ornaments, Pa. They look all shimmery from the candles shining on them."

Beside him, Alicia held the big Bible in her lap. She'd rescued it from the darkest corner of the parlor cupboard earlier in the day and dusted its cover with tender care. Now she waited for the right moment in which to open it and remind them all of the reason for this time of celebration.

"Are you going to read to us?" Jake asked.

"Do you mind?"

He shook his head. "I've always enjoyed listening to your reading aloud. I remember one night when I didn't pay attention to a single sentence of the story. I was so intent on the way you pronounced each word that I didn't connect them in any way. It was like music to my ears, hearing you speak and knowing you were mine."

She looked up at him in surprise. "I don't remember that."

"Don't you?" He smiled, and her thoughts turned back to the evenings they'd spent, thinking in a flash of recollection how the reading time on one particular night had become instead a time of learning to know Jake's body. A time in which he'd turned her from a reluctant spinster into his wife.

"Yes, I suppose I do, now that I think about it," she said, feeling a blush color her cheeks. He reached over to her and his fingers traced the line of her cheekbone and jaw.

"I didn't think I could still make you blush," he murmured. "I'd thought you were beyond that stage." His hand dropped to rest against her belly, where his child lay beneath the layers of her clothing, hidden and cherished within the depths of her body.

"Alicia, I don't know if I've made it clear to you, but I'm so pleased you're going to have my child. I've been wondering if we should tell Jason," he murmured in a low voice.

"I've thought the same thing," she told him. "Maybe it would be a good idea before it becomes obvious. Though I don't think I'll show my pregnancy any too soon. There's enough of me to hide it pretty well."

"I like you just the way you are, Alicia. I don't yearn for anything different than what I have, what you've given me. I hope you know that by now."

"I suppose I do," she said. "Just sometimes, I think I'd like to be small and slim and more feminine."

His laugh was dark and mischievous to her ears, with a hint of invitation. "You can show me just how feminine you are, later on tonight. I don't think I could stand it if you were any more a woman than you are, my dear."

She blushed again, unused to the sort of compliments Jake offered on occasion. "I look in the mirror every day, Jake. I know what I look like."

"No, I don't think you do," he said, disagreeing with her in a gentle tone. "You only know what you see, not the picture you present to me."

It was late when the Christmas story had been read from the Bible, later yet when Jason made his way up the stairs to bed. Then came the time of sharing and loving, which Alicia had looked forward to all through the evening. She lay in Jake's arms, the darkness of midnight surrounding them, and her heart seemed to sing a melody of its own.

And yet there was another melody missing from this house, and she felt a sense of loss as she reflected on the joy that had once been his in those days when music had been central to his life.

As sleep overtook her, she vowed to somehow restore to him the pleasure to be found in the world of music he'd so long denied.

CHRISTMAS WAS OVER, and Alicia sighed as the last of the ornaments were packed away in the attic. There was a certain sadness in the retiring of the majestic tree, and as she and Jason hauled it outdoors she remembered seeing an abandoned tree another time. Children had set it upright and decorated it with bits of bread and seeds for the birds.

Within an hour, they had secured the tree and spent a joyous time decorating it in a new and productive fashion, then watched as the birds flocked to eat the offering they'd provided. Somehow it made the day seem brighter, the sun gleamed high in the heavens and she hugged Jason tightly to herself as they shared the sight of the cardinals and blue jays fussing with the sparrows who gathered in the tree.

She smiled as she prepared supper, for there was in her an anticipation of what loomed on her horizon. She looked forward to spring and the time of renewal as never before. There would be increased newness of life in the months to come, when she would find her dearest dream come true.

Thinking of the workbasket beside her chair in the parlor, she smiled. Filled with small bits of clothing, it almost overflowed onto the wooden floor. The plans for the days to come were many and fruitful. She had only just ordered a bolt of outing flannel from the general store, to be turned into diapers. Without a doubt, the news that the McPhersons were in the market for such a thing would be all over town, if it wasn't already the subject of supper table conversation.

She'd thought that Jason would catch on to the fact she was doing a lot of handwork, but he seemed oblivious to her sewing, and she'd not yet decided how to let him in on the secret. "Maybe tonight," she said to herself, drying the dishes and putting them away in the cupboard.

She thought of the plan she'd hatched during the night when sleep had eluded her and Jake had held her close. In accordance with her plotting, she'd been to the lumber mill earlier in the day, making her purchases and arranging to have them carted to the house tomorrow. She thought of what Jake would do—what he would say, and her shiver was involuntary. It was the only fly in the ointment today, she decided, this telling him of her plan.

Then there was the gentleman who had halted her progress as she'd left the lumber mill, drawing her to one side of the walkway to introduce himself. It was then, in those few moments, that her resolution became a solid plan.

"I'll take care of it," she'd said brightly, even as she wondered at her impulsive behavior. Now she would face the moment of truth. Now would come the time of reckoning with Jake.

She left her boots by the kitchen door, snow melting from them, and hung her coat on the rack before she made her way to the parlor, aware of rosy cheeks and cold hands. She solved the problem of her chilled fingers by nestling them against Jake's throat, then laughed at his shivering response.

"I met a gentleman in town, Jake," she said eagerly, settling next to him on the couch. "He wants to come visit with you. I said it would be all right." Even to her own ears her words sounded artificial, she thought; then she noticed his frown and doubted her wisdom. "You don't mind, do you?"

"Who was it?" he asked shortly.

"His name is Baldridge. He said he knows you from several years back, that you used to work for his company."

"I won't see him," Jake said bluntly. "You had no right to make an appointment without checking with me first, Alicia."

"I'm sorry," she said quietly. And she was. Sorry she'd been impulsive, sorry she'd taken for granted that Jake was ready for this to take place.

"I didn't mean to overstep. I'll walk to town and find him and tell him you're not available." She rose from her seat and would have been halfway to the parlor door, but he reached out to grasp her wrist and halt her in her tracks.

"Sit down, Alicia. You don't need to be out and about in this weather," he told her. "Send Jason."

She shook her head, disappointment making it imperative that she leave the room before she embarrassed herself by shedding the tears that threatened. "I made the appointment. I'll be the one to break it," she said, tugging at his grip, then stepping away from his side. "Besides I have some things to do in town."

"What?" he asked suspiciously.

"I've ordered some wood to be delivered to the house tomorrow," she told him, "and I've got to buy the nails I need to start my next—"

"What are you planning now?" He interrupted her, quite rudely she thought, and she was certain he was terribly suspicious. "I don't want you starting any more building projects before the baby comes. You need to take care of yourself."

"Building projects? All we did was build a doghouse for the new puppy," she said with a tentative smile.

"You fixed the gate and the front step and put a railing on the back porch," he reminded her. "Not to mention overseeing the building of the shed and lean-to."

"That was all a long time ago!" she said lightly, her fist clenching as she assumed an easy pose.

"Well, what have you planned now?" he asked, and she felt hesitation slow her response, fear of his reaction making her draw away from him.

"I'm going to build a ramp. So you can go out once in a while," she said carefully. "Jason will help me, and Cord agreed to come in next Saturday and lend a hand."

"I won't be going anywhere," he told her bluntly. "I have no need of a ramp. There was one out there before and I had it torn down."

"I know," she said. "I heard."

"Then I'd think you could figure out that there wasn't much point in putting up another."

"We'll talk about this later," she said, turning away from him and walking toward the door. Her hands trembled, her eyes burned with unshed tears, and she concentrated on the kettle of soup simmering on the stove. For surely, she needed some sort of distraction in order to set aside the pain of Jake's refusal.

"Come back here!" Jake roared, and she ignored him, continuing out the door and down the hall to the kitchen.

He followed her, as she'd known he would, and the kitchen door banged loudly as he slammed it open. "I won't have it, Alicia. You've gone too far this time."

"I beg to differ, sir," she said staunchly, recognizing that her dreams were worth fighting for. "I haven't gone nearly far enough. I'm tired of you being a recluse, Jake, and me along with you. There are things to do in this town, things we could enjoy together, if you only would. I refuse to let you sit here in this house and become a hermit."

"You don't have anything to say about it," he told her flatly. "This is my choice, and I don't have to answer to you."

"I'm aware of that," she said. "I know my opinion is of little value to you, but—"

"Just stop right there," he roared. "I've never denigrated your opinion. I've bent to your will more than once. I've done what you've asked of me, even to opening up the damn piano."

"I won't be happy until you're *playing* the 'damn' piano," she said sharply. "And let me tell you, Mr. McPherson, that day will come. I won't rest until you sit down and play for me. I don't think it's fair that almost everyone in town has heard you perform except for your wife."

"What are you talking about?" he asked, his mouth turned down in a sour expression. *"Everyone in town, indeed."*

"You gave a concert some years ago," she reminded him, "then you played for several performers at the opera house the following years. In fact, you were already working on another concert when Rena died, Jake."

"Well, someone's been busy filling your ears with my past exploits, haven't they?"

"Is that what you call it?" she asked. "I wasn't aware that your music was such a big secret."

"It's not a secret. It's just in the past," he told her. "You might as well forget the whole thing, Alicia. It's not going to happen. Not ever."

"You won't give me the joy of hearing you make music?" she asked, her heart aching as she recognized his fury with her.

"You've interfered for the last time," he said. "You can tell them to keep the damn lumber at the sawmill, and just forget the nails. This isn't going to happen, I told you."

"I'll go now and undo the damage I've done, Jake. Then I'm going to come back and pack my things and begin to sort out my life."

"Pack your things?" His eyes were wild now, dark and dangerous, as if he would leap from his chair to halt her progress. "What the hell are you talking about? You're my wife, Alicia. You're not going anywhere."

But he was too late to halt her progress as she sailed across the kitchen, snatching her coat from the peg and picking up her boots as she reached the door. She halted on the back stoop, sliding her feet into the heavy footwear, slipped her arms into her coat sleeves and was halfway around the house before the tears began to fall.

CHAPTER EIGHTEEN

SHE'D BEEN GONE the better part of an hour when he heard the front door open quietly and then close with a soft snick of the latch. His chair had never moved so slowly, he thought, his callused hands spinning the wheels as he shot through the parlor door and into the foyer.

Alicia stood beside the door, removing her coat, then bending to slip her feet from the heavy boots she wore. Her gaze was averted, her face pale, and for a moment he felt a tug of remorse at the pain he'd caused her. More than a tug, he thought, more like an avalanche that threatened to bury him in guilt.

"Alicia. We need to talk about this," he said quietly, even as his heart pounded in a wild rhythm in his chest. "Come into the parlor, please."

She sighed, the whispering sound conveying a sadness too great to be borne. He searched out her eyes, and flinched. Swollen and reddened by tears, they refused to touch upon him and he reached for her, grasping her hand, attempting to halt her progress as she headed for the stairs.

"Where have you been?" he asked quietly.

Her spurt of laughter was harsh, unlike the woman who had bent to his will in other times, whose only goal in life had seemed to be his happiness. Now she leveled on him a look of mockery, and he knew a moment of fear.

"I went to the sawmill and canceled my order, and then stopped by the hotel and told Mr. Baldridge you wouldn't see him. Just as you told me to, Jake."

She tugged at his hold, her fingers peeling his from their grip on her, and backed from him. "I've done as you asked, Jake. Now I'm leaving you to sort out your life," she said. "You don't need me. You were doing just fine before I walked in that door the first time, and you'll no doubt be happier without me here to disturb your routine."

"I do need you, Alicia," he said forcefully, aching to make her aware of his pain. "I simply have a problem with going back to the life I led during those years when Rena was alive. I've gotten used to the way things are now, and it's—"

"Safe?" she asked, cutting him off as he groped for a word to describe the situation. "Do you feel comforted by the grief and sorrow you've worn like a blanket over the past years? Have you found peace and happiness in the life you've forged without Rena here?"

He looked at her, feeling the anger rise within him. "You always dig deep, don't you?" he asked bitterly.

"You enjoy throwing up those early days, trying to make me feel appreciative to you for the changes you've made in my life."

"And do you?" She watched him from swollen eyes, her face reddened by the cold, and he thought he'd never seen her look more appealing. Alicia had a rare beauty of her own. She was a woman who feared nothing, not even the man who had made her life so difficult over the past months, the man who even now was speaking harsh words that flew from his mouth with the precision of an arrow seeking a target.

"Hell, yes. I appreciate everything you've done for us, for Jason and me. We eat regular meals and the house is in order. Jason has turned the corner finally and is managing to keep his nose clean. A goal that seemed impossible a year ago."

"And you, Jake? What have I done on your behalf?" He thought her eyes glistened with fresh tears, or perhaps it was the glow of hope. If ever he'd spoken words that were important, now was the time.

"You've brought life to my existence, Alicia. You've given me happiness."

"And what have you given me?" she asked, prodding him.

He was silent as he considered her question, then he spoke haltingly. "A home, a son and another child for you to love as you've loved Jason. I hope I've given you the knowledge that you are needed and wanted."

She stepped back from him, her fingers fumbling

for the newel post, one foot rising to touch the bottom step of the long stairway. "What about love, Jake? Have you offered that? Or have I missed something?"

He was astounded at her words. Of course he cared about her; the declaration was on the tip of his tongue as he watched her climb the stairs. *Cared about her?* Such pallid words to describe the overwhelming power of love. For the first time, he recognized the depths of his feeling for the woman. He'd coasted along, content to allow her tender care of him, falling more and more each day into the routine she'd set, the hours of intimacy they'd shared.

If she walked away—he'd have lost the light at the end of his miserable tunnel.

The door to the upstairs bedroom clicked shut, and he envisioned her searching out her valise, thought of the collection of clothing she'd left upstairs. She'd have to come back down in order to pack the things she'd installed in his bedroom. Her brush, her comb, the mirror she seldom peered into. Then there was the nightgown she wore on occasion, the wrapper she donned each morning before she went to the kitchen. Her house shoes that peeked from beneath the bed.

He closed his eyes. Surely she would not leave him, would not walk out that door and never look back. His brow furrowed as he considered what his life would be without her, and pain such as he'd never known filled his breast and overflowed, almost strangling him with its aching presence. His eyes blurred and he rubbed at them distractedly. He'd wait until she came down. Then he'd persuade her to stay.

The image of Alicia, carrying her valise, coming toward him with resolution written on her features was more than he could stand. He'd have to stop her, make her understand that he needed her. Make her aware that he wanted her in his life.

Make her realize that the love he'd denied in his heart was filling him now with an aching, burning urgency he could not contain.

"Alicia." He spoke her name in broken syllables, rolling his chair to the insurmountable obstacle of eighteen-stair steps, curving in an elegant rise to the second floor of his home.

No, not a home—not once Alicia walked out the door. It would become, once more, a house, an empty shell, barely resembling that which she had made of it.

And he would forever mourn her leaving.

He slid from the chair, kneeling on the first step, balancing himself on the stump of his left leg and reached for the gleaming spindles that attached to the banister. The pain and pressure against his thigh almost undid him, but he set it aside as nothing, for the aching need for the woman at the top of the stairs was by far the greater agony.

The second step took but a moment—the third a bit longer, for sweat broke out on his brow, and he gritted his teeth against the force of his stump grinding into the bare wood.

The door of her room opened. He heard her footsteps in the hall. He chanced a look upward, knowing already what he would see. She stood at the top of the stairs, her eyes wide, her mouth forming words that were not forthcoming. The heavy valise hung from her right hand, then it hit the floor with a thump as she dropped it beside her foot.

"Jake! What are you doing?" Her tone was incredulous, as if her eyes were playing tricks on her. "Stop, Jake. You'll hurt yourself!" she cried, even as he forced his way to the fourth step. She descended the steps lightly as she sped to his side, and her hand touched his head, her fingers wide-spread against his crown.

Then she was there, settling on the step above him, allowing him the comfort of her lap upon which to place his head. He knelt there, swaying a bit as he steadied himself against her, and his arms circled her, clutching her as if she were the only life preserver on-board a sinking ship.

"Alicia. Please don't leave me," he whispered, knowing no shame, only sorrow at the thought of losing her. "I love you, Alicia. I don't know what I'd do without you. Please don't leave."

"You love me? Since when, Jake?"

Wasn't that just like her, to strike to the heart of the matter without any pretense. He laughed, a rough sound that shook his body. "Since when? Maybe since you came into my house and read me the riot act. Or perhaps when you made Jason go and repair the damage he'd done. Or," he continued, "it might have been when you made me open the piano and give Toby lessons."

He looked up at her and knew a moment of such pure need he could hardly bear it. "I don't know when I loved you first, Alicia. It might have been the night you came to me and gave me…gave me the gift of your body. Do you remember that first time?"

She nodded, her face pale, her eyes shadowed. "I remember, Jake. It was the most wonderful night of my life."

"If I change…if I promise to make amends, will you stay? I'll try, Alicia. I'll do whatever you want." And then he frowned. "Perhaps we'll have to negotiate on a few things, but for the most part, you can have things the way you want them."

She smiled. "I should have known that you'd make restrictions on me, that you wouldn't go whole hog, Jake." Her hands cupped his face, and she bent low to press her lips against his.

"Will you let me build the ramp?"

It seemed to be the crux of the matter, he thought, for she held her breath as he considered the bargaining tactic she'd chosen to home in on. "No," he said with finality, and watched as the light faded from her blue eyes. "I'll let you supervise while Cord and Rachel's brothers tend to it. Or I'll hire someone to do it."

Her face lit from within as he spoke, her eyes filling with a brilliance he was now familiar with. He stretched upward to find the warmth of her mouth, his hand pressing against her nape to bring her closer. "What else, Alicia?"

She hesitated, and the joy that had almost come to dwell in those blue eyes seemed to fade as she made her request. "Will you play for me? Not for anyone else, Jake. Only me? I won't ask more than that."

And she wouldn't. For as he well knew, this woman was as honest as the day was long. Could he do as she asked, could he live with the pain of once more bringing to life the music that had been missing from his soul for so long?

For there would be pain in this endeavor, *that* he knew without a doubt. He would suffer again the loss of his legs as he struggled to once more conquer the pedal and make his fingers stroke the keys with even a semblance of his former ability.

For Alicia? Could he do it for this woman who had given him a second chance at life? The answer came clearly.

"I'll do anything you ask of me," he said quietly. "Including that."

"I feel as though we're sitting on opposite sides of a bargaining table," she said softly. "I don't want it to be that way. I want us to be two halves of a whole, Jake."

"We can be," he vowed. "I'll see to it." The old arrogance tinged his words and he recognized her smile as one he'd seen before.

"Invincible, aren't you?" she asked. "Determined to have your way."

"In this, yes," he told her. He tugged at her hand. "Come here, Alicia. I want to hold you properly and I can't while you're up there and I'm down here."

She obediently slid down two steps to rest beside him, and he settled next to her, his arm at her waist, his other hand tilting her face to his. "Will you say it again, please?" she asked, and he did not pretend ignorance, his answer coming readily.

"I love you. I love everything about you. You're the most important thing in the world to me, sweetheart." He felt the pain of failure slice through him as he thought of the past.

"I put my music ahead of everything else when Rena was alive. She took second place, and she allowed it. Because she loved me, I suspect."

"Ah, but she knew that you loved her in return," Alicia said quietly.

Jake nodded. "Yes, I did. But not as I should have." He touched her lips with his, and the kiss was a promise. "Not as I love you. It's as if I've learned what the word means, Alicia. As though I've changed."

"You have," she stated flatly. "You're a different man than you were. More of a man than the one I saw the first time I walked through that door." She nodded toward the wide front door, and then frowned as a movement in the narrow glass panel caught her eye.

"Someone's outside," she said quietly. "Let me go see who it is."

But the door opened before she could move, and Jason came in on a gust of wind, his gaze immediately shooting to where they sat on the staircase. "What are you doin' there, Pa?" he asked in amazement. Then he looked more closely at Alicia. "Have you been crying, Mama?"

It was the crowning touch, Jake thought, the final bit of the puzzle coming together. For though Jason had announced his intentions, the word had not passed his lips. He'd bypassed it in several ways, mostly by not using a title at all when he spoke to Alicia. Now his concern apparently overcame his reticence and he rushed to the stairway, climbing to where they sat, kneeling before Alicia.

"Did my pa make you cry?" he asked belligerently. "Did he?"

"Yes, I did," Jake admitted. "But I've kissed it and made it better, son. She won't be crying anymore."

Jason looked doubtfully at him and sought Alicia's opinion on the matter. "I don't like it when you cry, Mama. You won't do it anymore, will you?"

She shook her head, reaching to touch the dear, dark curls that needed the taming of her comb and scissors. "I won't do it anymore," she said, repeating his words.

He looked up at her hopefully, and his smile was beguiling as he asked the question that was obviously foremost in his mind. "What are you cookin' for supper?"

Late spring—1881

THE ARRIVAL OF SPRING brought about changes in the
big house. A Saturday in May found a whole crew of
men busily pounding nails, putting together a ramp
that would add considerable ease to Jake's life. He sat
in the shade on the porch, watching, his coat draped
over his shoulders to keep away the chill.

Beyond the porch was sunlight, bright and strong,
as was the woman who directed the proceedings. She
was heavy with the child she would bear sometime
within the next two weeks, if her calculations were correct. But her strength was formidable, and Jake smiled
as he watched her supervising the building of his route
to the future.

He would need the mobility the ramp provided, for
he would once more be occupying the office in town
he'd given up four years ago. Cord was making arrangements for Jake's transport and, understanding
his brother's need to help, Jake had only nodded his
approval.

He watched Alicia now as she approached the stairs
and grasped the handrail. Her gaze touched on the
fresh paint with which Jason had liberally coated the
risers, and she smiled as if a particular memory had
pleased her. Then, her eyes on Jake, she climbed toward him and bent to press her lips against his brow.
Her words were audible only to his ears, but it was

enough to send him into a state of readiness he'd planned for over the past months.

"Are you sure?" he asked, looking up at her sparkling eyes.

"I'm sure," she said. "At least as sure as I can be. I've never done this before, you know. I'm thinking I need Rachel here, Jake."

He roared out his brother's name, and Cord looked up in alarm. "What's wrong?" he asked, long strides bringing him to the porch. His gaze touched Alicia. "Are you all right?" As if his keen gaze had caught the air of expectancy on her face, he nodded in answer to his own question. "You'll be all right once things get under way, won't you?"

"Will you go and get Rachel?" Jake asked him.

"I've done better than that already," Cord replied. "I've asked her to be here for dinnertime to give Alicia a hand."

"She may be stuck with fixing dinner by herself," Alicia said, wincing as if something had caught her unawares.

"How far apart are your pains?" Cord asked quietly, his gaze narrowing on her.

"They're getting there," she said agreeably. "Maybe five minutes."

Jake felt sweat break out on his forehead. "You need to be in bed," he said roughly. "We need to call the doctor."

"In a bit," she said blithely. "I've a ways to go."

"Alicia." He spoke her name with the stubbornness he kept in store for just such an occasion. "We're going into the house *now*, and Cord will send in Rachel when she gets here. This is not a matter up for discussion."

She shrugged and smiled in Cord's direction. "This time I'll let him win the argument," she said.

"I'll send for the doctor," Cord said. "Although I think she's right. It won't be anytime soon."

As it happened, they were both wrong, for it was just before dusk when Jake's daughter was born. Dark hair and eyes gave her the appearance of a tiny sprite, and her howl of awakening could be heard throughout the house as she made her entry into the world.

The bedroom was a hive of activity, with the doctor tending Alicia, Rachel washing the baby girl, and Jake swinging onto the bed to lift his wife in his arms, holding her close. She settled against his chest, weary, her features wan from the time of labor. But her eyes were bright, her mouth smiling as she looked toward the tiny bundle in Rachel's arms.

Then she transferred her attention toward Jake, and her whisper stilled the anxiety he'd been beset with over the past hours. "Thank you, Mr. McPherson, for my daughter. I think she looks like a tiny flower, don't you?"

He could only agree, nodding as she announced the name she'd chosen. "I'd like to call her Rose," she said.

Jake nodded. Whatever Alicia wanted, he was willing to bow to her wishes. At least for tonight.

From the doorway, a worried voice begged entry

and, as the doctor pulled the sheet up over Alicia, he called permission.

"What are you doin', Pa?" Jason asked. "Is Mama all right? I heard the baby crying, and Uncle Cord said I could ask to come in now."

"I'm hugging your mama," Jake said, tackling the most important issue first. "And yes, you may come in and meet your sister, son. We've named her Rose. Does that please you?"

Jason's eyes sought out the tiny face as Rachel offered the baby for the boy's inspection, and his eyes were wide as he took in the red face and the squalling infant. "She won't bawl like that all the time, will she, Pa?" he asked anxiously.

"No," Jake assured him. "Only when she's wet or hungry or wants to be held." He grinned at the boy. "You were the same way, Jason. All babies are alike."

"Maybe I could hold her sometime," the boy said wistfully.

"Jason, come here," Alicia said, patting the bed on the other side of her. She nodded at Rachel, and in moments the new baby girl was in the midst of a three-way hug, her mother's arms cradling her as Jason bent to touch his lips to her head, Jake reinforcing Alicia's hold on his daughter.

"Wow, she smells like—" Jason wrinkled his nose. "Kinda sweet, and kinda different."

"That's what all newborn babies smell like," Rachel said. She looked with tenderness at Alicia. "Cherish it while it lasts, sister dear. The particular scent will wash off quickly, but you'll never forget how marvelously sweet it is."

Jake thought Rachel looked just a bit wistful as she watched the three of them, then she turned aside as the doctor issued instructions for Alicia's care.

"I'll be here for a day or so," she assured him. "Then Jake will take over."

"I haven't forgotten how to tend a baby," he said stoutly. "And Alicia will need my guidance."

She rolled her eyes at him. "Some things never change," she said flatly.

His smile flashed and he agreed with her readily. "You're right there, my dear. The most important things in life are steadfast and solid…unchanging in a changing world all around us."

"Like loving me, Jake?" she asked softly, and he nodded his reply.

Then he underscored his meaning with the words she still needed to hear, even though they were a regular part of his vocabulary these days.

"I love you, wife of mine," he whispered.

"I love you, too, Mama," Jason whispered. "And Rose." He slid from the bed and headed for the door. "I hafta go and tell Uncle Cord about the baby now. But I'll be back right shortly."

"He's going to need your attention while I'm busy with the baby, Jake. I fear he will run you ragged," Alicia said with a smile.

"I can handle it," Jake told her. "I can handle anything these days, sweetheart."

Her laughter rang out, the sound of a woman pleased with herself, with the knowledge that her life was complete. With the confidence that she loved and was loved in return.

NIGHT HAD FALLEN and the parlor was lit by a single lamp, shedding its glow over the form of mother and child. Alicia rocked gently to and fro, looking out the window, awaiting the surprise Jake had promised. She looked up as he rolled into the room, noting the look of peace he wore, the firmness of his jaw, the brilliance of dark eyes that flashed in her direction.

"I wrote something for you, Alicia," he said quietly. "I'd like to play it for you."

"You wrote a song for me?" She thought of the times when she'd heard his touch on the piano keys while she was in the yard, or arriving home, only to have the sound cease at her approach. Wisely, she'd allowed the secrecy he'd put in place, knowing that eventually he would come to this point.

And yet, for him to have written a piece of music with her in mind was more than she'd expected.

Jake smiled at her from across the room. "It has no words. Toby would call it real music, as opposed to songs with words." He slid from his chair onto the piano bench and set the pedal in place near his right knee. His glance at her was fraught with a tension he could not hide. "I may not be very good at this. I've only practiced it a couple of times when you were out."

His fingers touched the keys, tentatively at first, then with a strength and purpose she could not mistake. It was the touch of a master, of a man whose talent superseded that of any other she'd heard at the keyboard. Her parents had taken her to concerts as a part of her education, but never in the fanciest concert hall had she heard the depth of feeling that was now brought to life from Jake's gifted fingers.

"What do you call it?" she asked, content for the moment to listen, wrapped up in the intricate harmony of notes he created.

He glanced at her with an all-encompassing look and she felt the message he conveyed as if it were whispered aloud.

"I call it simply 'For Alicia,'" he said softly. "It speaks of all you are, sweetheart, of all you mean to me, of the love we share, the beauty you shed about you."

His head bent as his hands moved gracefully over the keys and the music he played sounded like a choir of angels in her ears.

For Alicia.

HQN™

We *are* romance™

Don't miss out on the return of a steamy classic
from *New York Times* bestselling author

CARLY
PHILLIPS

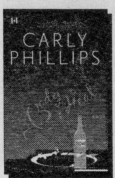

Massage therapist Brianne Nelson has fantasized about sexy,
injured detective Jake Lowell since they first met. And thanks to
his wealthy sister, Brianne is about to become Jake's personal
massage therapist for the next month! Only, Jake isn't in any
hurry to return to the police force just yet...not until he finds
the man responsible for his injuries; but in the meantime, he's
going to enjoy all the therapy he can get....

Body Heat

When wildest fantasies become a wilder reality...
available in stores in January.

www.HQNBooks.com

PHCP143

HQN™

We *are* romance™

New York Times bestselling author

MERYL SAWYER

The stares of the citizens of Twin Oaks don't scare
Kaitlin Wells. Falsely jailed for a theft she didn't commit,
she's back to prove her innocence, although it's clear that
someone doesn't want her disturbing the peace or getting
close to new sheriff Justin Radner. But some laws can't be
ignored, and soon Kat and Justin are risking love and life to
expose what lies beneath this sleepy little town.

Half Past Dead

Thrilling romantic suspense...coming in January!

www.HQNBooks.com

PHMS063

If you enjoyed what you just read,
then we've got an offer you can't resist!

Take 2 bestselling
love stories FREE!

Plus get a FREE surprise gift!

Clip this page and mail it to Harlequin Reader Service®

IN U.S.A.
3010 Walden Ave.
P.O. Box 1867
Buffalo, N.Y. 14240-1867

IN CANADA
P.O. Box 609
Fort Erie, Ontario
L2A 5X3

YES! Please send me 2 free Harlequin Temptation® novels and my free surprise gift. After receiving them, if I don't wish to receive anymore, I can return the shipping statement marked cancel. If I don't cancel, I will receive 4 brand-new novels each month, before they're available in stores. In the U.S.A., bill me at the bargain price of $3.80 plus 25¢ shipping and handling per book and applicable sales tax, if any*. In Canada, bill me at the bargain price of $4.47 plus 25¢ shipping and handling per book and applicable taxes**. That's the complete price and a savings of 10% off the cover prices—what a great deal! I understand that accepting the 2 free books and gift places me under no obligation ever to buy any books. I can always return a shipment and cancel at any time. Even if I never buy another book from Harlequin, the 2 free books and gift are mine to keep forever.

142 HDN DZ7U
342 HDN DZ7V

Name	(PLEASE PRINT)	
Address	Apt.#	
City	State/Prov.	Zip/Postal Code

Not valid to current Harlequin Temptation® subscribers.

Want to try two free books from another series?
Call 1-800-873-8635 or visit www.morefreebooks.com.

* Terms and prices subject to change without notice. Sales tax applicable in N.Y.
** Canadian residents will be charged applicable provincial taxes and GST.
   All orders subject to approval. Offer limited to one per household.
   ® are registered trademarks owned and used by the trademark owner and or its licensee.

TEMP04R   ©2004 Harlequin Enterprises Limited

HQN™

We *are* romance™

Fan favorite award-winning author

MARGARET MOORE

pens a new historical that will
sweep you off your feet!

In this sequel to *The Unwilling Bride*, handsome knight
Sir Henry defies the warnings of his family to assist
Lady Mathilde resist the efforts of her enemy—her nefarious
cousin Roald. Amidst dangerous political intrigue and shifting
loyalties, both cannot deny their forbidden attraction to each
other, and what began as a simple bargain leads to something
neither could ever have hoped for.

Hers to Command

Available in stores in February.

www.HQNBooks.com

PHMM095

HQN™

We *are* romance™

Chocolate can make a girl do the craziest things…

By *USA TODAY* bestselling author

JENNIFER GREENE

Lucy Fitzhenry has just discovered the best chocolate in the world…and it makes her do the craziest things. How else can she explain sleeping with her boss? Nick is so far out of her league that she's determined to forget that night and act the professional that she's supposed to be. Yet every time they taste test her brilliant recipe, they wind up in each other's arms and there can only be one explanation…

Blame It on Chocolate

Available in stores in January

www.HQNBooks.com

PHJG145